We hope you e[…]n or renew it by the

You can renew it at www.norfolk.gov.u[…]braries or by using our free library app.

Otherwise you can phone 0344 800 8020 - please have your library card and PIN ready.

You can sign up for email reminders too.

The Johnson Sisters

Tresser Henderson

www.urbanbooks.net

Urban Books, LLC
300 Farmingdale Road, NY-Route 109
Farmingdale, NY 11735

ISBN 13: 978-1-62286-540-6
ISBN 10: 1-62286-540-5

First Mass Market Printing October 2017
First Trade Paperback Printing June 2015
Printed in the United States of America

10 9 8 7 6 5 4 3 2 1

Distributed by Kensington Publishing Corp.
Submit orders to:
Customer Service
400 Hahn Road
Westminster, MD 21157-4627
Phone: 1-800-733-3000
Fax: 1-800-659-243

Acknowledgments

As always, I'm going to start out by thanking God for all of His many blessings. Without Him, nothing would be possible. God is the head of my life, and I thank Him for what He has done, what He is doing, and what He will do in my life.

Five years ago I dreamed of getting one book published, and here I am coming out with my fourth. All I can say is God is good. Never give up on any dreams you have, because they can come true. All you have to do is have faith. Please trust, even now my faith waivers. I doubt this gift that has been granted to me, and I still question if I should be doing this. Don't you know God has sent individuals my way to let me know not to give up? As soon as you are ready to throw the towel in on something, God shows you to keep striving because He has a plan and a purpose for our life. I know writing is my love, but even the things we love don't always turn out quite the way we want them to go, you know. My mother tells me all the time, "In God's time, not your time."

I want to thank my husband, Wil, for standing by my side and being my motivator. He is the man God has connected me to, my companion, my high school sweetheart, my lover, and my partner through thick and thin. Babe, I'm so blessed to have you in my life. I love you. I appreciate you. You are a wonderful man, and I can't say this enough.

To my children, who are growing up so fast: I love you. The older you get, the more you are interested in what I do, and it's funny because I find you guys are sometimes my motivational speakers during this journey. It's in those moments when I know I have to be doing something right with you. I see your personalities shine and wisdom being spoken, which makes me so proud of you. "Out of the mouths of babes."

To my parents, Clarence and Rebecca Atkinson, what can I say but thank you? Thank you for always being here for me no matter what. Anything, and I mean anything I need, you are always there for me, and I never take for granted the gift of having you as my parents. I can never repay you enough for what you have done for me. I love you so much, and I'm blessed to have you as my parents.

To my sister, Sabrina Atkinson, who always gives it to me straight, no chaser: you could be a character all by yourself (LOL), and sometimes you have inspired some of the characters I write about. You are hilarious and a joy to be around because you keep me in stitches from laughing so much. I love you, and I'm proud of you.

To my brother, Clarence Atkinson, A.K.A. Duddy. (That's right, Duddy): you are six foot four and my baby brother who I have to look up to. You are so sweet and kind. Please don't let anybody change that about you. You are going to make some woman a wonderful husband one day, but don't rush it.

I want to acknowledge some ladies who've played a major role in my life, who have picked up a phone, texted me, come by my house, took me to the side to talk to me, given me an uplifting card, or just said "I'm here." These ladies have done that for me, and maybe I shouldn't be writing this when I'm so emotional about this, but I'm going to do it anyway. As women we have to uplift one another, and I'm so thankful to God that he saw fit to place me in the position to receive blessings from these ladies. I don't like to list names because I feel like I always forget somebody, but I'm going to try.

To Rochelle Cicero, Crystal Townes, and Tina Walker: you ladies are the best friends ever, my ride or die as they say, and I love you very much for always being here for me. Not once have I doubted your friendship, which I don't take for granted. You are who I turn to and also the ones who are first to see what's up with me. I love you ladies.

To my wonderful aunties, Patricia, Thelma, and Rosaline: I love you for always supporting me for my entire life. You ladies are so fun to be around. I look forward to our family gatherings just so I can be around you. Although they are few and far between due to the distance, I still appreciate you. Thank you for always supporting me.

To Ms. Patricia Liggon, Ms. Wanda Hester, and Ms. Cheryl Boyd: you ladies exemplify grace with a smile and wisdom galore. I feel like I need popcorn and a soda when I talk with you because I learn so much from you. I love our talks, and I love you very much. Thank you for being here for me.

To Tracey Hodges: I love you. You are the epitome of greatness. You have had some challenges that would defeat the average person, but you have risen above it, and that was because of your faith. During your struggle, you still picked up the phone and checked on me. You don't know how much of an inspiration you are to me. I know we are cousins, but you are like my sister. Even miles apart I know you love me and I love you. Thank you for always being here for me.

To Angela Henderson, my sister from another mother: thank you for everything you do for me. You may not think it's much, but it's more than I can explain. You are such a strong woman. You bend but you don't ever break. That's your faith in God, knowing He will always see you through. You are an amazing woman and I love you.

To authors Ni'chelle Genovese, Victoria Christopher Murray, and Ashley Antoinette: thank you for your patience when I have questions about a business I sometimes don't understand. Not only are you amazing authors whose work I love to read myself, but you are also humble enough to help me. A lot of authors don't do what you guys have done for me, and I thank you and appreciate your guidance.

To Sonia Gravely, Tammie Earick, Catherine Settles, Danielle Johns, Sha-Nae Mack, Rico Gill, and Shannon Brown: you all are wonderful individuals. You don't know how much you have touched my life. Who said work couldn't be fun? I think we spent more time together at work than we did with our families at times, but having you all around made work great. Thank you so much for being here for me.

To Ashley Kasey, who said she wanted her own paragraph because she crazy like that. She stood and watched me type this, and if you knew her, you know she meant it. (LMAO) Thanks for being here for me, keeping me laughing and in trouble at times at work because you know we can never be together because you know they think the two of us are troublemakers. I'm not. I can't speak for you. (LOL) Thanks for keeping a smile on my face and for being a great friend.

All of you at some point during this challenging time in my life have been there, said something, allowed me to vent and even cry without question. You pushed me when I didn't think I had the strength to continue trying. Sometimes somebody can say the right thing that's like a bell going off in your spirit, and I know God sent you and continues to send some of you my way as confirmation for me. You have helped me in ways you can't imagine. I'm so blessed to be surrounded by greatness. They say watch the company you keep, and I can say the company God has positioned around me are definitely some prayer warriors. If I forgot anyone, please don't think I did it on purpose. As they say, blame it on my mind and not my heart.

Special thanks to Carl Weber and Natalie Weber. Carl, thank you for this opportunity. I told you I was going to continue to bring it, and I'm doing that. Without you, I wouldn't have had my start. And Natalie, thank you for continuing to put up with all my e-mails. I feel like a pest sometimes, but you always respond to me and help me when I need it, and I thank you for that.

A special thanks to the editing staff and graphic designer, Lonnie Baskerville, on this book. You are amazing, and I appreciate what you have done. Thank you.

I want to thank Randi Jo Wines and everyone with the Gainesboro library in my area for always supporting me. You all are amazing.

And last but certainly not least, I want to thank all my family members who have supported me and encouraged me. A special thanks to my fans, who have supported me since book one. You all are awesome. Thanks for your feedback and support. To all the readers who took a chance on Tresser Henderson books, to the booksellers who carry my books, to the book clubs who have chosen my books, to all the other libraries who include my books in their establishment and to the online Web sites who've supported me, thank you.

Chapter 1

Vivian

I was sitting behind my mahogany desk when an administrator walked in, handing me a folder on a case I needed to call on and resolve. Being the director of underwriting for a major insurance company was daunting. I loved my job, but like anything, at times it really became too much for me to handle. Today was that day. I hadn't had a chance to breathe since I walked into this place. One issue after another walked in or called needing a resolution.

I knew I needed to hire a new manager to handle things ASAP. It had been a week since my manager quit on me. I mean, she just walked into my office, placed her badge down on my desk, and walked out. I ran after her, wondering what was going on. This was so sudden and done in such an abrupt fashion that it caught me off-guard. I needed to understand why she was choosing to make this decision.

"What's going on, Samantha? Why did you put your badge on my desk?" I had asked, stepping outside my office, looking at her saunter away.

"I'm quitting," she said, stopping and turning to look at me with frustration written all over her face. As nicely dressed as she was in her deep coral short-sleeved sateen jacket with matching straight-leg pants with black pumps, Samantha looked vibrant. Her outfit brought happiness to the space, but her demeanor was one of being overwhelmed.

"Why?" I asked.

"Vivian, I appreciate you taking a chance with me and offering me this position but I can't do this anymore. I'm not cut out for this."

"But you are doing so well," I said. And she was. Samantha had managed to move from mail clerk to manger in three years. Anything she worked on was done with flawless determination. I mean, she did make some mistakes, as most of us did, but she would correct them with no problems and keep on with her day. Sometimes when you gave feedback to someone on what they did wrong, they took it badly. Some believed they never made mistakes. Some blamed someone else for their mistakes, but Samantha took hers in stride. She was harder on herself than I ever had to be on her. So, for her to give up like this was surprising to me.

"I thought I could handle this job, but I can't. I've never been this stressed out in my life. Then I hear they are going to give me another team to manage," she said, putting her finger on her temple.

"I've heard the same thing, but nothing has been set in stone yet," I said.

"I already have forty-seven people under me, Vivian. I don't think I can handle another twenty-four. All of this downsizing and putting more work on the ones who are here just to save more money for the bigwig's pockets is bull."

"I know this job is stressful," I agreed. Everything she was saying were exact things I had thought about and argued to the higher-ups about myself, but in a business like this, you had to take one on the chin, do your job, or you could be without one.

"I don't want you to leave. Let me see what I can do. Give me two weeks. This way you can put in your notice and exit the right way. If I can't change things within that time, I will not stand in your way of leaving if you still choose to do so," I offered.

Samantha stood looking down at the gray carpet tiles , pondering what I was saying.

"Two weeks. That's all I ask. This will also give you time to find something else if you still feel like you need to leave."

She nodded, saying, "Okay. I'll do that."

Two weeks came, and as much as I had hoped I could change things, I couldn't. My power was useless when it came to downsizing and the overworking of individuals. Samantha never changed her mind, and she did leave the company. I can't say I blame her. Her last few days here, she seemed relieved with her decision, and a part of me envied her. She left despite the great money she was making, but this goes to show money isn't everything. Happiness most of the time outweighed finances, especially when it came with the cost of losing yourself.

Right now I didn't mind the stressful distraction. It wasn't like I had someone to go home to. This lifestyle afforded me the life I always wanted for myself. I grew up in the small town of Chase City, Virginia, a town known for having only two street lights. I grew up on five acres of land in a three-bedroom, one-bath house in which my five sisters, my mom, and dad lived.

Three girls slept in one bedroom and two in the other. So, needless to say, we had an argument about something every day. The one bathroom situation was enough to cause World War III because we would battle to be the first one in. Most times we had to do our hair sitting on the edge of our bed, holding a mirror between our knees in order to get ready and be out the door on time. Bathroom time had to be timed. We only had twenty minutes each to do what we had to do in the bathroom, and that time flew. You were always reminded your time was up when you heard a tap at the door letting you know it was time to get out.

We didn't have running water for seven years of my life. I can still recall having to go to my aunt's house, who lived down the road, to get water in as many jugs as we could. Water needed to be heated on the stove in order for you to take a bath. There was no central air, so when it was hot as hell, we had to fight over who was going to sit directly in front of the fan to cool off. We heated the house in the winter with a wood-burning stove, which still to this day I consider to be the best source of heat. My dad would get it so hot in the house we had to open windows to cool off.; but when morning came and no one got up during the night to refill the stove, it felt as if we were lying outside in the snow, and it was then we wished we had that heat we let escape once we opened the windows to get some reprieve from the heat.

Back then, I didn't think we were poor. My parents never let me feel as though we were. We always had a roof over our heads, clothes on our backs, and food. Most of the vegetables were grown in the very large garden my parents planted every spring. You name it, we grew it. My mom cooked every night, and most times there were no leftovers. As many mouths as she had to feed, you can see why.

I am the oldest of our clan. Then comes Renee, Shauna, Dawn, Serena, and Phoenix, who was the spoiled baby of the bunch. I have to say we were all close. Unfortunately, about seventeen years ago Renee was killed. Her death was so devastating to our family. She was only sixteen and the one I was closest to growing up, since we were only a year apart. I miss her so much. There isn't a day that goes by that I don't think of her beautiful spirit.

We, as sisters, vowed on the day of her funeral to always remain close, no matter how hard it got at times. All we had was each other. To keep the closeness we even moved to the same city of Roanoke, Virginia. I was surprised by that. I thought Phoenix would be down in Atlanta, or somewhere trying to act in California. I'm still waiting on the day when she was going to break the news to us that she was moving away. You never know what to expect with the Johnson sisters.

Chapter 2

Phoenix

I was so excited about tonight. Two of my favorite things were about to come together as one: a party and sex. Now, I know what you're thinking. You think I was having some type of swinger party, but I was not. I was having a sex toy party. This was the first one I was hosting, but I had been to a few before. I think I was invited because most of my friends and some of my family members considered me to be one of the biggest freaks they knew, and they knew I would buy the products, which got them closer to getting as much free merchandise as possible. Now tonight was my turn to see how much free stuff I was going to get.

I looked at the table I positioned in my living room against the wall. It looked great covered with a black cotton tablecloth and red napkins.

I thought about breaking out my dishes, but I didn't want these heifers tearing up my stuff, so I opted to use red square plastic plates for them to eat off of. I picked up one of the plates and loved the look and feel of them. I purchased the plates online and thought they looked terrific. They were disposable, but these bad boys might be washed and saved to use for other occasions. I might as well get my money's worth.

I stood back and was happy with the way everything looked. A cheese, fruit, and veggie tray, along with finger sandwiches surrounded by a chocolate fountain raining down luscious goodness adorned the table. A few bottles of Moscato were also chilling on ice. This was just for starters.

I picked up a strawberry and held it under the drizzling chocolate and let it cover half of the fruit. Holding the berry over a napkin, not wanting to drip anything on my outfit, I brought it to my mouth and took a bite. Oh, my goodness, it was so good. I closed my eyes, savoring the flavor. Strawberries are my favorite fruit, and to combine that with this russet liquid almost made me have an orgasm.

I finished the fruit, walking away so I wouldn't stand there and eat the entire tray by myself. I had to leave some for the guests, who should be arriving in about thirty minutes. Thinking about that, I thought the girl showing the products tonight should have been here. I hoped she hadn't forgotten.

I went into my dining room and looked at the meal I'd had catered. I decided to go with filet mignon with bacon-wrapped asparagus and seasoned, grilled potatoes served with brioche. For dessert we were having mini cheesecake bites. You thought I was excited about the strawberries and chocolate? The several different arrays of cheesecake excited me the most. The flavors consisted of plain, key lime, amaretto, chocolate, marble, and strawberry cheesecake, of course. I know all of this sounds extravagant, but I liked to go all out like this when it came to any event I threw. I was a diva for real. Nothing but the best, depending on the crowd. And I know what you're thinking: filet mignon served on plastic plates is going all out? Hell yeah, for me it is. Again, I didn't like people who tore up my things. Just because I had it didn't mean I had to show it off all the time. I worked hard to get everything I had, even if I did get men to supply most of my needs.

I went to my bedroom and looked at myself one last time in the mirror. Damn, I looked good.

I snapped my fingers at myself as I twirled to make sure I looked good at all angles. "In the words of Kenya Moore, I'm *Gone with the Wind* fabulous," I said to myself, twirling.

With my long hair sophisticatedly curled and makeup done to perfection, I knew I looked hot. This was a casual event, but I couldn't help but put on my black-and-white form-fitting mini with one shoulder exposed and a cutout at the waist making it super sexy. Hell, I was sexy. I am five feet four inches, weighing 130 pounds, with measurements equaling 34-26-36, and yes, my butt is my main attraction. I'm talking about fastening your seat belt and enjoying the ride type of attraction. I am a walking rollercoaster of thrills and spills, if you get my drift. Being as beautiful as I am comes with a lot of advantages. One of them is the lifestyle I lead now.

I stood in the mirror thinking, *Damn, look how far I have come.*

I can remember when I was in high school, I was considered a rail. I was a stick figure. The boys used to hold up a pencil to me and compare me to it, laughing like it was so funny; but I didn't find a thing to laugh about. It hurt my feelings. Now those same boys were men who salivated over me. Most of them I dissed, but some I had to have just because I'd had a crush on them in high school.

One in particular scratched my itch on a regular. His name was Von. In school he was the quiet athlete who hung with the popular kids but still didn't want to be seen with the unpopular. Now he was an NFL football player with all the right moves. He still wasn't much of a talker, but that was fine with me, since all I wanted was his money and his dick, which both suited me very well.

The doorbell rang, snapping me out of admiring myself. I pulled my dress down a bit and went to the door, opening it. The consultant who would be showing us the products tonight was standing in front of me.

"I'm so sorry I'm late. I had a flat tire," she said, panting like she had run all the way here.

"Oh, you are fine. No one has arrived yet. Come on in," I said, watching as she pulled in two large suitcases.

"Good. I hate to be late. It takes me a little time to set this merchandise up."

"Do you have anything else to bring in?" I asked.

"I do, but I'll get it," she said.

"Okay. If you insist," I said, not really wanting to help her in the first place. I was trying to be nice.

She went back outside and proceeded to bring in a table for setting everything on and a briefcase, which held the order forms along with the pamphlets of products.

I picked up one and scanned through it, thinking I needed 85 percent of what she had in this booklet. New products came out so often that it made the old merchandise you previously purchased look prehistoric. These companies were on top of their game when it came to finding the many different ways to sexually please someone.

As she took each tool out of her suitcase piece by piece, I was getting eager. I looked at the clock to see that as usual, all these tricks were late. I'd said arrive at seven. I should have said six. That way they would have been on time.

It wasn't long before the representative had everything arranged on the tables. After she did that, she placed a folder in each space I had available, which consisted of my sofa, love seat, and twenty chairs I had in my spacious living room. Then she turned her attention to me.

"So, I'm ready."

"I am too. I don't know why my guests are late. Forgive them," I said.

"No problem. It actually worked in my favor today," she said, breathing a sigh of relief. "Now, you know the more you sell, the more free products you get. You get ten percent of total sales."

"I know, and I hope these women buy, buy, buy."

When I said that, the doorbell rang. The first to arrive was my oldest sister, Vivian, and middle sister, Serena.

"Hey, you guys," I said with glee, giving them both a hug as they walked in.

"Sorry we're late," Vivian said. "Multiple outfits here delayed us," she said, pointing at Serena.

"I didn't know what I wanted to wear. I still got this baby belly," she said, grabbing her gut.

"It's almost gone," I said, rubbing her almost flat stomach. She only had a little pudge, and I believed if she took a dump, it would go down.

"I still need to lose another fifteen pounds, and then I'm good," Serena said.

"That will make you smaller than you were before you got pregnant," I said.

"Exactly. I'll feel better about myself. Looking at you in that dress is not helping either. I thought this was a casual event. Where the hell do you think you are going?" Serena asked.

"Girl, this old thing?" I joked.

"Please, Phoenix. Every time I see you, you got something on I haven't seen you wear before. Where the hell are you getting the money to afford so many clothes?"

"Serena, don't worry about my finances," I said, giggling. "It's none of your business."

"Y'all make me sick," Vivian interrupted.

"Why?" I asked.

"Y'all know why. Look at me. I'm the plus-size sister."

"And you look good every time I see you, too, Vivian."

"You do look good, sis," Serena cosigned.

"I know, but y'all skinny bitches always find a way to make me feel bad standing here with your perfect shapes. Serena is talking about losing more weight. Any more weight loss and you are going to disappear on us."

"Whatever, Viv. I'm doing this for me. This kangaroo pouch ain't cutting it," Serena said, jiggling her belly.

"That ain't a kangaroo pouch. This is a kangaroo pouch," Vivian said, lifting her shirt to reveal the Spanx she had on pulling everything in. Vivian rolled the garment down and let her belly expand outward. Serena and I giggled. "You see. So can y'all shut up about weight?" Vivian said, pulling the Spanx back up and fixing her clothes.

"You did not have to go that far," I said.

"Yes, I did, so y'all could shut up," Vivian said.

"Okay, you guys. Enough about our bodies. Where is everybody?" Serena asked.

"You two are first to arrive," I said.

"We can see that," Vivian said.

"Wasn't this supposed to start at seven?" Serena asked, picking up an appetizer off the table and putting it in her mouth.

"Yep. You know how black folks are," I said.

"Don't put this on black people. Kimara is Puerto Rican. Mayumi is Japanese. Bella is Italian, and Hanna, Mackenzie, and Paige are white. You should say this is a woman thing, or mother thing, or even diva thing, but not a black thing," Vivian corrected, walking over to claim the space she wanted for the party. She sat down on the sofa.

"Well, I didn't mean to offend black women," I said jokingly, checking out what Vivian was wearing. Even though she was considered plus-size, she could dress her behind off. She looked good in her red skinny-leg jeans with black dolman top and black stilettos. You would think that red would make her look bigger, but it didn't. It flattered her body nicely. With Vivian's thickness, she carried it in her hips, butt, and breasts, so I didn't really see what the issue was.

"Is that an apology coming from Phoenix? Because I need to voice record this on my phone," Vivian said, pulling out her cell and typing something. "You never apologize about nothing, and that's as close to one as I've ever heard you come to."

"Shut up," I said, playfully hitting her.

"I'm just saying."

Serena went over and sat on the sofa next to Vivian, yawning, leaving a space to her left for someone else to sit.

"All right, sleepy head. We can't have that. You got to get ready to have some fun tonight," I said.

"Phoenix, I'm tired. Nevaeh still isn't sleeping through the night. I know I get up every two to three hours. But when the sun rises, that girl sleeps for hours. Why do babies do that?"

"I don't know, and I don't want to know," I said seriously. "I don't want kids. Hell, I don't really like them. All that crying and throwing up and changing Pampers and always needing someone to care for them. Naw. Y'all can have that, because I don't want it."

"You just don't want anybody stealing your spotlight," Vivian chimed in. "Selfish is what you are."

"True," I agreed with her.

"At least she owns it," Serena defended.

"All I know is this party better be good. I worked ten hours today, and it was taxing. A guy got fired today and lost his damn mind. Security had to come and get this fool. They literally dragged him off our floor and out the building.

He was screaming many threats of what he was going to do when he came back."

"When he came back?" Serena questioned. "I hope they called the police on his behind. Disgruntled employees go on shooting rampages all the time. I hope the company is taking his threats seriously."

"I hope so too. The only positive thing on my end was I tried to fight for him to keep his job. Hopefully he remembers that if he decides to come back and go crazy. Still, I hope human resources was smart enough to disarm his badge so he can't get back in the building, because he looks like the type who would come shoot up the place," Vivian said.

"I bet you he was white," I said.

Vivian sighed, saying, "There you go again with that race crap."

"Well, am I right?"

Vivian didn't say anything.

"See, I knew it. Only white people snap and want to shoot everybody and then turn around and shoot themselves. Why not just shoot yourself when you get home and eliminate all the tragedy?"

"You know what? I'm done with this conversation. I'm going to the bathroom before you find something else crazy to say," Vivian said, getting up and leaving the room.

***

It was around eight when most of my guests arrived, including my other sisters, Shauna and Dawn. Shauna was feeling good when she walked through the door. Probably that joint and beer she had in the place of bacon and eggs with some orange juice this morning. I wished she would calm down on her drinking and smoking, but I had to say she was fun to be around when she was tipsy. When that heifer was sober, she was hell to be around.

The only people who hadn't arrived were my best friends, Kimara and Mayumi. I texted them and they said they were pulling up. As soon as they arrived, my posse was complete and it was time to have fun.

It was good to see everybody mingling with each other. Drinks were being poured and appetizers were being eaten. Everybody knew each other already, which made things easier. The only two who might've had an issue with one another were my sister Dawn and my guest Paige. I could see the two of them giving each other the evil eye every now and then. They had a history and it wasn't a good one. I hoped this evening would go on without any hiccups.

"Ladies, have a seat. It's time to get started," I said as the women shuffled to their seats. "I want to first thank y'all for coming to my sex toy party, even though all y'all bitches was late."

The ladies laughed along with whooping and hollering with excitement.

"I'm going to introduce you to the woman of the evening. This is Ashley, and she is our consultant and educator for the next hour, so pay attention, get involved, and let your inner freak be your guide to purchase some sex goodies," I said, clapping and giving Ashley the floor. I sat next to Serena on my sofa.

"Hi, ladies," Ashley said and everyone greeted her back. "It's so good to see so many of you. I'm excited to be here tonight. I can't wait to show you all my merchandise. I made sure to place a folder in each of your seats. The folder contains a booklet, an order form, my business card for future parties, and also a sheet on how I did my showing. On that sheet, it also has a box to check yes or no if you would consider being a consultant like me. The job is very fun. I get to travel, make good money, and make women happy all while selling them products that bring them joy.

"I have a few items with me—not all, because we would be here all night. If you see something you like, put a checkmark beside it. If you decide to make a purchase, some of the merchandise can be taken home tonight, but it is first come, first served. I have a limited amount. The rest of your orders should be back in a week. Most of the things I'm going to show you are our bestsellers, so sit back, enjoy, and please know no question is wrong to ask."

Chapter 3

Phoenix

Ashley started out by showing us creams and lotions. Some were used for moisturizing and massaging, and some were used for licking. We tasted nipple drops and warming oils that tasted like candy. There was chocolate for the body, and primer to suck off the man's penis. There was not a woman in there who didn't get her savor on. I have to say I thoroughly enjoyed the tasting too. I could have sucked down a bottle of that apple-flavored warming oil. It tasted like a Jolly Rancher.

Ashley proceeded to show us a bottle of spray to numb the back of your throat for oral sex. She introduced this product along with giving each of us a flavored condom. Along with the condom, I stood to hand out bananas.

"What are we supposed to do with this?" Dawn asked.

For somebody who thought they knew everything, my sister was sitting here acting like she didn't know a damn thing. Common sense should come into play sometimes. If you are holding a condom and a damn banana, what do you think you are supposed to do with it? But maybe I shouldn't think that way. Maybe she's never used a condom before. Yeah, that's it.

"You supposed to take the condom you have and roll it down the banana."

"Oh, I can do that," Dawn said.

"But the catch is you have to use your mouth to put it on, and then you have to suck it," I explained.

"I'll be damned," Dawn said, causing everybody to laugh. "I'm going to put this condom on with my hands."

"That's fine too," Ashley said.

"If y'all would like to see if the spray works, try it," I said, squirting the elixir into my mouth. "Who in here likes giving head?"

"You," most of the women said, causing laughter to permeate the room.

"Like I'm the only one. Please. All y'all give head, so don't play innocent," I countered.

"I don't," Serena said, smiling devilishly, knowing damn well she was lying. She and Tyree had been together for a minute, and I knew that man looked like he wouldn't have stayed with Serena if she weren't giving him some head. My sister must have been thinking the same thing, because she called Serena out on her bull.

"That's a damn lie. You don't have that baby for nothing," Vivian joked.

"That's right. All of y'all are freaks to the tenth power. I know this because none of you ladies would be here if you didn't have some inner slut buried inside you," I joked.

"And you are the biggest slut of us all," my sister Shauna said, sipping on her glass of wine.

It was funny watching these women take these bananas into their mouths like it was their man. I was no exception. I joined in with them. Why perpetrate? I gave head and, honestly, I liked it. Throwing a flavored condom in only made the act tastier.

I looked over at my good friend Paige taking the entire banana down her throat. I mean, she made it disappear. She only had the tip of the banana's stem showing, and these weren't tiny bananas. I purposely picked the longest ones I could find, just so I could see how much these tricks could take.

Paige held her hands out by her side like she had performed the circus act of swallowing a sword instead of a banana. I was astonished.

Homegirl didn't even bother to use the spray to eliminate the gag reflex. She wasn't choking. There weren't tears running down her face. She looked totally unfazed. Then Paige reached in and pulled the banana from her throat with no problem. There wasn't one blemish to the banana. None of her teeth had clipped it, and it didn't break during its journey down her throat.

"Damn, girl. Remind me to keep you away from my man," one of my guests said.

"I know, right? They do say white girls give the best head," another said. Paige didn't mind the joke. She knew it just like we did. She just made it factual by her demonstration.

I saw Dawn watching her and knew she was getting heated. How ironic it was for Dawn to watch this woman down this banana like a damn champ, knowing this same woman slept with her man and probably did this exact thing to his dick. Talk about adding insult to injury. After seeing what Paige did, I would be intimidated too. If swallowing that banana was any sign of how good she could suck a dick, Dawn's man still might be seeing her. I knew if I was a man, I would be.

After the room calmed down from the banana tricks, Ashley went on to show us some sexual position books and massage books. She passed them around for us to get a better idea of what the books entailed.

"I think I have done all these positions," Kimara said, taking a sip of her wine.

Scanning through the book, Vivian said, "If you did all of these positions, then you are truly the master at this craft, because I don't see some of these positions as humanly possible. Who thinks of this stuff?"

"Like we aren't already performing acrobatic moves in the bedrooms," Shauna said, looking in another book alongside Dawn. "Spin around on the dick. Put your legs behind your head and finger your ass. Now finger my ass. Lick your nipple while you squeeze my butt at the same time. Do a handstand while I eat you out. Twist your head this way so you can touch your toes with your tongue. And my favorite, can you Luke dance on my face?" Shauna joked.

Everybody burst into laughter. Tears were streaming down many faces as they laughed at the truth. Men did think we were gymnasts.

"You crazy, girl," I said, dabbing at the tears so as not to mess up my makeup.

"No, these men are crazy. If we could suck them, fuck them, and fix a sandwich at the same time while watching a ballgame, men would think we were goddesses, or should I say magicians," Shauna kidded. "How about they reach down and suck their own dicks? Show me that so I can be amazed for once," she said.

"You know they had a man from Africa whose dick was so long he could do that," Kimara said.

"I heard about him. They said his dick went to his knees," Bella agreed.

"See. They trying to outdo us again," Shauna said. "They are sucking their own dicks now. We have to perform our due diligence before all men figure out it's best to do one another," she said.

Everyone laughed at my crazy sister. One thing about the Johnson women, we damn sure speak our minds. Shauna and I are the two who are so much alike when it comes to our mouths. I am the diva version of Shauna, where she comes off more hood. I have to also admit she is as pretty and shapely as me. Out of all my sisters, we look the most alike. Sometimes people think we are twins, which makes me mad sometimes, since Shauna is four years older than me. Either they think I am old as hell, or she looks young. I'm going with Shauna looking young.

The party that was supposed to last one hour turned into two hours. Everybody had something to say about most of the merchandise and was having a ball. Where the excitement hit the fan was when we got into the toys. I have to say I could hardly contain my anticipation either.

"This is the bullet," Ashley said, holding up the rubber-covered bullet, which was black and had a remote control hooked to it for speeds specific to your pleasure.

"I've heard of this thing, and if it does what I heard it do, I want you to ring me up now," Bella said.

"It does work, girl. I have one, and it's the best investment ever," Kimara said. "I haven't hit high yet. I'm scared if I do, I'm going to blast off into orbit."

Everybody chuckled. Several "I'm getting that's" rang out, and all I could do was think about all the free merchandise I was going to be getting for myself.

"Do you have something like this that will benefit both the man and woman at the same time?" Mayumi asked.

"We sure do," Ashley said, turning to her table and picking up two toys. "This toy here is like a condom with benefits. You slide this down on your man's member."

"What's that big thing on the tip, where the man's head is?" someone asked.

"These little fringes are meant to massage and tantalize your insides when he goes in and out of you," Ashley explained. "This is the least expensive of our partnering toys."

"Will that thing come off, though?" my sister Serena asked.

"I'm pretty sure it will if the man has a little dick," Kimara said. "Ain't nothing worse than getting a condom stuck up in you."

Laughter erupted again.

"Most times it stays on, but there's always a chance it can come off," Ashley said. "I am going to show you another partnering toy. This one is our highest in price, but also one of our top sellers."

"Are those bunny ears?" Vivian asked.

"Yes. This is like a cock ring, which goes around the base of the man's member. The bullet comes with it and vibrates the both of you. The ears are meant to tickle your happy spot, and this part vibrates his ball region," Ashley explained.

"To get the best bang for your buck, ladies, you need to ride him. Get on top and ride until you can't ride no more. I have that, too," Kimara said.

"You're just filled with spiciness, aren't you, Kimara? Is there anything you don't have?" Vivian asked.

"I'd rather not go into my repertoire of freak-nasty toys," she joked, causing more giggles.

Finally we were getting to the nitty-gritty of the toys— the vibrators. Ashley picked up this chocolate dildo that looked so much like a black man's dick I had to wonder if she was into black men. From the way she was holding that seven-inch dildo, homegirl looked like she was. Regardless, I was in heaven.

"This is the part I've been waiting for," someone said.

"Me too. I need something that's going to satisfy me when a man ain't around," another said.

"Well, ladies, if I don't have it here, then shame on our company, because we usually have the best of the best," Ashley said. "Our rotating vibrators seem to be the bestsellers. With any of these, you can't go wrong. But in our traditional, this seven-inch is very popular," Ashley said, holding up the chocolate brown vibrator.

"Y'all skimping on some inches when it comes to this one, aren't you?" Shauna asked. "I've seen some chocolate ones at least nine inches or more."

"Me too," I concurred.

"Most women might not want something so big up in them," Dawn said, and the room erupted into mayhem. Most of the women were disagreeing with Dawn. I thought they were about to jump her.

"Girl, the bigger the dick, the better," I said.

"Hell, pain is pleasure," Shauna said, taking another sip of her wine.

"There's not a woman I know who wants a little-dick man. We need something to fill us up," Paige said. I had to wonder if this was said for vindictiveness. Regardless, Dawn didn't take her remark too well.

"We know how you like to get filled up. It's with dicks that already have girlfriends," Dawn said angrily.

"Well, if the dick was satisfied at home, then the dick wouldn't have to fill me up in the first place," Paige retorted, flicking her long, golden hair over her shoulders, causing a hush to go over the room.

Even though Paige is white, she's no pushover. A lot of black women think they can jump at a white woman and expect to win, but in this case, they might catch a beat down. Paige is a beast when it comes to fighting. She had to learn how to defend herself because she was always getting jumped on by somebody who hated the fact that she dated black men. Black women despised her. I saw it as more of a jealousy thing, and they had every right to be jealous due to Paige's beauty. It doesn't help that she also has nice boobs, a big behind, and long, blond hair that makes her blue eyes pop. She is my version of an urban Barbie. Paige doesn't care who she sleeps with.

Dick is dick to her, regardless of where it had to go once it was done pleasing her. Too bad one of those dicks happened to be engaged to my sister.

"I punched you in your face one time, trick," Dawn said, standing to her feet. "I don't have a problem doing it again."

Also standing, Paige snapped back with, "It was a sucker punch, and your ass got punched right the hell back, didn't you? As I recall it, I punched you multiple times. I'm not scared of you, Dawn. Bring your ass over here if you want to; you will catch a beat down identical to the one I gave you before."

"Ladies, calm down. You are not doing this here, and definitely not in my house," I said, getting up and standing between the two of them.

"I don't know why you invited her in the first place," Dawn said with an attitude.

"Because I'm her friend, that's why," Paige yelled.

"Y'all sit down and be quiet. Ashley doesn't need to see this side of us, okay? Let her finish her showing so we can place our orders, eat, and go home," I said with a raised voice so they knew I meant business.

Paige sat back down with the help of Kimara. Vivian pulled Dawn back over to her seat. Even though neither wanted to back down, they kept their cool. It still didn't stop either of them from giving each other evil glares. That was fine, as long as they didn't tear up my place.

Serena changed the tension in the room by asking, "Do you have something for men? You know, something they can stick their dicks in besides us."

"Yes," Ashley said, giggling as she turned to the table and picked up this ivory concoction. "This is a masturbation sleeve, but I would like to call it a pocket coochie. It resembles the lips of the woman. He would be amazed at how real it feels. It should be used with our lubricant, of course, for easy penetration. I'm going to squeeze some lube inside and pass this around for each of you to stick your finger inside to see how realistic it feels. And the lube is warmed for more appeal."

"This toy hasn't been used, has it?" Shauna asked, frowning up her face.

"All of my products are not used," Ashley said with a smile.

"Some of us might not know what it's supposed to feel like, because we've never stuck our fingers inside ourselves," a guest said. All heads turned to her in shock.

"You haven't fingered yourself?" Shauna asked bluntly.

"No," my guest said.

"I have heard it all," Vivian said. "One doesn't like big dicks, and now we have one who doesn't know what her own coochie feels like. I'm done," my sis said, throwing her hands up.

"Imagine this would be how you feel," Ashley urged. "If you don't want to do it, then you don't have to."

Each woman, including my guest who said she never felt herself, slid her finger inside the sleeve, frowning her face in disgust.

"Damn, this feels real. I'm sold," Serena said. "I might get two, in case Tyree wears one out."

Everybody laughed.

Vivian looked at Kimara and asked, "Does your man have this?"

"Of course he does. Once I slid that thing up and down his dick, that fool went crazy. And to enhance his pleasure, I stuck the bullet in the other end of it to make it vibrate his head when he went deep into it," Kimara explained.

"You know, you would be a great consultant," Ashley suggested.

"Damn right she would. She's a walking billboard on these products," Vivian agreed.

The last product Ashley ended up talking about was the swing, and of course it was brought up by freak-nasty herself, Kimara.

"Yes, we do have the swing, but I don't carry it with me due to the fact that I can't assemble it in someone's home. Once it's up, it's up. But, I do have the box, which has a picture of it and the different positions that can be done with it," Ashley said.

Ashley passed the box around the room, and most of the women didn't want to let the box go. They were impressed with the many positions that were possible.

Once Kimara got the box, she asked Ashley, "So, have you tried it?"

"I haven't, but I have associates who have, and they loved it," Ashley said, giggling.

"Forget swinging from the chandelier. We need this," Shauna said.

"How much is it?" a guest asked.

"It's two hundred dollars," Ashley answered.

"Damn. That's a lot of money to figure out what else we can do when it comes to sex," Vivian said.

"This coming from the one who would like to put a stripper pole in her house," I said.

"Okay, you got me," Vivian said. "Great point. Maybe I should invest in one of these bad boys, too."

"First you got to get a man," I joked.

"Who says I don't have one?" Vivian countered.

This got me to thinking. Did Vivian have a man we didn't know about? She was private like that.

Finally it was the end of Ashley's showing. Now it was time for her to go into a separate room to take us one by one to place our orders. This way no one knew what the other ordered. Privacy first and foremost, but most of them told what they were buying, especially my friend Kimara.

"I need some nipple drops and some more of that edible oil that heats up when you put it on your skin. I need another pocket coochie. I want some anal beads, and some of that lubricant for the anus. And I'm getting that fishnet garter set. I've wanted that thing for a minute. And you know what? I think I'm going to get that swing, too. That position with her in the swing and the man eating her out . . . hell, I'm getting the swing for that position alone. He can do the front and twirl me around and lick the back," Kimara said.

"You are so nasty. You let a man lick your anal region?" Dawn asked her.

"Damn right. I'd rather have that licked than my poon poon. You never had that done before?" Kimara asked.

"Hell no," Dawn blurted.

"Girl, you don't know what you missing. It's a different type of climax. It tickles at first, but once you get used to it, it's amazing."

I told the ladies to help themselves to the food I had catered. While they were getting their eat on, I was going to go pick out what merchandise I wanted. I went back last, because Ashley had to total up the amount of sales in order to figure out what my percentage of free merchandise would come to.

"So, how did we do?" I asked Ashley with enthusiasm.

"We did very well. The total came to $3,378," Ashley said, and I almost fell to the floor.

"Wow. I knew my friends and family were freaks, but not this freaky," I said happily.

"So you get to order $377 worth of merchandise for free."

There was nothing better than hearing the word "free" come out of her mouth. That's how I liked my life: receiving things that didn't cost me nothing but some fun and a nice reward in the end.

"You can give me your first item, and we can write up your order," Ashley said.

I made sure to start with the bullet.

Chapter 4

Vivian

I had to admit tonight was a lot of fun. I was glad Phoenix talked me into attending because I told her I wasn't coming at first. I didn't feel like being around a bunch of people, particularly my sisters. I loved each and every one of them, but I couldn't seem to get away from them. We would be together every day if we could, but I didn't. Our once a week dinner get-together was starting to get a bit much for me. I don't know why I was feeling this way, since after the death of Renee we promised each other we would at least be with each other once each week, even if it was to have coffee together.

After ordering my merchandise, I quickly left the party. Phoenix didn't want me to leave, but she didn't push it too much since I did show up. Since Serena rode there with me, she had to leave when I did, and she wasn't ready. She ended up asking Dawn to give her a ride home. Dawn didn't want to, but gave in, telling her she would. I was tired and was ready to get in my bed, the faster the better, so I said my good-byes to everybody and jetted home.

I don't know if I kicked off my shoes first to relieve my feet, or unsnapped my bra to take that restraint off. All I know is I wanted to get into a comfortable state. It didn't matter, because once those items came off, I was free. My Spanx was my next constriction to be removed before taking my shower. My bed was calling me, and I was answering it by saying, "I'll be right there."

No sooner than I put my legs under the cover and turned the television on, my doorbell rang. It could only be one person, and I wondered why he didn't use the key I gave him.

"What the hell do you think you are doing?" were the first words that fell out of my mouth as I looked into the face of my ex-boyfriend, Eric, standing on the other side of my door. I had thought it was my best friend, Sheldon, but I was wrong this night.

With his manhood hanging out, Eric had each hand propped up on the base of the door, with this smirk on this face, trying to lick his lips like LL. He looked down at his growing extension and looked back up at me.

"You are going to get arrested for indecent exposure," I said, giggling.

"Then you better let me in before I get in trouble."

I crossed my arms, asking, "What do you want?"

"It's not obvious?" he asked cockily, looking down at his manhood still hanging to the left.

"And what makes you think I want you or your dick?"

He looked down at his pride and joy and said, "Oh, you want this. I bet your thighs are wet with envy now."

I didn't say anything. I looked down at his manhood, which was beginning to become erect. I didn't get sex often because I didn't believe in sleeping around, but tonight I needed to get my coochie worked. After that sex party showed me all the different things that could be used to enhance my sex life, I was raring to go. And I didn't want to use a vibrator, even though I had just purchased a new one to use on myself tonight. Now I had the real deal and could use a hot, throbbing dick inside me.

I stepped to the side, giving Eric the signal to come in. He walked past me, and I shut the door. When I turned around, Eric was stroking his manhood like he was priming it for me. I didn't feel like doing much talking, so I jumped right on him. I don't know how we managed it, but in a matter of minutes we were in my bedroom, butt-ass naked.

Eric was hitting me from the back like he hadn't had pussy in quite a while. He gripped my hips, pulling my substantial buttocks into his adequate plumpness. I didn't know why I allowed myself to get screwed by this man since he dumped me months ago for being too fat. It wasn't like I had lost much weight. I wasn't skinny enough to be on his arm, yet my pussy was good enough for him to dip his manhood inside me. Damn hypocrite. And yes, I must be a hypocrite too. I didn't have to allow myself to be used like this.

I thought about this after I climaxed, which didn't take long, since Eric knew my body and how to please it. I'd climaxed three times already, while he kept trying to reach his pinnacle. After six months of batteries buzzing between my thighs, I needed to nut from the real thing. But now that I had, I didn't think it was even worth it. I actually pitied myself.

As Eric pounded and grunted, I tried to hold back tears for a minute. He might have thought he was bringing water to my eyes because he was that good, but feeling unworthy was the reason for my sorrow. Where in the hell was my self-esteem right now? As soon as I saw this man on my stoop, I should have slammed the door in his face and told him to never bother me again, but here I was playing booty call and being used yet again by a man who didn't respect me.

I dropped my head into the sheets as I went on an emotional rollercoaster. One minute I was confident and the next I hated myself. I let the tears soak deep into the fabric of my sheets as Eric continued to pound, probably thinking he was doing me a favor.

"You like that, baby?" he asked.

I didn't respond. How could I when I felt the way I did? His pounding increased like he was trying to get a reaction out of me. I pulled my head up from the sheets and frowned a bit, and he took this as me enjoying it.

"Oh, you like it, don't you. I can tell."

I couldn't take it anymore. I turned, pushing Eric off of me.

"You want it a different way?" he asked. "You want to get on top," he said, positioning himself on his back like I was going to climb on top of him. Eric was fine as hell and his body was worthy of the ride, but I couldn't bring myself to continue.

"No. I want you to leave," I told him, pulling the crinkled sheet around my body.

"Leave?" he asked, surprised, as his manhood glistened with my juices.

"Yes, leave," I said, getting up from the bed and putting on my pink silk robe.

"What the hell is wrong with you? Do you see this dick? I haven't cum yet," he replied, pointing to his extension.

"And you won't with me," I said, tying my robe closed.

"Come on, Vivian."

"You can beg all you want to, Eric, but I'm not finishing this."

He climbed from the bed angrily. He snatched his boxers off the floor and attempted to put them on, losing his balance and falling to the floor. I smirked a bit. He didn't find this funny as he got up from the floor.

"I can't believe you. You asked me to come over."

I frowned as I shook my head in disbelief before replying to his statement. "Don't get it twisted, Eric. You were standing on my stoop. Don't try to make it look like I begged your ass to come over, because I didn't. You were the one who just showed up unannounced," I said, pulling my long hair back in a ponytail.

"You knew what it was going to be when you saw me standing outside your door," he argued.

"I did, and I got mine, so we are done."

Eric picked up his blue jeans and shirt from my maple hardwood floors. Each movement was done with irritation.

"I knew it was a mistake messing with you, but I was doing you a favor," he said.

"Me!"

"Yes, you. I mean, look at you. Who wants to sleep with somebody who looks like you?" he said rudely, scowling at me.

"You, that's who! How many times have you begged to get all up in this?" I retorted, pointing between my legs. "I know this is good for you to keep coming back for more," I fired back.

"Please. I didn't have another honey to get with tonight, so I decided to slum with you," he dissed.

"This coming from the man who is the biggest whore around. You sleeping with sluts was the demise of our relationship, but I'm the one slumming. If I am, it's because I'm dealing with your trifling ass."

"Your weight was the reason I went out and got other pussy. I got tired of you squishing me when you got on top," Eric said.

"As hard as you're trying to make this out to be about my weight, I know it's about you being a damn dog. I let you mentally abuse me for months, but now I know better," I lied. His words did cut me to the core, but I wouldn't let him get the satisfaction of knowing it. I told him, "You miss me."

"Like hell I do."

"Then why be mad at all? If I were nothing to you, then you wouldn't be mad. You could leave here and get a nut elsewhere."

"And I am," he said, sitting on the side of my bed after searching on his hands and knees for his shoes. He looked up at me.

I knew I touched a nerve. Little did he know he had touched several in me months ago, making me second- guess the person I thought I was; and here he was trying to do it to me again.

"You know what, Eric? This is the last time I submit myself to you. As much as I loved you, having you come in and out of my life isn't worth it, so hurry up, get your shit, and get the hell out my damn house." I pointed to my bedroom door.

He stood, straightening his jeans. He reached down in his pockets and felt for his keys, but they weren't there. He patted both front and back pockets, and still there were no keys. I pointed at my dresser where they sat. He glared at me before walking over and snatching them off.

"Good luck with your weight," he snarled.

"And good luck with your blue balls," I retorted, watching Eric walk out of my life again.

The confidence I tried to maintain while he was there instantly diminished like someone letting air out of a balloon. His words had deflated me yet again.

Yes, I'm what you would call voluptuous, or at least that's what I call myself instead of fat, obese, or just plain huge. Voluptuous sounds so much better, and I see that word as sexy. I'm that, too. I feel that most days, and today was one of them. Skinny skanks might not think so, but that's okay. They ain't supposed to think it, because I don't like holes. I like my poles. They're jealous of me anyway. They wouldn't worry about me if they didn't see me as a threat. I may be five feet five inches, 223 pounds, but I carry it very well. A hundred pounds of that weight is in my breasts, thighs, and behind. My stomach isn't as flat as I would like, but a few sit-ups would help that.

For the most part of my life, I considered myself to be a confident woman. I didn't care what people thought of me. I was skinny, about fifteen years ago, weighing 124 pounds; and no, I'm not carrying baby weight. This is the weight of life's stress, which ended up being diagnosed as depression. Food became my peace, and that peace accumulated onto my body.

It has taken me a long while to accept I have depression. I thought any medication being taken for something mental made you crazy, especially in my family. They drown their issues in food, alcohol, weed, and sex. I have members in my family whose medicine are all four of those things. Yet, when I say I take medication for depression, they look at me like I'm getting ready to pull out a gun and go postal.

Actually, that is a plus for real. The more they think I am crazy, the more they know not to mess with me. Still, I don't want to be the one they think should be admitted into a rubber room. I'm not crazy. Life made me this way, and I have to wonder at what point things changed for me. I used to be my biggest cheerleader. Now, I am all cheered out. I needed to find that spirit to celebrate myself, but after Eric's visit, I would find it more difficult to look at myself as valuable at all.

Chapter 5

Phoenix

My house was finally empty, except for a few stragglers. I had put up everything that wasn't toted up out my house from the dinner. These hungry heifers made sure to take plates, but I couldn't blame them, because I did have an amazing spread. With her attitude still evident, Dawn questioned me on where I was getting my money to be able to afford all this food.

"None-yah," I told her. First it was Serena, and now her.

"Filet mignon. Cheesecake bites. What you do, rob an upscale restaurant?" Dawn asked.

"No, I paid for it with my money," I stressed, cutting off the chocolate fountain and toting it to my kitchen with Dawn following me.

"You can't have money and no job, Phoenix," Dawn said.

"Again, you're all up in my business. Go home to your man. Use some of those products you purchased on him," I urged, hoping she would leave me alone. For a split second, I almost called Paige to come into the kitchen, knowing this would irritate the hell out of Dawn and shut her conversation down. As fate would have it, Paige showed up like a champ without me having to call her.

"Girl, you need some help?" she asked, looking at Dawn and rolling her eyes. Here she was, asking to help me when my very own sister didn't offer to lift a finger. All she was interested in was where my money was coming from. I couldn't lie; I was happy to see Paige, and the look of disgust on Dawn's face was enough to make me smirk a little bit. She was busy worried about my money. She needed to be worried about where her future husband was laying his pipe.

"You can if you want. I'm not going to turn it down," I said, looking at Dawn, who seemed noticeably pissed.

"I'll help some, but I have to get home and get me a piece. This poon poon ain't had a dick in me in a week," Paige boasted.

"Who's your conquest tonight?" I asked, not thinking as I poured the chocolate out of the fountain into a large container.

"I can't say," she said sarcastically.

"You see. That's the shit I'm talking about," Dawn blurted, pointing her finger at Paige.

"You talking to me?" Paige asked, putting her hand on her chest.

"Yeah, I'm talking to you. You've been saying slick shit all night."

"Girl, this is a fight you don't want," Paige warned.

"Oh, really?" Dawn asked.

"Really! Why you mad?" Paige asked.

"I'm mad because you a whore," Dawn said, walking closer to Paige.

"If you keep stepping to me like you want some, I'm going to give it to you again," Paige cautioned.

I thought my sister would heed the warning, but I guess the bad blood between them two was worse than I imagined.

"Bitch, I will whoop your. . ." Dawn said, not finishing her sentence as she went over to Paige and swung on her. Paige retaliated by punching her back, and before I could get to them good, they were fighting. I dropped the fountain, spilling some of the chocolate all over my counter. Trying to break them up, I ended up between them. Paige was reaching over me and punching Dawn in the back of the head as she held a handful of her long hair.

"Let her go, Paige," I yelled.

"Bitch, I told you not to mess with me," Paige screamed, steady landing punches to my sister's head.

Shauna and Serena ran into the kitchen and grabbed Paige, who wouldn't let go of Dawn's hair. I turned and grabbed Paige's hand to pry her fingers from my sister's hair. One by one I struggled to lift her fingers as she jerked with all her might to rip Dawn's hair from her skull. Once her grip was released, Dawn stood pushing her hair away from her face. I jumped in front of Dawn, pushing her away from Paige, because she looked like she was going to go in for some more.

"Stop it," Shauna yelled.

"She shouldn't have put her hands on me," Paige said, panting.

"And you shouldn't have slept with my man," Dawn shrieked.

"Check your man, not me. If you had any type of common sense you would see that, but nooooo, you want to play dumb wifey, thinking you can punk me. But you wrong, trick. Your ass got played. Jump again and I will whoop that ass again," Paige threatened.

Dawn breathed heavily as she defiantly scowled at Paige with so much rage. My sister knew Paige was right, but she would never admit it. Corey was the one who needed to be checked for real. Paige wasn't the only woman he had slept with during their relationship together. Her man was a dog, and I knew he would sleep around on her again. Why wouldn't he? Dawn always took him back. You teach a man how to treat you, and Corey knew he could treat Dawn like crap and she would be dumb enough to deal with it.

"I'm leaving," Dawn said, pulling her mangled hair back in a ponytail. "Come on, Shauna and Serena," she yelled.

Both my sisters looked at me. Shauna shook her head.

"She's yelling at me like I slept with her man. I don't want him," Serena quipped.

"I'm getting pissed off now. They done made me lose my buzz," Shauna said, walking out of the kitchen behind Dawn with Serena following her.

I couldn't help but laugh at them.

"I'm sorry, Phoenix. I didn't mean to be fighting up in your house like this, but you know me. I don't care where I am; if someone wants to check me, then we going to handle the damn thing wherever," Paige said, fixing her clothes, which were hardly messed up since she was in control of the fight.

"I understand. And I'm sorry for my sister's behavior."

"You can't help who your blood is. I'm glad you are not like her. Talk about total opposites," Paige said. She ain't never lied.

Dawn was somewhat quiet, so to see her get bold and jump knowing she couldn't fight, from what I could see, was another side of her I hadn't seen before. It was almost like she was homie.

She isn't into clothes like me or trying to look her best at all times. For goodness' sake, she came over here in a jogging suit tonight. Don't get me wrong; a jogging suit is great for leisure around the house or running to the store or gym type thing, but not for gatherings. If she was going to wear a jogging suit, she could have at least put on a cute one. The one she was wearing was too oversized for her body and didn't hug her nice body at all, and it was an ugly pea green color that made me think of throwup for some reason.

As gloomy as she looked, I was waiting for her to pull that hood over her head and call it a night. She should fix herself up sometimes. She used to dress. I didn't know what had happened. Well, I did know. Corey happened. Ever since she'd been with him, Dawn had lost her own identity. She had been too busy playing private eye investigating what the hell Corey was doing.

I used to feel sorry for her, but now I didn't. You make your bed, you lie in it, and she was lying beside a cheating dog. She was way too pretty for him. She could get any man she wanted, yet she chose this punk.

There was no excuse why Dawn should settle for the life she had. Dawn has a shape with just a tad bit more weight than me, but it is in the right places. Her skin tone is like mine, caramel but lighter. She has the best hair out of all of us, taking it from our great-grandmother. It is long and silky.

I love my sister dearly, but we don't get along that well. We tolerate each other because we're siblings. I always wished our relationship would get better, but as long as she was in denial about herself and her relationship, our relationship would remain like it was: tolerable. I knew after this episode with Paige, any type of rapport we had may be severed, just for the simple fact I was friends with the enemy.

Chapter 6

Dawn

Two things went wrong tonight. One was going to the sex party at all, and two was the fact that I trusted my sister, who knew my situation but still was selfish enough to invite the enemy. How shocked was I to see my nemesis, Paige, already there laughing with the woman next to her? My blood instantly began to boil.

How could Phoenix do me like this? She should have known only one of us should be there, and that one should've been me. When I found my seat with a tipsy Shauna behind me, Vivian spoke, giving me the look like, "Are you okay?" I stretched my eyes, letting her know I wasn't. My night went from sugar to shit real quick. I'm not sure everyone in the room knew the beef Paige and I had, but I didn't like being there with the ones who did know. Some women were giving me the eye, looking back and forth between me and Paige. I almost told them, "Either say something or get out my face."

Then when Paige and I made eye contact, she gave me this smirk like, "Yeah, I slept with your man. What are you going to do about it?" I wanted to run across that room and snatch that blond hair out of her head. I glanced over at Vivian, who sensed my anger. She held her hand out flat and lowered it to let me know to calm down. That was easier said than done.

That lady showing us toys reminded me of the sex Paige had with my man. Oh, and the damn banana down the throat thing was icing on top of an already rotten cake. Paige made sure to demonstrate in great detail how to force a banana down her throat. I wished she would have choked on it.

The entire night my irritation was building, until I lost it on Paige. I would do it again if she thought every time I saw her she could drop little innuendos about my man. I was surprised Phoenix intervened, but the worst part of the whole situation was my sister seemed to be on Paige's side and not mine.

Still steaming at the altercation between me and Paige, I roared into the garage of my two-story colonial, hitting the button to let the garage doors down. I sat in my car for a minute trying to gather myself. The harder I tried to calm down, the angrier I got. Picking up my purse from the passenger seat, I got out and stormed into the house, slamming the door closed.

Corey walked into the kitchen as I was taking off the jacket to my jogging suit. "How was the party?" he asked.

I thought that was stupid, because Corey should have recognized I was distraught. The slamming of the door should have clued him in along with the frown lines in my forehead. I guessed he was too busy trying to be cute dressed in black slacks and a black striped collared shirt.

"The party was terrible," I belted.

"Why? I thought all sex toy parties were supposed to be exciting," Corey said.

"It was humiliating, especially since my sister decided to invite Paige."

The smile on Corey's face dissipated. He asked, "She was there?"

"Hell yeah, and it felt like that bitch was taunting me all evening."

"What did she say to you?"

"What didn't she say? All night she kept saying things and doing things that were pissing me off, Corey. I knew she was doing this on purpose. Finally I confronted her, and from then we started fighting."

"Fighting. Dawn, you too old to be doing that."

"I was tired of her. I lost it."

Corey walked up to me and hugged me, saying, "Well, try to forget about her. We have plans. Let's go out and have some fun, just me and you."

"I don't know if I feel like going anywhere," I said, trying to push myself back out of his arms.

"But you said we were going. Are you telling me you don't want to do this now?" Corey asked.

I wanted to say yes, but I knew the reason why I didn't want to go was because Paige and Phoenix messed up my evening. All I wanted to do was crawl up on my couch and relax. I'd had enough excitement for the night, and I really wasn't in the mood to do anything else. As much as I didn't want to get dressed to go out, I had to. Me and my husband-to-be had been planning this for over two weeks now, and I couldn't allow the madness that happened earlier to interfere with a wonderful evening with Corey.

"Give me a few minutes and I will be ready," I told Corey, whose smile returned.

He kissed me on the lips and said, "Hurry up," smacking me on my butt as I walked past him.

After showering, I put on a sexy black strapless dress and my five-inch black heels. When I went to brush my hair, I got upset again when pieces of my hair came out in clumps from Paige jerking on it earlier. I pulled the clumps of hair out of the brush and took in a deep breath, trying to calm myself. I was not going to let that trick mess up my night. I brushed my hair down, letting it sweep my shoulders, and tucked my hair behind my ears. Despite the hair she succeeded in pulling from my scalp, I still had plenty. I was ready to go.

When I walked into the living area, I saw Corey had put on the jacket to the black slacks he was wearing. He was standing at the door looking at his watch. When he saw me, his smile returned to his lips.

"Honey, you look good enough to eat," he said, walking over to me and embracing me. He nibbled on my neck.

I had to smile at my fiancé. As many issues as we had in the past, I knew I was the woman he wanted to be with. "Maybe you can do that later," I teased.

"Maybe I will," he retorted with a smirk.

"So, you ready?" he asked.

"I am if you are."

I still wasn't in the mood, but I was going to push through my frustration and try to enjoy a memorable evening with my man.

Chapter 7

Phoenix

Finally I was getting me a piece, and it was so damn good. Von pounded into me, giving me exactly what my body craved: an orgasm. I bucked and I yelled. I screeched with satisfaction, enjoying the weight of him on top of me. This man was nothing but the truth. I didn't need him in me to get off, because I would just look at this luscious man and get quivers throughout my body.

All was going great, until Tobias walked in. I saw him enter out of the corner of my eye, but I didn't bother to stop, and neither did Von, who was so wrapped up in my good pussy that he didn't notice Tobias come in the room.

Tobias stood there gawking. Nothing was falling out of his mouth. Not a "stop it" or "what the hell is going on?" He stood there like a knot on a log and watched as I got pounded by a man who wasn't him. My plan went down exactly like I wanted it to, with the exception of him not going off about the situation.

I arched my back and dug my nails deeper into Von's back, yelling louder with pleasure, hoping this surge of my desire would ignite a rage in Tobias. Von buried his face in the crook of my neck as he gripped my butt and lifted it to his manhood to enter me deeper and deeper. There were no sheets covering us, just our arms and legs intertwined for Tobias to see. I moaned and wailed, getting annoyed because Tobias still wasn't saying anything. I threw some words in to make matters worse.

"That it right there, baby. Pound this pussy. That's right. Like that," I urged as Von obeyed my orders and deepened his penetration, pleasing my center.

Now is when Tobias made himself known by clearing his throat. Von was so deep in me he didn't hear him. Tobias cleared his throat louder, and this time Von heard him. He looked around to see Tobias standing in the room, and then he looked down at me.

"What are you doing here?" I asked Tobias.

"You told me to come by."

"No, I didn't," I lied.

"Yes, you did," he said slowly.

"Well, I don't remember," I said as Von got off of me and sat on the side of the bed saying nothing. He was good. Even though Tobias interrupted, we both had reached our peak. I reached mine several times. Tobias had just walked into the second go-round.

Boldly, Von stood and pulled his boxers up on his magnificent frame. When he did this, he made sure to turn around so Tobias could get a good look at what he was working with. There was no smirk or frown on Von's face when he did this. He was straight-faced as he took his time getting himself together.

Tobias stood there looking like a damn punk. If he was supposed to be my man, then why wasn't he flipping out right now? There is not a man I know who would be calm about what Tobias just walked in on. I was confused and in utter shock at his reaction, which was none.

Once Von was completely dressed, he leaned down and kissed me on the cheek. "I'll holla at you later," he said to me as he stood back up and glanced at Tobias. Von casually breezed past Tobias, who still stood watching.

Maybe that was his thing. Maybe he liked voyeurism and this scene turned him on. Well, it wasn't turning me on. If anything, it was weirding me out even more and further let me know this was why I didn't want to be around this man anymore.

"So you're just going to stand there?" I asked sardonically.

"How could you do this to me?"

Now I was getting a reaction, even though it was still a composed one.

"What are you talking about?" I asked, playing stupid, pulling the sheets around me and leaning back on the headboard like I didn't have a care in the world.

"This. You and this man."

"Tobias, we are not together," I said loudly, trying to get this through his thick skull.

"Yes, we are," he argued.

"No, we are not. I broke up with you three months ago, but you keep coming back. You keep showing up thinking I still want you."

"You do. You want me enough to screw me," he said.

"And? I like to have sex. That doesn't mean I want to be in a relationship with you. If that was the case, I would be with Von. Did you see what that man was working with?" I asked.

He rubbed his head, saying, "I can't believe this. You have really hurt me."

Now, mind you, when he was talking, it was not done in an angry tone. He was standing there looking like a wimp. If this were me and I caught the person I wanted to be with fucking somebody else, I would be going the hell off. But not Tobias. He was cool as a cucumber, which made no sense to me. Who would be calm at a moment like this? I swear I didn't understand this man, but I really didn't care to.

"I wish I could say I'm sorry, but I'm not, Tobias. You needed to see this in order to know whatever you thought we had we don't have anymore. No matter how many times I tell you this, you don't believe me. I'm hoping this incident will convince you I've moved on to bigger and better."

"It has opened my eyes up a bit about you," Tobias said, looking like he was getting ready to cry.

"Good. Now maybe you can give me back my key and get rid of the copies you have made."

"Phoenix," he said, pausing.

This punk was really getting choked up by what I was saying. I rolled my eyes. I mean, what the hell? *Get a damn backbone already and handle your business. Leave me alone,* I thought.

"What, Tobias?" I asked in frustration since it was taking him so long to speak.

"I'm willing to forgive you for this," he said.

What he said almost made me fall out my damn bed and hit my head on the corner of my nightstand to knock myself out. Was he kidding me? “You are going to forgive me?” I asked in shock.

He walked over to the bed and sat down on the side Von just had me sprawled out on. I knew he had to be sitting on our wet spot. He went to reach for my hand, but I moved it before he could touch me.

“I forgive you. You needed to get this out of your system, and now that you have, we can start fresh in our relationship.”

“What relationship? I don’t want you!” I yelled.

This frustrated me, because even after catching me with another man, Tobias still couldn’t see how bad I wanted him out of my life. I knew I was good, but damn. This man had lost his ever-loving mind over me.

“Actions speak louder than words, Phoenix, and our actions the other night were pure love and ecstasy.”

“It was only sex,” I shrieked.

“Which I love more than life. Phoenix, I love you so much, and I want to show you how much you mean to me.”

Tobias reached down in his pocket and pulled out a black velvet box. He then got down at the side of my bed on one knee. Opening the box, he asked, "Phoenix, will you marry me?"

Was he kidding? I mean really. He caught me screwing another man, and now he was asking me to be his wife minutes after Von extracted his dick out of me. Was he serious right now?

I looked down at the ring, curious to see how much Tobias claimed to love me, and for a moment the diva in me almost said yes as a two-carat princess-cut diamond was sparkling back at me. He had excellent taste, but he was not my cup of tea.

"Phoenix, did you hear me? Will you be my wife?" Tobias asked again, begging me with his eyes to say yes.

I got out of the bed on the other side, away from him. I couldn't take it anymore. I grabbed my robe and put it on, wrapping it tightly around my naked body. "Look, Tobias, I don't want to marry you. I don't want to be your wife. I don't even want to be your girlfriend or your friend at this point. You need to leave," I told him. I didn't bother to hear what he had to say because I walked out of my bedroom and headed downstairs with him following me.

"You have to say yes," he begged.

"No, I don't. I want you to get out of my house and never come back. If you try to use your key, you will find my locks will be changed again," I said.

I began to remember how he got the key to my new locks. He removed my key when I was asleep and made a copy before I had a chance to realize it was missing. I was getting my locks changed again, even though this would be the third time.

"You can't do this to us."

"Like hell I can't. Get out, Tobias."

"But, Phoenix—"

"Now, before I call the cops on you," I threatened.

"You wouldn't do that to me," he said ignorantly.

I sighed and walked over to the phone, dialing 911. "Yes, I need the police. I have an intruder in my house who refuses to leave."

Chapter 8

Serena

I had to think of other ways to please my man, and I used to let my lips do the talking, but after that party tonight, the first purchase I made was that pocket pussy thingy. As much as Tyree wanted to get deep inside me, I couldn't let him, because I had to wait at least six weeks before we did anything, since I had just given birth to our daughter, Nevaeh. My scared behind was paranoid, because I didn't want to get pregnant again. I had a couple of friends who let their men sweet talk them into doing it, and when they went for their six-week checkups, their behinds were pregnant. So I wasn't going to be doing anything. I was going to wait. This toy would have to suffice.

Tyree was against it at first, but when he stuck his finger into that toy, his eyes lit up with curiosity. I laid that man back and slid that rubbery toy onto his manhood and watched as my man climaxed with pleasure minutes later. Before this, I was licking this man into a deep coma, but my jaw muscles could relax for a change. Nothing worse than giving and not being able to receive. My monthly was still present, so I had to suffer until I had the go-ahead.

The banging at my door woke me up out of my sleep. I had just dozed off good and was not happy my slumber had been disturbed. Unlike me, Tyree didn't budge. He was dead to the world.

The person banged again, and I hoped the loud knocking wouldn't wake Nevaeh up like it did me. I nudged Tyree to get up, but he moaned, never waking from his sleep.

Pushing him again, I said, "Tyree, get up. Somebody is at the door."

He never budged. He just moaned again, but never awoke from his sleep. I didn't understand how he couldn't hear this loud knocking. Whoever it was really wanted to get in, but I didn't want them on this side of my door. It was after two in the morning. I didn't feel like leaving the comfort of my bed. It was a cool night, and I was snuggled beneath my warm covers with the ceiling fan above giving me the light breeze I needed to sleep even harder.

The banging on the door persisted. I sighed as I slowly willed myself out of my comfort zone and to this door to see who in the hell had the audacity to wake me up this time of the morning. I prayed it wasn't Tyree's baby mama, Juanita. I swore if it was her, we were going to have a problem. She would do something like this. The last time she showed her face on our doorstep, it was after two in the morning, and the trick came over because Zamir, Tyree's son, was running a temperature of 99.7. She wanted Tyree to go with her to the hospital to have him checked out. At the time I didn't have Nevaeh, but even I knew a 99.7 temperature didn't warrant an emergency room visit. All it was was she was jealous Tyree didn't want her trifling behind anymore, and she was doing any- and everything to make our lives miserable and using their child to do it.

The knocks became more tenacious, and I prayed this crazy woman wasn't on the other side of my door. When I swung the door open, my sister Shauna ran in my house. She pushed me out of the way and slammed the door to my place like some maniac was chasing her.

"What the hell is wrong with you?" I asked, looking at a hysterical Shauna. For a minute I didn't care about the state of mind she was in. I was pissed that she pushed me back, almost causing me to fall, and slammed my damn door.

"Are you going to answer me or not? What the hell is going on, Shauna?"

She still didn't answer. She put her face against my door, hugging it like it was her lifeline. I could see she was trembling. Then I could hear her crying uncontrollably. This stunned me to the point of fear, because Shauna didn't cry. She was so hardcore it wasn't funny. This was the same sister who fought guys in the street and didn't give a damn about nobody, so to see her like this frightened me.

I placed my hands on her shoulders, and Shauna jumped, causing me to back away. Once I paid full attention to how she was looking, I noticed she looked a hot mess. Her face looked like she rubbed Vaseline all over it. It was so shiny. I think it was actual tears that had encased her face as water poured from her eyes. Shauna was always the talker of our family. There was never a time she had nothing to say, so for her to stand there and not say anything caused my panic level to increase an octave.

"Is it Mama? Is she okay? Shauna, tell me what's wrong," I said as my sister came over to me. She dropped to her knees, wrapping her arms around my waist, and she sobbed loudly.

"Shauna, you can tell me anything," I encouraged as water filled my own eyes to see my sister like this.

Shauna continued to weep hysterically. I tried to bring her to her feet and managed to do so as I walked us over to my sofa. Sitting her down, I sat beside her. She pushed her long, untamed hair out of her face, asking, "You don't see it?"

"See what?" I asked.

She kept pushing her hair back from her face, saying over and over again, "Look at me, Serena. Look at me."

I did as she asked, but I couldn't see anything. Really I was still trying to wake up, so I didn't have my wits about myself to focus clearly on what was going on.

"How can you not see this?" she asked desperately.

"See what?" I questioned, feeling like maybe Shauna was losing it. She was not the emotional sister. Well, let me take that back. She was, but most of the time her emotion was anger, not hysteria.

"Look at me. Look at me," she yelled repeatedly, looking at her body, and it was then I noticed she was in my living room in a T-shirt and socks. I couldn't tell if she had on underwear because the shirt was long.

"Why are you over here like this?"

Shauna didn't answer as she broke down in tears again. She dropped her head, causing her hair to fall down around her face. I tried to push her long hair from her face, but when I attempted to do so, she began to shriek.

"Ooooouuuuuch." She winced. She smacked my hand away as she tucked her hair behind her ear.

That's when I saw it; a huge knot was near her temple. It came into view because she turned her head, giving me a better visual as the knot protruded from her head. I reached out and touched it, not thinking, causing Shauna to recoil in pain.

"What happened to you?" I asked worriedly, feeling the tears she had shed start to dwell within me.

"Cal tried to kill me tonight."

"He did what?" I asked as rage entered me. And then my thoughts immediately went into beat down mode.

"I told him I was tired of his crap and if he didn't like what was going on with us, he could leave. Evidently he didn't like me telling him to get out my house, since he doesn't have a pot to piss in. Yet, I guess he expected me to kiss his ass and beg him to stay or something, but you know me, Serena. I don't beg no man to stay with me. Hell, I prefer to be by myself. Next thing I know he just snapped."

"What did he do to you?" I asked, trying to listen calmly, all the while thinking how I was going to get at dude. He put his hands on a Johnson sister and Cal had to pay.

"I was sitting there smoking my cigarette, and all of a sudden he punched me in my face."

"He did what?" I belted, not believing, or maybe it was the fact that I didn't want to believe this man had the nerve to do this.

"Look at my lip," she said, but nothing was showing. It was then Shauna pulled her lip out. I could see where her tooth cut into her inner bottom lip.

"What did you do?"

"I couldn't do anything because he jumped on me. He picked me up off the bed and slung me across the room. The way I fell, I hit my head on the corner of my dresser," she said, reaching for the area where she'd hit her head.

"I hit the floor, and Cal jumped on me again. He straddled me and punched me in my face I think three times; I can't remember. It could have been more because I was still stunned after hitting my head on the dresser. He was yelling he was going to kill me. I tried to scratch at his hands, chest, and face to get him off of me, but it was like he didn't feel anything. Then he tried to choke me," she said, touching her neck.

"He choked you?" I yelled, moving her hand out of the way. I saw some cuts, like his nails dug into her skin. There was some slight swelling and some discoloration to her skin. Fury began to grow within me.

"He kept squeezing and squeezing, still telling me he was going to kill me. I tried to beg him to let me go, but he wouldn't. I guess when I didn't pass out or die, he began to bang my head into the floor over and over again."

I sat there listening intently, already getting in my head the cousins I was going to call to go beat this punk down. First I was going to call our cousin Big Ray. Then I was going to call Gerald and Pookie. All I needed was them three and I knew the job would be done. Pookie was going to come strapped. He stayed strapped and had no qualms about putting a bullet in anybody. At this point, I didn't care. He could shoot Cal and I wouldn't care. Cal had hurt my sister and tried to kill her tonight, and I wanted the punk to get dealt with.

"Serena, I must have passed out, because the next thing I remember is waking up on the floor and seeing Cal stepping over me with his packed bags. I just lay there like I was still passed out until I heard him go out the front door. As soon as I realized he was outside, I got up and ran to the front door, closing it and locking it."

"He has a key, don't he?" I asked.

"He does, but he doesn't have it to the deadbolt."

"How did he leave? He doesn't have a car," I said.

"He didn't. He was still there when I left."

I shook my head at this story, not knowing what else to say. Shauna continued, "He tried to come back in the house but realized he couldn't get in. I sat in my room, trying to wrap my mind around what had just happened. I could hear him outside screaming at me to let him in so he could apologize."

"Apologize. It's too late for a damn apology. And he's screaming at you to let him come in so he could do this. That sounds really sincere," I said sarcastically.

"He kept tapping at my bedroom window for me to open the door so he could come in, but I wouldn't. I just wanted him gone. After I didn't hear him anymore after a while, I figured he had left."

"How did you get away?"

"I ran to my car thinking he was gone. Once I got in I locked the doors, and that's when I saw him sitting in the yard chair outside my house."

"Did he say anything?" I asked.

"He came over to the car and started banging on the window, saying he was sorry and to open the door. I ignored him and pulled off."

My sister began to cry again. My anger hadn't diminished. I really wanted to get this man, or shall I say coward, who thought he could put his hands on a woman.

Shauna gathered herself enough to say, "I wonder if he planned to do this."

"Why do you say that?" I asked.

"You know the bat I keep beside my bed?"

"Yes."

"It was gone. I think he moved it knowing that would be the first thing I would go for. My blade was in my purse, but I wasn't able to get to that. I guess that's a good thing, because I could be sitting here telling you how I murdered this fool."

"He would deserve it. It would have been self-defense. But you don't have to worry about revenge, because I'm calling Big Ray," I said, getting up off the sofa. Shauna grabbed me by the wrist, stopping me.

"Don't," she belted.

"Don't what? This man tried to kill you tonight. He needs to get the same beat down he put on you tonight so he will know how it feels," I said assertively.

"But Big Ray and them will kill him."

"And?"

"And I don't want him to die," Shauna said.

"You just sat here and said if you could have got to your blade you would have stabbed dude to death, so why you worried about his livelihood now?" I asked irritably.

"It's different, Serena."

"How? Dead is dead regardless of how it's done," I argued.

"Why should Big Ray and them get in trouble for somebody like Cal? You know Big Ray probably already on parole," she said convincingly.

"If Big Ray is involved, no one is going to know about it. You know that. He's been around way too long to not know how to get away with beating this punk down."

"Please, Serena. Don't call him. Then he's going to get Gerald and Pookie, and you know any one of them will shoot Cal."

I had to laugh at her saying it, since I had just thought it.

"Please sit down with me for a minute," Shauna begged, still holding my wrist so I wouldn't dial up the entourage.

"Shauna, don't you know you could be dead now?" I said, causing tears to cascade down her face again.

"I know," she said, dropping her head in shame.

"The thought of that scares me, sis," I said with tears welling up in my eyes. "You are my sister and I couldn't stand losing you. Not after . . . Not after . . ." I got choked up and sat down beside my sister. We looked into each other's eyes and understood the pain the other felt.

She nodded and said, "I have done a lot of foul things in my life, but I've never had a man beat me like this. I still can't believe I allowed it to happen."

"You didn't allow this to happen. Now, if you stay with him after this, then yes, you are allowing it, but now, it's not your fault, Shauna."

"I can't believe this," she said, massaging her scalp through her hair. "My head hurts so bad."

"I think I need to take you to the emergency room to get checked out," I suggested.

"I'm not going. I don't feel like telling nobody else what happened, especially a damn doctor."

"Fool, what if you have a concussion?"

"My head is hard. I'll be all right," she said, grinning for the first time since she got there.

"I know that, but even hard heads can get damaged. The knot on your temple is enough for me to worry about the injuries you could have," I said.

"All I need is some ice and some sleep."

"You can't go to sleep. You have to stay up for at least a few hours to make sure you don't slip into a coma or something," I said.

"What are you, Dr. Serena?"

"Yes. I got my PhD from the school of common damn sense," I said jokingly.

"Funny."

"Sis, I think you really need to get checked out seriously," I said.

"Serena, I don't feel like dealing with any doctors, nurses, or cops for that matter. Besides, I've been drinking and smoking."

"And? What does that mean? You also been battered," I said.

"Just leave it alone. I'm not going and that's that."

"You have to do one or the other. Either go to the doctor or let me call Big Ray. You choose."

"You know what? I'm leaving," she said, standing to her feet but stumbling a bit with dizziness.

"You see? You can't even stand up without stumbling."

"I'll be all right," she said, walking to the door.

"And where are you going?" I asked.

"Home."

"You know what? Something is wrong with your head if you making all these crazy decisions. You are not going home. What if that fool is still there? Do you expect me to let you go back to that?"

"He won't be there," Shauna said confidently.

"And how do you know that?" I asked.

She said nothing. She gawked at me.

"Exactly. Look, you are staying here tonight. No ifs, ands, or buts about it." I held my hand out, saying, "Give me your keys."

"I'm not going anywhere."

"I know, but I'm making sure, so hand them over," I said, wiggling my fingers in the "come here" fashion.

Shauna put the keys in my hand even though she didn't want to give them up. I knew her. If I didn't take those keys away from her, when I woke up in the morning, Shauna would be gone.

"You can rest in the guest room next to Nevaeh's room. But don't go to sleep."

"Okay," she said dejectedly.

"And, Shauna, if you decide to be hardheaded and leave here without me knowing, I'm going to call Big Ray to handle things with Gerald and Pookie in tow."

Shauna didn't say anything. She walked out of the living room, heading for the bedroom. I knew I would be up for a while, because there was no way I was going to be able to sleep knowing there was a possibility my sister wouldn't wake up.

Chapter 9

Phoenix

Don't you know that fool thought I was playing a joke on him? He thought I was talking to a dial tone and hadn't called the police on him because my love for him wouldn't do that to him. Well, that punk realized I did call when he saw the cops pull up. He looked at me in disbelief.

"Maybe this will convince you I mean what I say. I don't want to be with you, Tobias."

"I still don't believe you. We are having a rift right now, but eventually it will get solved."

The cops walked up to my open door waiting on them. "Ma'am, did you call about an intruder?" the tall, well-built officer asked as he glanced at Tobias, who was acting like he lived there.

As striking as this cop was, I almost forgot Tobias was there. This cop was fine as hell.

"Ma'am," the handsome cop called out, snapping me back to why he was here in the first place.

"Yes, I'm sorry," I apologized, smiling at him like a shy schoolgirl. But there was nothing girly about me. I was all woman, and I was getting immediately turned on by the magnificence of the chocolate brother.

"Officer . . ." I paused, looking at him questionably as I searched for his name on his uniform.

"I'm Officer Winn. And this is my partner, Officer Taylor," he said, pointing to the dainty brunette woman standing behind him.

She was eying me in a way that made me want to check her. She was giving me a look like I shouldn't be ogling Officer Winn at all. Maybe she was jealous because she was trying to get it or had already gotten it, and that was the reason why she was giving me the stank eye.

"Ma'am," Officer Winn called out again, and when I made eye contact, his stern face changed into one of ease.

"Yes, Officer," I said sweetly.

"Why are we here again?" he asked.

"This man will not leave my house," I said, changing my tone to one of urgency.

"Did he touch you?" Officer Winn asked.

Instantly I wished Officer Winn would touch me. He could have his way with me any kind of position he wanted, because this man was so fine.

"Did he touch you?" Officer Winn asked again, snapping me back from daydreaming about his attractive behind.

"No, he wouldn't be dumb enough to do that. He just will not leave my house," I said, looking back at a pathetic Tobias.

"Is this true?" Officer Winn asked Tobias.

"Officer, this is a misunderstanding. My girlfriend is mad with me right now. I don't know why she called you all."

"First of all, I'm not your girlfriend. Second, I called because I want you out my house," I said, pointing to my door. My robe loosened a bit, almost causing one of my breasts to come tumbling free.

Officer Taylor frowned, but Officer Winn smirked, giving me the impression he didn't mind as his eyes looked as though he wished he got a free look. His partner eyed him and shifted uncomfortably.

Pulling my robe closed, I said, "Get out!"

"I live here too," Tobias said, surprising me with this bit of information.

"Is this true, ma'am? Does he live here?" Officer Taylor interjected.

"No!" I belted.

"Please calm down," the female officer warned.

"This is my house and my house only. I'm the only one who stays here," I asserted, ignoring this woman telling me to calm down. Just because she was behind that badge and police uniform didn't mean I had to respect her.

"Stop lying, Phoenix. My clothes are upstairs in your closet. My shaving kit is in your bathroom."

"No, it's not," I said.

"Ma'am, if he lives here—" the female officer attempted to say, but I cut her off in annoyance.

"But he doesn't! I pay this mortgage. I pay all the utilities."

"Well, that's a lie too, babe," he said softly, like this wasn't an issue. "I've been paying your mortgage, electric, and water. Officer, if you would allow me to show you, I have the receipts and my account information showing I paid it," Tobias said, going over to my console table and pulling out his checkbook and receipts.

When did he put his things there? And if he put that there, he probably was right about having some clothes and his shaving kit upstairs. Had this man slowly moved his things in my place without me even knowing?

"See? I made sure the clerk wrote down I paid and my information," he said, walking back over to the officers and pointing at the slips of paper.

"Ma'am, this does show he's been paying the bills at this address. If he didn't live here, why would he be paying your mortgage?" Officer Taylor asked, leering at me like she was happy I was caught in a lie.

I wanted to put my hands on this woman. She was getting a kick out of making me look stupid. The snide smirk on her face let me know that.

"He helped me out a few times. So what? That doesn't mean he lives here," I disputed.

"I can take you upstairs to show you my clothes and other items. I even bought the food for her dinner party she had tonight," he said, bringing out yet another receipt.

I wanted so bad to snatch all of those pieces of paper out of his hand and stuff them all in his damn mouth so he could choke on it. How dare he make me out to look like a liar? If I would've known he kept track of him helping me out, I wouldn't have had anything to do with this punk. To me, this was looking like a setup that I allowed to happen because I was too busy enjoying the fruits of his labor. But the cops couldn't believe this, could they?

"Ma'am, I'm sorry to tell you we can't make this man leave. It appears that he does reside here, and by law, regardless if his name is on your lease or not, he has tenant rights. All the evidence is here," Officer Taylor said, taking over this little interrogation.

"You got to be kidding me," I said, putting my hands on my hips in frustration. I peered at Officer Winn, who stood back watching as his partner did all the work. As good-looking as he was, he was there to do his job.

I asked him, cutting off his partner, "Is this true?"

Officer Winn nodded, saying, "If you want this man to leave, Ms. Johnson, you have to give him at least a thirty-day notice to leave your residence. If he doesn't leave within that time frame, then you will have to file an eviction notice with the court," Officer Winn explained.

"Eviction notice, on my own damn house?" I questioned.

"Yes, ma'am," he said.

"Even if he hit me?" I tried to lie.

"You said he never put his hands on you. Your exact words were . . ." Officer Taylor said, looking down at her notepad. She proceeded to read, "'He wouldn't be dumb enough to do that.'" She looked up at me, happy at my humiliation right now.

I was mad at myself at this point. Why did I say that? I could have said he hit me and he would be gone and I would be back in bed getting some sleep. As usual, my mouth worked faster than my brain. Now Tobias was the one who had rights over property that was mine. I was pissed.

"If there's another problem, please feel free to call us," Officer Taylor said to Tobias like she was on his side. I didn't bother to say anything else. I did get one last glance at Officer Winn as he proceeded to leave my stoop.

"Thank you, Officers," Tobias said in his chipper voice.

This just made me cringe with resentment.

"You all have a good night," Officer Taylor said, and I slammed the door in her face.

"Phoenix, you can get arrested," Tobias said.

"Why, for closing my own door? She lucky I didn't do more," I bellowed. "I can't believe you lied like that," I said through clenched teeth.

"Honey, I didn't lie. Everything I said was the truth."

"I'm going to get you out of here if it's the last thing I do," I said, stomping up my stairs and slamming my bedroom door closed, locking it.

Chapter 10

Shauna

Serena ended up staying up with me until she thought it was okay for me to fall asleep. I slept in the third bedroom they had. When I woke up, the first person I thought about was Cal and what he did to me. My second thought was how my head was killing me. I had a hangover without the drunkenness. I knew this pain came from Cal slamming my head into the floor. For a minute, I didn't want to move for fear the pain would increase. I lay there looking up at the speckled ceiling, wishing things were different. I never thought I would have anything like this happen to me.

I managed to sit up, making sure to move slowly, and was happy the pain didn't escalate. I was more sore than I thought. I threw my feet over the side of the bed and sat there for a bit.

I still had on the T-shirt and panties I ran over here in. I looked at the side table next to the bed to see my sister put a change of clothes there for me to put on. I picked it up to see she put a pair of gray jogging pants and fitted white V-neck tee with a pair of socks and underwear. I ran my hand through my tangled hair, wincing a bit, and when I brought my hands back down, I saw clumps of my hair came out in my hand. Tears threatened to escape as I recapped the night and wondered how in the hell this had happened.

Here I was thinking I had to worry about my sister calling our cousins, and I never considered what Tyree would do once he found out. I knew I should have kept what happened to me to myself. Cal beating me was the least of my worries. Now that Tyree knew too, it was enough to stress me the hell out.

All because of the simple act of Tyree going to the restroom in the middle of the night, and that's when he realized Serena wasn't in the bed with him. He thought she was with Nevaeh but quickly found out she was with me, since the spare bedroom was right beside my niece's room. When Tyree saw me, he knew something was up. As much as I didn't want to tell him, I had to. Seeing him standing before me caused me to burst into tears again. Needless to say,

Tyree was heated by what happened, and he immediately began calling his boys, letting them know to serve Cal with a pretty ass-whooping if they saw him.

I could stop Serena, but Tyree was another story. He was the brother I never had, and he acted the role of one, too. Tyree let me know way back he didn't like Cal. He only dealt with him because he loved me, so for this to happen, he was ready to stomp a hole in him.

Really Cal was hated by many men in the street. He always thought he was big and bad all the damn time, running his mouth like he couldn't be beat. All mouth and little action was what he was. "I'm from Jersey, yo," he would say all the time, like that was going to make somebody back down. I had family in Jersey, but none of them bragged like he did. I guess since Virginia was more down south than upstate, he thought everybody from here was supposed to be punks. Boy was he ever wrong.

He learned one lesson when his ass got stabbed in his back on the basketball court four months ago for running that mouth. It was through the grace of God that the blade missed his spinal cord and he lived. That alone should have been enough to clue him in on keeping his mouth shut, but if anything it made him cockier because he survived the stabbing. He walked with his chest stuck out more than ever now, with not one damn lesson learned. All he got out of it was he had street scars, and the fact that he survived proved his toughness. This punk really began to think his ass was invincible.

Like a dummy, I still stayed with him. Look where that got me. I could have lost my life at the hands of this fool. He couldn't beat a dude, so he thought it was fitting to make himself feel better by beating me. I was the only one he had in his corner. A lot of his own family didn't have his back, so now he was going to stand alone, and I knew this was the time he would run to them. The only one who seemed to have his back was his mother. She was a good woman. Out of this entire situation, she would be the one person I would miss.

The shower I took made me feel a hundred times better. The hot water helped ease my aching bruises, and I washed my hair, pulling it back in a ponytail. With clean clothes on and feeling refreshed, I felt good.

The aroma of sausage swarmed the air, and I knew Serena wasn't in the kitchen. Tyree was. He was the one who did the cooking most of the time between the two. I also smelled coffee, and for once I craved to have a cup with lots of sugar and cream.

When I got downstairs, to my dismay, my sister Phoenix was sitting at the island in the kitchen. I heard her say, "Cal needs to start counting his nine lives, because Big Ray and them getting ready to take what's left away from him. I promise you that."

She was always so damn loud and dramatic. And they said I was the crazy sister.

Serena was sitting beside Phoenix. Both were drinking the coffee I smelled earlier. I turned to see, like expected, Tyree at the stove preparing breakfast.

"Why did you call her?" I asked Serena as I walked into the kitchen painted a sunny yellow. It wasn't overpowering at all. It made you feel like happiness should always be within this space; but I wasn't feeling any type of happiness right now, not after seeing Phoenix here. If anything I was feeling dread at the days ahead, knowing I would be the brunt of conversation between my sisters and whatever other family they decided should be brought into my troubles.

"Phoenix called me this morning because we were supposed to go walking so I can start losing this baby weight," Serena said, grabbing her little pouch from having Nevaeh.

"And you couldn't wait to tell her what happened to me," I said, crossing my arms in frustration.

"She is our sister, Shauna. Don't you think she should know?" Serena asked.

"If I wanted her to know, I would have run to her house. I thought I could trust you, Serena," I said, walking around the island to retrieve a mug from the cabinet.

"Shauna, you can be mad all you want. Serena's right. I should know about this," Phoenix chimed in.

"Why? What business is this of yours?"

"We're sisters. How many times do we have to say this to you? Cal stepped way over the line when he thought it was okay to disrespect you like this. And with him disrespecting you, he has disrespected us. That's why I called Pookie and Gerald over."

"You did what?" I blurted in the middle of pouring the hot elixir into my mug. I halted my coffee-pouring midair, trying really hard not to drop the pot onto the granite countertop.

"You heard me," Phoenix said.

I looked at Serena, who stretched her eyes and picked up her own cup to take a sip. The mug was so big it looked like it was covering her entire face. Maybe she was trying to hide from me.

With Phoenix at the reins, I knew this situation was going to get worse, which was why I knew Serena told her instead of any of our other sisters. To be as pretty as she was, Phoenix was *boughetto*—bougie and ghetto. Yesterday she was high-class snooty; now she was ready to scream whooty-who. Just call my sister Phoenix the diva of the family. She was the type to start trouble and then finish it, even if it meant somebody else was fighting her battles. Don't get me wrong; Phoenix fought. She had to, as many times as she slept with somebody's husband.

My sister let her beauty work for the good of her pockets. Where she got that behavior from, I don't know. Her attractiveness managed to get her a house, a brand new Range Rover, and monthly installments of money given to her. Whoever her sugar daddy or daddies were this time, they were definitely taking good care of her. Still, I had to wonder at what cost.

"You see why you shouldn't have told Phoenix," I said to Serena, putting some sugar into my coffee.

"Don't be mad at her. Be mad at me," Phoenix said.

"Oh, I am. I wish y'all would let me handle this on my own," I said.

"Just like you handled him last night? From the looks of your damn eye, it looks like he handled you good," Phoenix responded, taking a sip of her coffee as she eyed the bruise on my eye.

"Phoenix," Serena called.

"What?" Phoenix asked, looking dumbfounded.

"Really? You had to talk about the bruises."

"I'm pretty sure she saw them when she looked into the mirror this morning. Maybe that will further help her decide not to go back to that punk."

I rolled my eyes, saying, "You see why I don't ever want to come to y'all with anything."

"Why you trippin'? You lucky to be alive from what I heard from Serena, and you complaining," Phoenix said with a sneer.

"Phoenix, don't start with me today. You know you don't want none. I might have got caught off-guard last night, but this morning I'm more than lucid enough to know how to whoop your ass."

"I'm trying to help," she blurted like she was doing me a favor.

"But I didn't ask you to, did I?" I said, leaning forward for her to read my lips and hear me good.

"Get your panties out your ass and be happy you got family willing to be there for you. All you have to say is thank you and leave it at that," Phoenix countered.

I sighed my frustration, asking Serena, "Did you call Dawn and Vivian, too?"

"No, I didn't. I figured we would see them later at our dinner."

"That's if I go," I murmured.

"Why aren't you going?" Phoenix asked, frowning.

"I don't need to hear why I let this happen. It's bad enough having to deal with you two."

"Are we that bad?" Phoenix asked.

"Hell yeah," I shouted.

"Shauna, I know I come off hard sometimes—" Phoenix began to say.

"You think?" I responded.

"And I acknowledge that, but I act crazy when it comes to the people I love."

"Not only with the people you love," Serena said under her breath.

Phoenix nudged her with her elbow, causing Serena to say, "Ouch."

"Like I was saying before I was rudely interrupted," Phoenix said, side-eyeing Serena, "I love you, Shauna. I hate this happened to you. Yes, I have overreacted, but I want Cal to get dealt with for what he's done to you."

"But why is this any of your business?" I asked.

"It's my business because you are my sister. Plus, this has struck a nerve in me because it's happened to me too," Phoenix confessed.

"Really?" Serena asked in shock.

"Yes," Phoenix said warily. "I went to this get-together with a guy I was seeing, and he thought he could smack me in front of a bunch of his people because I talked to him a certain type of way and came out my face wrong."

"He smacked you?" Serena asked.

"Yep," Phoenix said, nodding.

"What did you do?" I asked.

"I blacked the hell out."

Tyree giggled as he took the biscuits out of the oven.

"It took four of his family members to pull me off of him. By the time I was finished with him, it looked like a cat had attacked him. Plus, I gave him a black eye."

"Dammit," Tyree said.

"He was lucky I wasn't toting my pistol. I swear on my mama I would have shot him dead," Phoenix said, holding her right hand up like she was being sworn in by a court officer.

"You would have shot him?" Serena asked, giggling.

"You damn right I would have. A man putting his hand on this pretty face? Please. And to do it in front of people trying to prove he had some kind of control over me," she said with eyebrows raised. "I think what triggered my departure–"

"Departure?" Serena asked, frowning.

"My mind leaving the building," Phoenix said.

"Oh. Okay."

"I snapped because this jackass had the nerve to laugh after he slapped me. I think that's what made me lose all sense of reality."

As much as I loved my sisters and family members, we tended to be a little crazy. No. Let me scratch that. We were a lot crazy. I mean crazy in the sense of some members having papers showing they've been in a mental institute. I had to sometimes question our stability. None of us were quite right upstairs and I knew this.

Just when I didn't think my morning could get any worse, I saw Big Ray walk in the kitchen. He hugged Serena and Phoenix and then went over to Tyree, giving him the brotherly handshake. I was last on his journey of affection. After he hugged me, he pushed my hair back gently and took my face into his massive palms. He tenderly moved my head back and forth, looking at my developing bruises. When he let go of my face, I could see him clenching down on his teeth, causing his jawbone and temples to flex. I knew what this meant. It meant things were about to get real.

"Big Ray, you don't have to do this. I'm okay," I said, looking up at my six foot five inch cousin built like a brick building, weighing about 320 pounds. His size alone was intimidating, but when it came to the women of the family, he was a big teddy bear. Trying to convince him everything was okay, I said, “I think Cal knows not to let this happen again.”

“I don’t know about all that, cuz. He messed up when he touched one of ours,” he said with his deep baritone voice.

“I know he’s not crazy enough to try anything else with me,” I said, changing my words.

“How do you know that, Shauna? He hasn’t had to deal with any consequences behind this,” Big Ray said, looking sincerely into my eyes.

I could see the pain and anger within him. I still tried to smooth things over so he could leave it alone. “Ray, by the time he hears about all y’all looking for him, he’s going to be long gone. He ain’t dumb enough to stick around for an ass-whoopin’,” I said.

“He violated you. No man ever violates my peoples. Y’all are like my sisters. Your mama help raise me when my mama was cracked out in the street, so to see you hurt like this, it pains me, Shauna,” he said, visibly upset.

I wanted to cry so bad, but I held back my tears. That would have only added to him wanting to hurt Cal. As bad as Cal deserve whatever he got, I didn't want Big Ray to risk himself for someone as sorry as Cal.

"So I can't change your mind?" I asked Big Ray.

"I'll tell you what; we won't go looking for him. The word will be put out in the street. But, Shauna, if we see him, he will get dealt with."

I nodded.

"I'm serious, Shauna. I can't lay eyes on this punk and not do what I say I'm going to do if I see him," Big Ray stressed.

"I understand, Ray," I said, smiling at him.

"I don't know what you saw in him anyway," Phoenix said, ruining the loving moment I was having with my cousin.

"For goodness' sake, sis," Serena said, but Phoenix kept talking.

"He ain't cute. His breath stank, and his grill is busted. I still can't believe that punk thought he was the prettiest thing walking."

"Well, I did care for him," I replied, wishing she would shut up.

But that would be too much to ask of Phoenix, so she replied back, "Love wouldn't have allowed him to kick your ass. I hope you are done with him. From the looks of that eye, you need to take a picture for it to be a constant reminder of what he did to you so you won't take him back."

"Taking pictures is a good idea, Shauna," Serena agreed. "I'm going to get my camera," she said, hopping down from the stool and jetting past us to go upstairs.

"Bump the camera," Phoenix said, taking out her cell phone. "I'm going to snap this right now," she said, taking numerous pictures of my bruises. "This is evidence."

"I better not see this on Facebook or any other Web site, Phoenix. I know you."

"Why not?"

I scowled at her, and she said, "Okay. I wasn't going to do that anyway."

It didn't matter how many pictures they took of me; the emotional toll of this situation was enough to wound me for life. I was done with Cal. As much as I hated agreeing with Phoenix, love wouldn't allow something like this to happen to me. I came to the realization that what he had for me wasn't love at all. It was straight-up abuse.

Chapter 11

Serena

My house was finally empty of my family. Shauna decided to go home, and Big Ray and Phoenix decided to follow her to make sure that fool Cal wasn't still waiting outside her house.

I expected to be exhausted from going on my walk with Phoenix this morning, but I was worn out mentally by the drama my family brought into my home. Don't get me wrong; I loved my family, and yes, I would have welcomed Shauna into my house anytime, but this was a bit much for me to deal with because I hated drama. I always tried to avoid it, but somehow drama was always brought to me.

Maybe it was because I was a nice person. Maybe it was because I was that person people loved to confide in. Either way, sometimes it was a bit much. Still, I've learned to deal with it because being a Johnson sister comes with its fair share of tumultuous situations.

The day went by so fast, and now it was time for me to go over my sister's house for our dinner we had together. Tyree walked into the bedroom soaking wet with his body dripping with sweat. He had just come from playing basketball with his friends. I was mad because he was supposed to be here thirty minutes ago to get Nevaeh while I went over my sister's house. He knew this before he left but, like Tyree, he did whatever he wanted, only thinking about himself.

"You're late," I said, sliding on my gold-and-orange bangle.

"The game ran long," he said.

"I don't care. You knew I had something to do. You should have cut your game short," I snapped.

"Serena, please don't start."

"Don't start? Don't start what?"

"This," he said, holding his hands out to me. "I'm not in the mood to deal with your attitude."

"Fine, Tyree. You won't have to deal with it once I leave. Hell, I'm thinking about leaving permanently. Then you wouldn't ever have to worry about my attitude again," I said angrily.

"Do what you got to do. I'm tired of you threatening to leave me. If you are going to go, then leave already," he said, peeling off his soggy shirt.

"Don't tempt me," I said, glaring at him.

"Do me the favor," he shot back, walking to the bathroom.

"Oh, so you want me to leave?" I asked, getting angrier by the minute.

Sometimes I wished he wouldn't be so damn nonchalant about us. Why didn't he ever fight for us? Like now, he could have apologized and left it at that, but no, he had to push me further away from him. This unnerved me and made me wonder why I was trying. If he could give up on what we had so easily, why shouldn't I leave? It was always the same thing with him. He came with the "whatever" attitude like he could be with or without, and that always hurt me.

"I wouldn't stop you if you did want to leave," he said.

"Why wouldn't you? I'm not worth fighting for?" I asked, rushing to the bathroom behind him and getting up in his face.

"Seriously, Serena. Why would I try to keep you somewhere you don't want to be?" he asked.

"At least show me you want me by fighting or begging me not to leave, or apologize to me sometimes when you do stupid things like this," I retorted.

"You are not making any sense. I'm not going to beg nobody to stay where they don't want to be. That's crazy. And can you say that if I didn't want to be here anymore, you would try to get me to stay?" he said, frowning.

I thought about what he said and instantly understood his thinking process. As much as I hated to agree with him, Tyree was right. If he wanted to leave, I wouldn't beg him to stay either, so how could I want him to do something I knew I wouldn't do myself? I dropped my head as I got caught up in my feelings. Tyree saw the sadness on my face and came closer to me.

"Babe, come on. You know I love you, but you are not going to keep threatening to leave me. You've done it way too many times, and now I'm numb to it," he explained gently.

"I get it," I said solemnly, trying to hold back my tears.

"Is this stemming from the fact that I won't marry you?" he asked, turning his back to me as he reached in the linen closet and pulled out a baby blue towel and washcloth.

"Maybe. I still don't understand why you won't marry me."

"You knew going into this relationship with me, Serena, that I never wanted to get married. I told you about my parents and how their divorce destroyed our family," Tyree explained.

"But your parents are not us," I tried to argue.

"Again, you knew going into this relationship what it was. I never hid that from you, so for you to try to get me to do what I told I would never do pisses me off," he said, reaching into the shower to turn on the water.

"And it pisses me off you can't get past a past that wasn't your fight in the first place. That was your parents' fight. I'm your right now, Tyree. You do love me, don't you?" I asked.

"Of course I do," he said, turning to look at me honestly.

"But not enough to put a ring on it," I said, holding up my left hand, pointing at my fourth finger.

"I'm sorry, Serena, but I can't."

"You know what? Maybe we do need to take a better look at our situation," I said seriously.

"Maybe we should. All I know is I'm tired of talking about this. Nothing is going to change," he said, sliding his shorts off. "You know as well as I do both of us have issues to work through with us and our past. Yours is checkered too, Serena. I think you want to break this curse you think has plagued the Johnson women for generations. I don't see it as a plague. I see it as women choosing their situation that dictates their destiny. I also believe women teach men how to treat them."

"So I taught you how to treat me?" I asked.

"Yes," he said convincingly.

"What? Did I teach you to make me feel unworthy, unloved, what?"

"The love is there and it's real. Your worth is something you have to find within yourself. I can't do that for you. Nor did I ask for that job. As for the lesson to be learned here, you chose to go down this road with me, and that road was clouded. I cheated. You cheated. We knew what it was. You know about my baby mama, my son, and other women I've been with. I know about you and the men you been with. It is what it is," he said, pulling the curtain back farther. He took off his boxer briefs and was standing in front of me naked before stepping into the shower and closing the shower curtain.

"So, just like that I'm supposed to accept this?"

"You don't have to accept anything, Serena," he answered. "I know I want you in my life."

"But only as your girlfriend, not your wife?" I asked.

"Exactly. Even though I love you, I haven't gotten over you cheating on me, and I'm pretty sure you haven't forgotten about me cheating on you. You want to take all of this baggage into vows said before God like it's going to make our situation better. I'm sorry, but I'm not about to do that."

"It would make me feel better. All I've asked for is the ring. We can wait a couple of years to get married to see where our relationship takes us."

"You say that now. As soon as I give you the ring, then you will be hounding me about when are we getting married."

Tyree might have had a point.

"I know you, Serena. As soon as you get what you want, you find something else that's wrong and beat me over the head with it until you get that, and then so on and so on. It never ends with you."

"You don't know that," I lied because everything he was saying was the truth still. For some reason I couldn't get out of my head that the ring would prove his love to me.

"Who are you trying to kid? I wasn't born yesterday. You and I have a dysfunctional relationship, and I refuse to commit to that for the rest of my life. I always knew if I ever got married, it would be 'til death do us part. I'm not ever going into it lightly. Babe, I don't want you to leave me, but you are not going to scare me into giving you a ring. I fear God more than I fear losing you, and I will not play around when it comes to marriage."

What could I say to that? Even I knew I could not compete with God. Not that I would ever try to, but what Tyree was saying made sense. It angered me that it did, because I wanted what I wanted and that was the ring and then us getting married to one another.

I don't know how long I stood there thinking about what he said, but I finally snapped out of my thoughts and spoke to him.

"I'm leaving, and I'm taking Nevaeh with me," I said, giving up on this conversation, knowing it wasn't going anywhere.

"I thought you said you wanted me to watch her," Tyree said, cutting off the water and opening the shower curtain. He reached for his bath towel and wrapped it around his waist. As mad as he made me, Tyree looked so sexy with the water trickling down his dark chocolate skin. His muscles rippled as the water made its way down his body.

"I changed my mind. My sisters would love to see her."

"Can I get a hug before you go?" he asked with outstretched arms and a smirk on his face.

"No."

"Come here, baby. You know I love you."

"But I'm not wifey material," I shot back.

"In my eyes you are my wifey."

"But not officially. It's only in your meek little imagination. Hug that imaginary wifey, because your girlfriend is leaving."

With that I left him standing with his arms still outstretched to embrace the fact that one day I might not be there for him to hug at all.

Chapter 12

Dawn

I could not wait until I got over to my sister Vivian's house for our weekly dinner. This time it was Vivian who would host the dinner, so I knew we were going to have something scrumptious to eat. Out of all four of my sisters, Vivian was the best cook. I didn't know if it was because she was the oldest or what, but homegirl could throw down.

The last time she made spice-rubbed barbecue ribs with homemade coleslaw, broccoli salad, cornbread, and sweet potato casserole. You're talking about good. Vivian slow-grilled those ribs so long the meat was falling off the bone.

We made pigs of ourselves as we chowed down with BBQ sauce all over our hands and faces, even though she provided kitchen towels for each of us to wipe our hands with. She had enough food to feed an army, so it wasn't a problem for any of us to leave there with Styrofoam plates filled with food to eat the next day.

When I got to Vivian's, I didn't bother knocking as I walked into her house.

"Knock knock. It's me, Viv," I yelled.

"I'm in the kitchen," she replied.

When I walked in, Vivian was standing at the stove, stirring something in a huge pot. "Hey, sis," she said.

"Hey. How it's going?"

"I can't complain, or rather, there's no need to."

"True. You look good," I complimented her, looking at Vivian wearing a pair of black jeggings with a red off-the-shoulder top and leopard-print wedges.

"Thank you."

"Where did you get those shoes, girl? They are so damn hot," I said, admiring the wedges.

"I ordered them off the Steve Madden Web site. Feel them," Viv said, walking over to me.

I bent over and rubbed the shoe. "Is that fur?"

"It feels like it. I love these shoes, and they are so comfortable."

"They don't look comfortable," I said, looking at the five-inch shoe.

"The platform helps. All I buy is shoes with platforms these days. It takes inches away from the actual heel height, but still makes it look like you are rocking high heels. You can try them on if you like," she said, stepping out of the shoes.

I giggled as her height shrank dramatically. I was curious and stepped into the shoes. "Wow. I like these. They are comfortable," I said, pleasantly surprised as I looked down at the fabulous shoe.

"Told you," she said.

"I'm going to have to get me a pair. How much were they?"

"Please don't ask," she said as I stepped back out of the shoes and watched as she walked over and put them back on.

"Seriously, how much?" I asked again.

"With shipping I think I paid close to one hundred and forty dollars."

"Vivian!" I yelled.

"I know, but they were cute and I love shoes, so here I stand," she rationalized. "But that's nothing compared to the price of other shoes I've purchased," she said.

Vivian never lied. She had a nice collection of shoes. My sister had shoes she hadn't worn yet. I would have expected this type of glam from Phoenix, but Vivian even beat her when it came to how many shoes she possessed. I know many may think $140 for shoes is not bad, but when you came from the humble, or should I say poor, beginning like we did, you would understand why I frowned at the mention of the price. We used to think paying fifty dollars for shoes was a lot.

But I couldn't be mad at Vivian. She'd worked hard to get to where she was and rightfully deserved to buy whatever she wanted. Next, I would expect her to be stepping around in Giuseppes and Christian Louboutin. That's if she didn't have any already. Knowing my sister, she did. "I wish I could buy expensive shoes like you."

"You can," she quipped.

"Girl, I'm comfortable in my sneakers. I'm not trying to break my neck in shoes like that."

"Beauty is painful sometimes. I twisted my ankle last year, and it killed me to let my heels go for two months. Don't get me wrong; I do enjoy my sneakers, but I like to dress up sometimes too, unlike yourself," Viv said.

"I dress up," I defended myself.

"When?"

"When I go to church," I retorted.

"And when was the last time you did that?" Vivian asked, reaching into her cabinet and pulling out a bottle of spice. She took the cap off and shook it into the pot.

"Okay, enough with the interrogation. What do you have in the pot?" I asked, trying to change the subject.

Vivian knew what I was doing, eyeing me skeptically, but she went along by answering, "I made some gumbo. This is my first time making this, so I hope it's going to be good." She picked up a spoon and dipped it into the liquid, brought it to her lips, blowing it slightly, and sampled it. "It tastes good, but I feel like it's missing something. Come over here and taste it," she said, putting the spoon she used to taste her food in the sink.

Vivian retrieved a fresh spoon out of the drawer and dipped it into the pot, lifting the mixture to my lips. I blew it, holding my hand under the spoon so none of it got on my clothes, and then I consumed it. "Mmmmm. Girl, that's good. I should have known you couldn't mess up anything."

"But doesn't it need something?" Vivian asked.

"Maybe a little bit more salt. Other than that, I think it's great," I said, taking the spoon out of her hand and licking it before putting it into the sink.

Vivian pinched some salt into the pot and stirred it some more. "This is going to be as good as it gets," she said, turning off the eye under the pot and moving it to one that was cold.

"I see I'm the first one again," I said.

"Yes. You know you are always the first one, unless Sheldon is here."

"Is Sheldon coming tonight?" I asked, hoping he was, just so I could stare at his fine behind.

"No, not this time. He had plans," Vivian said.

Sheldon was Vivian's best friend, and damn, he was sexy as hell. Tall and dark like the deepest of chocolates, and built like a stallion. You could see his six pack through the fitted shirts he wore; his body was so chiseled. To top it off, he had dreads, which he kept looking and smelling nice all the time.

I thought I loved a man with a bald head, but damn, after seeing Sheldon with his locks, he made me take a second look at brothers with them. Every time I hugged Sheldon I dove my face into his tresses. He looked even sexier when he pulled them back off his gorgeous face. The man had a smile to die for, with the whitest teeth I'd ever seen on a man and a dimple in his left cheek. I swear Sheldon was one man that could make me cheat on Corey.

I always wondered how Viv and Sheldon became such good friends, and most of all why my sister hadn't taken that fine specimen of a man as her own. For a minute I thought he was gay, but Sheldon let it be known real quick he was a ladies' man. I then had to wonder what the hell was wrong with my sister for not jumping that man's bones. I then questioned whether she was gay. One day I asked her, and she damn near had a heart attack.

"Hell no," she screamed. "I'm strictly dickly, sis."

"I had to ask, as fine as Sheldon is," I told her.

"We're just friends," Vivian would always say, but I still couldn't believe it. They acted like an old married couple but weren't getting the benefits of being one.

As I stopped daydreaming about Sheldon, Vivian said, "I swear we need to make our dinner time an hour earlier just so our sisters can get here on time."

"I know, right? And you know who's going to be last."

"Phoenix," we both said simultaneously.

"Speaking of Phoenix, did you hear about the fight I had with Paige at her house?" I revealed.

"Do you mean fighting as in arguing, or fighting as in coming to blows?" Viv asked for clarification as she leaned against the granite countertop to listen.

"Both, and you know I don't fight unless I have to."

"What happened?" Viv asked.

"I got tired of all the little jabs Paige kept saying the other night. I was standing in Phoenix's kitchen when Paige comes walking in talking about she was getting her some but didn't want to reveal who she was getting some from. That did it for me, Viv. I pushed her. From there we started fighting."

Vivian looked at me like I was crazy.

"What?"

"You know you were wrong, right?" she asked.

"How was I wrong?" I asked, surprised.

"Dawn, you started it by pushing that woman. What did you think was going to happen?" Vivian asked.

"I don't like her, and I wanted to hurt her."

"The one you should be hurting is Corey."

"I had it out with him, too, about Paige," I said unconvincingly.

"Yeah, but you took him back. You handled Paige like you should have handled Corey. Paige doesn't have love for you, but your man supposedly does."

"He does love me," I said.

"He's had a funny way of showing it since he's been with you. You're not with Paige, yet you treat her worse than the man who betrayed you. Yeah, that makes perfectly good sense to me," Vivian argued.

"So you want me to be her friend?" I asked with an attitude, getting heated that Viv didn't seem to be on my side.

"I'm not saying that. What I am saying is Corey is the one you should have been smacking. Paige didn't do anything that Corey didn't allow, is all I'm saying."

There was a knock at the door and I was glad. I was getting tired of discussing me tonight, even though this conversation was my own damn fault for bringing up; but I figured if I didn't bring it up, Phoenix would. I had to get my side out before Phoenix contorted it into something that didn't happen at all.

"Can you get that for me?" Viv asked, pulling out the bowls from the cabinet to set the table.

I went and answered the door. When I opened it, I saw my sisters Serena and Shauna standing there. "It's about time," I said jokingly.

"We ain't late," Serena said, holding the baby carrier with our newest member.

"Maybe you are on time by your clock, but you are late here. Y'all were supposed to have been here at five, and it's five thirty-seven. I almost started eating without y'all," I said, taking the carrier away from Serena and toting my niece into the kitchen.

"You could have eaten," Serena said, dropping her purse on the sofa as she followed me. "I bet you we beat Phoenix here."

All of us burst into laughter.

"What do we always say about Phoenix? She is going to be late for her own funeral," I said, putting the carrier on the countertop.

"And that's because she probably hired her own personal glam squad to make her over after death," Shauna said, causing us to laugh again.

"Let me hold my niece," I said, unbuckling the straps across her little chest.

"Y'all are not going to spoil her. She hardly sleeps at night now. She thinks somebody supposed to hold her all the time," Serena quipped.

"I wonder why?" Vivian asked, giving Serena a sideways glance.

"It's not me. It's her daddy. Tyree holds that girl all the time. I'm surprised he let her come over here with me today," Serena said, climbing onto the barstool at the island.

"Aw, daddy's little girl," Vivian said, speaking in a baby voice.

"I know, right? He even sleeps with her on his chest. I'm so scared he's going to turn over and squish her. He sleeps, and she lies there just as content. But when it comes to putting her in her bassinette, homegirl isn't having it. I'm surprised she's 'sleep now," Serena said. "That's why I don't want you bothering her, Dawn."

"Well, I'm her auntie, so I want to hold her. You are just going to have to get mad at me," I said, picking her up and placing her little frame up on my shoulder.

"I wasn't supposed to bring her," Serena admitted.

"Why?" Vivian asked.

"I was going to have some me time and leave her with her daddy, but we got into an argument, which is why I'm late."

"What are y'all arguing about this time?" I asked.

"What else? The ring he refuses to give to me."

"You need to leave that dead horse alone. That man is not going to marry you," Shauna said.

"I want to get married one day," Serena stated.

"Then you need to decide if the love you have for Tyree is worth losing to find a man who will marry you. And please know finding a good man who's going to take on you and your child, with a job, a car, his own place, not abusive, and loves you, and is not gay, is going to be a task in itself," Shauna explained.

Me and my sisters giggled.

"Why does it have to be so hard? Why don't men want to commit?" Serena asked no one in particular.

"Because that means giving up any other chance at random women," Shauna said.

"But he's supposed to be faithful to me anyway. He isn't supposed to be cheating. So if that's the case, why not make it legal?" Serena asked.

"It's something about that piece of paper men are afraid of. You see comedians joke about it all the time. It's the lockdown. The ball and chain for life, the clink clink," Viv said, holding her wrists together, causing us to chuckle.

"Well, Tyree needs to get over it and soon, or else I'm leaving," Serena declared.

"Yeah, right. You are not leaving that man. If you do, you're a fool. Especially if he is faithful and has a job," Shauna said.

"And good sex. You said his sex was amazing, so where you going again?" I joked.

My sisters laughed, and Serena found herself amused too.

"All we are saying, sis, is think about it good before you make an abrupt decision. Don't let love go over legalities," Viv cautioned.

By now I had checked out of the conversation as I snuggled my face against my little niece, saying, "I love the way babies smell. She makes me want to have one."

"Help yourself. She makes me not want anymore. I love her, but giving birth hurt like hell," Serena countered.

"I thought you got the epidural?" Shauna asked as she went over to the table to claim her spot.

"I did, but it wore off by the time it was time for me to push. I asked could they shoot me up again, but they said no because I was fully dilated. Girl, when her head started to come out, I thought the doctor was blowing flames down there. The nurse said something like it's the ring of fire. I started to tell her then cool it off with some cold water or ice cubes, anything that would reduce the burning I was feeling. That pain was excruciating," Serena stressed.

"But once you saw this little face, you had to forget about the pain," I said, rubbing my cheek against Nevaeh's curly black hair.

"That's true. You do forget about the pain you went through, but the fear is still there. And now I'm faced with a child who hates to sleep at night."

"But that's normal. Most infants do that. It will get easier," Vivian tried to convince her.

"Easy for you to say; you are the one getting six to eight hours of uninterrupted sleep," Serena said, crossing her arms with a frustrated look on her face. "I would kill for an eight-hour nap."

"I can watch her for you one night," I offered.

"Is Tyree going to stay with you too?" Serena asked, causing all of us to cackle. "That man ain't going to let her stay nowhere until she's thirty."

"Don't you mean forty?" Shauna joked.

"Exactly," Serena said, pointing to her as we giggled together.

"He can stay too," I said, rubbing her tiny little head.

"Good. Then maybe he won't try to ride me all night."

"You keep it up, you are going to have another little Nevaeh," I said.

"What's with the shades, Shauna?" Vivian asked, staring at Shauna, whose head leaned against her fist as she looked at us around the island.

And just like that, the mood shifted for some reason. I saw Serena give Shauna this look, but she didn't say anything.

"I'm just trying to style and profile," Shauna replied.

"You can take your shades off in here," Vivian suggested.

"I'd rather not," Shauna countered, as her chipper mood changed to a somber one. All of us looked at Shauna then Serena, who dropped her head.

"Uh-oh. What's going on?" Vivian asked as her eyes darted back and forth between the two.

I was lost also and wanted to know what was going on.

"You see. I knew I shouldn't have come over here," Shauna muttered, turning to face the window.

Vivian put down the spoon after she stirred the gumbo, and she went to Shauna. She pulled the shades from her face. When she did, we both gasped. "What the hell!" Vivian yelled.

"It's nothing," Shauna said, rubbing her bruised face.

"So a black eye is nothing these days," I said.

"Serena, explain please," our matriarch, Vivian, demanded as she walked back over to the stove.

"Her and Cal got to fighting, and he got the best of her. That's all," Serena explained like it was no big deal.

"That's all. You saying it like that's nothing," Viv said heatedly.

"Why are y'all just telling us?" I asked, trying my best not to raise my voice since I was holding the baby.

"We figured we would wait until today. It wasn't any need getting anybody else involved," Shauna said, looking at Serena, who turned her head like she didn't know anything.

"Anybody else. Wait." Vivian held her hand up. "Who else was involved?" Vivian asked.

"Big Ray, Pookie, Gerald, Tyree, and Phoenix," Shauna listed.

"Y'all can call them, but you can't call us. That's messed up," Vivian said furiously, walking over to the fridge to retrieve the lemonade she prepared.

"It wasn't like that, Viv. I wanted to handle this on my own, but some people thought it was in my best interest to call the cavalry," Shauna said, eyeballing Serena.

"I didn't do anything. It was Phoenix."

"But you called her."

"No, I didn't, Shauna. I told you she came over because we were supposed to go walking. She saw your car and knew you were there. Y'all know I'm not good at lying. She questioned me until I caved in, and things happened from there," Serena explained.

"All I have to say now is that y'all are lucky I'm even here. I didn't want to come. I heard it all before. I don't need it today, too. I know everything I need to know, and the main thing is I'm not taking him back before y'all come out your mouth with it," Shauna snapped. "So leave it alone."

All of us held our hands up like we were done with the subject. We knew when it came to Shauna's business, she never wanted anybody in it. This was why we only knew what she wanted us to know. Really she was much like Vivian in that way. They liked their privacy.

"Fine. I guess it's wrong for us to care," Vivian said, scooping ladles of gumbo into a large bowl she took out of her cabinet. While she did this, the room was quiet.

I kept my attention on my niece as we watched Viv scoop the liquid into the bowl. Once she was done, she picked up the steaming hot gumbo and carried it to the table. "Let's forget about this for now and eat," Viv suggested.

"What about Phoenix?" Serena asked.

"I'm not waiting on her anymore. She knew what time to be here. I'm tired of Phoenix thinking the world revolves around her. So if y'all ready, let's dig in," Viv said, and we all gathered around the table to get our grub on.

Chapter 13

Phoenix

I had a good reason why I was running late to Vivian's dinner. It was a man, of course. My sisters might not think it was a good enough reason to be late, but I thought it was, especially when it benefitted me. My extra, Eldon, was over, and I had to get me some of his yum-yum first. Lucky for me, Tobias wasn't home to mess up my flow. He went to play golf with some buddies of his, and while he was gone, I got my workout on with Eldon.

Eldon called me to see if he could drop by, and his timing couldn't have been more perfect. He was leaning against the doorframe trying to be cool, but it looked odd on him. Cool was the last thing Eldon was. He stood six feet one inch, 190 pounds, wearing a tight pair of jeans with a button-down blue-and-white striped shirt with a red bow tie and black slick bottoms. He wore his red-framed glasses today, I guessed to match his bow tie. Who wears a bow tie in the middle of the day, with denim jeans, no less? As hard as he tried to be cool was as hard as he was a royal failure at it.

I almost burst into laughter at his attempt, but I managed to hold back my hilarity. He was a little out of the ordinary from the men I was used to dealing with. The men I messed around with were damn near thugs or the business-corporate type. It was hard to place Eldon in either of these categories. Maybe *nerdy* was a better term, but this nerd had stacks of money and didn't mind hitting me off with some of his hard-earned cash every now and then.

Eldon not only had money, but the man knew how to eat some pussy. The man stayed hungry for it, and I really loved that he stayed hungry for me. As soon as we got to my bedroom, I couldn't get my panties off fast enough before he was laying me down on the bed. He dove between my thighs, feasting like it was Thanksgiving, I was the turkey, and my liquid pleasure was the gravy that saturated his face. He acted like he hadn't eaten in days and I was the meal that would conquer his hunger.

I sent up a big thank-you to the heavens as he salivated over my nucleus. He licked and sucked and plunged his tongue and fingers deep inside me. I was ready to hand this man an award for best pussy-eater ever, and I had quite a few who made attempts. Some failed miserably. Some could hold their own, but after having Eldon lay down his proficiency, it was hard to think of any man who could make me feel like this with his tongue.

I could feel my gravy running rapidly, yet he consumed it like he was drinking from a gravy boat.

"You taste so good," he muttered through licks.

I moaned my approval by saying, "Yes, baby, eat. Eat me good, baby."

I know I climaxed at least five times before he came up for air. Not only could he eat, but he would stay down there for a long period of time. When he came up, he wiped his face as I lay back, thinking I could go right to sleep now. His job was done to excellence. I could see his Johnson angling to get inside me, but this was the time I was ready to end this feast fest of ours and send him home. As much as I enjoyed Eldon eating me out, when it came down to the penetration, he really didn't do a good job with his stroking performance. One gift took away from the other. As good as he could eat me was as bad as he could screw me. He was really bad at it.

Honestly, there were very few men who held the title of total package in my book, and that's a man who can eat and fuck me like a champ. In Eldon's case, he could only eat. It wasn't like he had a very small penis. It was average, but he just didn't know what to do with it. That "motion in the ocean" crap was true, because when he tried to ride the waves of my ocean, his paddle got lost and the next thing I knew, Eldon was crashing to shore, releasing moments after he entered my sandy beach. I guess I shouldn't complain when it took him a minute or two to reach his orgasm. That was all of him I had to endure.

Yes, I hesitated, not wanting him to enter me, but since I knew it wouldn't take long, I let him inside. Like I thought, Eldon was crashing to the shore of my sandy beach, and all I had to do was gyrate my hips to pull his explosion from him quicker.

I was running late and needed to get cleaned up so I could leave. Unfortunately, this time I think I showed my disapproval for his motion in my ocean.

"What's wrong?" he asked after he bust his nut, panting like a dog needing water.

"Nothing," I said nonchalantly.

"It's something. You don't look pleased," he said, unclogging himself from me.

"I was pleased until you put your dick in me," I said, not thinking.

"What?" he asked, frowning.

I pushed Eldon off me and got up, saying, "Eldon, I enjoy what we do, but—"

"But what?" he asked, sitting there like a bump on a log.

"But you can't fuck. I'm sorry to be so blunt about it, but you can't."

"Yes the hell I can," he defended himself.

"No, you can't, sweetie," I said, scrunching my nose.

"Then why are you involved with me?"

"I'm with you because I like the way you eat my pussy. From what you lack in your strokes, you totally make up in your tongue. I swear if I could make your tongue platinum, I would certify it today, so you shouldn't get too upset, because at least you got that going for you," I tried to say convincingly.

Eldon got up off the bed and began gathering his clothes like a kid who was picked last on the playground. "I didn't come over here to be insulted."

"It's better you hear it from me than somebody else," I said, standing there buck-naked.

"I haven't had any other complaints from women," Eldon said.

"What woman do you know will complain? Most just lie there and deal with it. I did for a while, but I've gotten tired of pretending. I like to get into what I'm doing, and if you're not doing it for me dickwise, then I have to say something. Hell, life is too short to fake the funk."

"I guess you think you are the total package?" he asked angrily.

"You're here, aren't you? Not only do I taste good, but my cooch moved enough to make you cum in less than one minute flat, so yes, I think I'm the total package," I said, giggling. "You got a nice-sized Johnson, but you couldn't keep it wet inside me long before you were losing it."

Eldon was putting on his shirt when he caught on to me laughing at him. From the way he paused, his look went from one of anger to one of pure rage. Next thing I knew, he came over to me and grabbed me by the arm.

"What do you think you are doing? Let me go," I demanded.

"You want to get fucked, I'll fuck you," he said, pushing me back down on the bed. I wasn't scared. I was actually excited by his take-charge attitude. Now, this was what I was talking about. To urge him on, I started taunting him.

"What? You're going to fuck me now? Please don't if you aren't going to last but one minute again. I don't think you can handle my wetness for five minutes."

Eldon flipped me to my stomach, pulling my hips in the air.

"Don't let my fat ass cause you to shoot prematurely now," I teased.

Eldon pushed his Johnson inside me, causing me to take note this time. Not only did it feel bigger, but it felt like it was in control this time.

"Is this good enough for you?" Eldon shot back, plunging in and out of me. I didn't reply, because I didn't think he was going to last long again. Talk was cheap. Eldon had to show me what he was made of.

"If you last five minutes, I might scream your name," I coaxed.

Eldon pushed deep, hard, and with vigor. That nerdy man who showed up had disappeared, and now a champion had emerged. I turned my head to the right to look at my nightstand at the clock and realized he had lasted two minutes. I guessed he noticed what I was doing and plopped his body on top of mine to get me from looking. He came down and tongued me. I turned my head away as he continued to slide in and out of me. There was nothing gentle about this, and I liked it. I could feel my body coming to the point of heightened exhilaration. Eldon was doing his damn thing.

Making a mockery out of Eldon ended up being the best thing I could have done for him. This man put in work, causing me to reach my climax three more times, something I had never done from his manhood. When he finally finished, I turned to look at the clock to see he lasted forty-six minutes. I turned onto my back and clapped my gratification for a job well done. He was sweating profusely. His anger had turned into animal magnetism, and I loved every minute of it.

When Eldon left, I had an extra $2,000 in my purse after I told the sad story about falling behind on my mortgage. I guessed he wasn't mad at me anymore, and I damn sure had to pay respects to him for doing a damn good job at pleasing me.

When I arrived at Vivian's house, my sisters were already eating. They were damn near finished.

"So y'all are just going to start without me? Y'all never started without me before," I said, sitting at my place at the table.

"If you get any later, we might be washing dishes and putting the food up next time you come late," Vivian said.

"Probably was a man who made her late anyway," Shauna interjected, being right, but I wasn't going to admit it.

"I overslept," I said.

"Until six forty-five this evening?" Serena questioned.

"Y'all, I couldn't help if I had company," I said, picking up the ladle to scoop the mixture into my bowl.

"Like I said: a man," Shauna repeated.

"Shut up and go put some ice on that black eye," I joked, but I knew she wouldn't laugh. And she didn't.

"Phoenix, don't make me—" Shauna started before Vivian interrupted.

"Please don't do this today. Let's have a nice dinner without the arguing, okay?"

"On that note, I have something to tell y'all," Dawn said. "I was waiting for Phoenix to get here before I said anything."

"Let me eat some of this gumbo so I'll be able to stomach whatever you have to tell us," I said, picking up my spoon and putting the mixture into my mouth. I savored the food and thought, *Damn, this is good.*

"You ready now?" Dawn asked sarcastically.

"Hold up. Let me take another bite," I said, picking up the spoon two more times, putting some of the gumbo into my mouth. I held up my thumb, giving her the go-ahead, but I wished I would have waited to swallow before she belted the words:

"I'm getting married."

Chapter 14

Dawn

The room fell silent as Phoenix's spoon halted midair. She coughed and started choking on her food. Shauna reached over and hit Phoenix on the back until her coughing fit got under control. No one was saying anything. They were looking at me like I had something bizarre written across my forehead. Serena got up from the table looking like she was mad. She went over to the sink and rinsed her empty bowl out before putting it into the dishwasher.

"Let me be the first to break the ice. Who are you marrying?" Phoenix asked with a perplexed look on her face.

"I'm getting married to Corey, that's who. Stop acting like you don't know who I've been in a relationship with."

Phoenix shook her head. I heard Shauna sigh like she disapproved. My sisters were known for saying whatever came to their minds, and now none of them had anything to say. This caused me to get heated.

"No congratulations. Y'all not saying anything," I said.

"Congratulations," Vivian said.

I couldn't tell if she meant it. Their silence put me in a place of being uncomfortable. I was beginning to take their reaction the wrong way. I studied Vivian to see if she was sincere, but she was stone-faced. She didn't look happy, but she didn't look upset either.

"Thank you," I said apprehensively.

Another silence fell upon the table, and I blurted, "What's the problem, y'all? What the hell is with the silent treatment all of a sudden? Are y'all not happy for me?" I asked.

"We are," Vivian said.

"Stop lying, Vivian," Serena said, drying her hands off on the kitchen towel as she stood over the sink.

"I'm not lying," Vivian defended herself.

"Yes, you are," Serena argued.

"Y'all tell me the truth. You never hold back, so don't do it now," I said, looking around at each of them.

Vivian was eyeballing Serena. Phoenix was still eating on her gumbo, and Shauna was shielding her eyes with those sun shades so I couldn't see her eyes at all. From her index fingers massaging her temples, I felt like she didn't like the idea of me getting married either.

"Is anyone going to say anything?" I asked, glancing around at each of them.

"Okay, here it is. Who the hell are you fooling?" Serena asked, walking over to the table, but she didn't bother to take a seat.

"What is that supposed to mean?" I asked, looking up at her.

"I mean, why are you getting married to a man who can't keep his damn dick in his pants? How many times has he cheated on you? Seven?" Serena asked.

"More like seventy," Shauna chimed in.

"But he's changed," I reminded them.

"Since when?" Shauna asked, still rubbing her temples. "Did he get some type of counseling or sex therapy teaching him how to remain faithful? Hell, he just cheated on you two months ago, and now y'all getting married."

"Sounds like a guilty proposal to me," Phoenix said, dipping her bread into the bowl.

"A guilty proposal?" I asked.

"Yeah. He's trying to take the negative tension off of himself for being a damn dog and bringing something like marriage to the forefront to throw you off. As you can see, it worked," Phoenix said.

"Did it work? She acting like she can't recall the type of man she's marrying," Shauna cosigned. "He pulled a Kobe."

"A what?" I asked.

"A Kobe Bryant. You know, cheat on your girl only to buy her the ring to keep her from acting a damn fool until things die down," Phoenix explained.

"Please. He had this ring for a while," I explained.

"That's the lie he told you," Serena said, picking up Shauna's empty bowl off the table and walking it over to the sink to rinse out.

"Hell, you just got into a scuffle with Paige over them sleeping together the other day, so if it didn't bother you, then that incident shouldn't have happened," Shauna surmised.

"I'm not going into this marriage blind, you guys," I enlightened them.

"Then let's get your ass a seeing eye dog, because your ass is blind as hell if you can't see how wrong marrying Corey is," Shauna said.

This caused Phoenix to spit her gumbo across the table laughing.

"Eeeww," Shauna and Vivian blurted.

"I'm so sorry, y'all. That was a good one, Shauna. I almost choked on that one," Phoenix said, holding one of her hands over her mouth while using the other hand to wipe the spewed residue with a napkin.

"Make sure you wipe all that juice off my table. As a matter of fact, Serena, can you reach under the sink and pass me the Lysol disinfectant wipes?" Vivian asked.

Serena walked over to the table, handing her the container. Vivian opened it, pulling out a couple of sheets for Phoenix to clean up her germs.

"Why can't y'all be happy for me?" I asked.

"We are, but we also don't want to see you walk into something we know is not going to work," Serena said, taking her position back over at the sink.

"You sure you're not jealous because you been with Tyree longer than I've been with Corey and I'm the one getting married?"

"Oh, no she didn't," I heard Shauna mumbled under her breath.

I kept on talking. "Are you mad because Tyree isn't trying to make an honest woman out of you? I thought marriage was supposed to come before the baby carriage," I said defensively.

"Oh, no she didn't," Shauna said again, this time louder than before.

"Yes, the hell I did," I responded angrily. "Y'all are being so damn honest with me. I think I should tell some truth too," I said with major attitude.

Serena took in a deep breath before saying, "First of all, ain't nobody jealous over you and your dog of a man Corey. If I had a man like him . . . Let me rephrase that," she said, walking toward me with her finger in the air, pointing at me. "I'm not going to have a man like him, because I love myself enough to not want to put up with a man disrespecting me by sticking his dick in every woman willing to spread her legs for him. Second, what Tyree and I have going on will still be better than what you have, even without the papers, so get the shit right, Dawn. Ain't nobody jealous of you."

"Please, Serena. You acting like your relationship is first rate. How's his baby mama doing?" I asked with my head tilted to the side like I was pondering this but I couldn't care less.

Serena was really pissed now. She was so mad she couldn't think of anything to say as she practically stood over me with her chest heaving in and out.

Vivian stood to stop her from getting any closer, but I wasn't budging. I looked at her like, "Please try something." I'd got to fighting once in the past few days; I would do it again if I had to.

"You dead wrong for saying that, Dawn," Shauna retorted.

"Why? Y'all can beat up my happy occasion, but you don't expect me to say anything," I responded furiously.

"Everybody is wrong by how they are coming off, but, Dawn, we are also right about how Corey has been treating you," Vivian chimed in.

"Y'all don't have to live with him," I said.

"And we don't want to. Lying piece of crap," Serena uttered.

"Y'all are always against me. You think I'm stupid."

"No one has called you stupid, Dawn," Shauna said.

"Well, I think you stupid," Phoenix agreed.

"Ever since . . . Ever since . . ." I kept pausing.

"Leave it alone, Dawn. It's not that. Plus, this is not the time to bring up the past," Vivian said, figuring out what I was going to say.

"I think it is. I think none of you have ever forgiven me for what happened. That's why I'm treated the worst out of all of us."

"Hold up," Vivian said, standing to her feet with her hands up. "I never once treated you bad, so quit with the damn sob story. You are starting to piss me off now. Quit your damn temper tantrum. Either take what we are telling you as sisters caring about your well-being and happiness, or leave it alone. If anybody here should be mad at you, it's me," Vivian said angrily.

I knew Vivian was right, and I should have left well enough alone. I didn't know why I continued to live in the past, but it was hard not to. I couldn't help the way I felt. I wondered if the feelings inside me would ever get to a place where I would be settled with myself.

"I bet you I know what's going on. Dawn wants to be the first to break this family curse of the Johnson women," Phoenix said, finishing up the last of her gumbo.

"What curse?" Shauna asked.

"You know, the one where there hasn't been a woman in our family to get married for at least four generations. She wants to beat us to the altar," Phoenix said. "Not that I want to get married. I want to be single forever."

"I'm getting married because I love Corey, not because I'm trying to break some damn curse. Why can't y'all see that?"

"You can't sit here and tell me you don't love the fact that you are having a wedding. You've talked about this since you were a teen. Now your dream is coming true," Serena said. "And Corey knew this. He's playing with your emotions, which is the reason why he asked you to marry him in the first place. He was counting on your love for a wedding to shield his need for cheating."

"All I can say is I think you should wait," Shauna warned.

"This coming from you," I said.

"Damn right. I told y'all I'm never getting married either. I agree with Phoenix. I don't need a damn piece of paper confirming my love or commitment to a man. I do love the idea of a wedding, but all I want to do is walk down the aisle in my wedding dress to say I did it and walk the hell up out of there."

"Without saying vows?" Phoenix asked, giggling.

"Exactly. That's what most women want anyway: the actual wedding," Shauna explained.

"Would you have the reception, too?" Serena asked.

"Hell yeah. That's the best part. I would dance in my dress and kiss my man and be happy we are not legally bonded," Shauna said. "Dawn, maybe you should do the same thing. Corey is not the man you supposed to spend the rest of your life with. You know it. I know it. All of us know it. So stop fooling yourself, because you damn sure ain't fooling us."

"Amen," Serena agreed, her lips tight with aggravation.

"Y'all need to leave Dawn alone. Let her have her wedding with the man she loves," Phoenix said. "She's already following in the footsteps of her mother."

"Watch it," Vivian said.

"What? You don't remember when Daddy couldn't keep his dick in his pants?"

"Phoenix!" Vivian yelled.

"Well, it's true. What fantasy world are y'all living in to not remember that? Mama would've been a damn fool to marry our daddy too. As much as we love him, he is a male whore," Phoenix let slip.

"Our grandmother and great-grandmother had cheating men too, and you see they didn't bother to get married either," Serena cosigned.

"Here you are starting your marriage off with the same kind of man who has already slept with multiple women, and you want to make him legal," Phoenix said, chuckling.

"Cheaters learn how to get better at cheating. I mean, come on. Like he's going to come and say, 'Baby, I slept with another woman last night. Please forgive me,'" Shauna said, trying to mimic Corey's voice.

"The one thing y'all are forgetting is our daddy wasn't the only one who cheated," I said.

The room fell silent then.

"Mama cheated on him also."

"Can you blame her, Dawn? She got tired of him doing it, so she did it too," Phoenix responded. "I would have too."

"Two wrongs don't make a right," I countered.

"True, but in the end, both of them forgave one another and that's all that matters," Shauna said.

"Is it? Has Cal asked you to forgive him for whooping your ass?" I asked sternly.

Vivian and Serena shook their heads. I knew then what I said was a low blow, but hell, I was mad. I was tired of them beating up on me and the decision I was making to marry Corey. Yes, in my anger I may not have said things the right way, but I was mad.

"Aw, you have done it now," Phoenix said, picking up her bowl and going over to the stove to scoop her some more gumbo out of the pot, since the bowl on the table was empty.

Vivian and Serena snickered nervously, but Shauna wasn't laughing at all. All of our tempers were bad, but Shauna's was the worst. I watched as her jaws tightened and she gritted her teeth. I knew she was getting ready to let me have it, but I wasn't prepared for how far this disagreement would go.

Chapter 15

Shauna

Was this Beat Up On Shauna Week? I had had enough of people thinking they could come at me any type of way. First it was Cal thinking it was okay to put his hands on me. Then it was Phoenix and Serena wanting to handle things for me and Phoenix telling me I better not go back to him. Then it was Viv mad because I didn't say anything to her at all. Now I had Dawn casting out low blows because she was insecure in her relationship. She was upset because she, in actuality, wanted our blessing and we didn't give it to her.

Now because she felt bad about what we were saying, she wanted everybody to feel bad like she did. I had enough misery of my own without Dawn kicking me when I was down, and she should have known I was the wrong one to come for.

Taking my shades off, I looked around the kitchen and saw my sisters eyeballing me. My temples throbbed. My heart sped up its rhythm as my wrath began to ascend in my throat to the point of choking me. I began to tremble. I bounced my knee anxiously, knowing I was on the brink of snapping.

"I think we need to end this conversation before more feelings get hurt," Vivian suggested, trying to pacify the situation as she sat at the head of her kitchen table.

"I agree. We need to let this go and talk about something else," Serena agreed, looking at me. She shook her head at me, knowing what was coming, but I didn't think I could hold my temper back. Serena mouthed the words, "Leave it alone," shaking her head again.

I closed my eyes and dropped my head into my hands, trying to listen to what she was telling me, but I couldn't. The more I thought about what Dawn said, my throat closed up even more with the pressure of me trying to maintain what yearned to be released.

"All I wanted was a peaceful evening with my sisters, but I guess that was too much to ask," I said with my head down.

"You forgot who your sisters were," Phoenix joked.

"Evidently, but I thought today would be better. I mean, I knew you all would get on me about my eye," I said, pointing at my discolored bruise, "and what happened with Cal, but for it to be used in the way you used it . . ." I lifted my head to stare at Dawn. "This is why can't nobody say anything to you. You sitting here playing Ms. Self-righteous by dissing what happened to me, not wanting to look at this fake-ass relationship you have."

"Oooh. Shauna said fake," Phoenix said, giggling more as she spooned more gumbo into her mouth.

"You sitting here bragging about my fight when you just got your ass whooped by Paige, who screwed your soon-to-be husband. By the way, did you enjoy the banana show?"

Phoenix was steady cracking herself up over at the counter, leaning over her bowl and listening. Dawn shot her an evil glance, but Phoenix rolled her eyes and kept on eating.

"I didn't ask to get beat by Cal like you didn't ask to get crabs from Corey."

Phoenix spit her gumbo across the room again when I said that. This time she was coughing, choking, and laughing at the same time as she went over to the sink and coughed up the rest of gumbo that had lodged in her throat.

"What is it with you spitting your food across my kitchen?" Vivian asked. "In my sink, Phoenix? Why don't you stop eating?"

"Would you rather it had been on your floor?" Phoenix retorted once she gathered herself.

"The only difference with me, Dawn, is I'm not going to take Cal back. A man putting his hands on me is a lesson learned. You, on the other hand, didn't you have to go to the doctor to get treated several different times for STDs Corey brought back to you?" I asked cruelly.

Dawn scowled at me without saying anything as Phoenix stood holding her chest, still trying to recover from her choking a second time that night.

"I think I'm done. Damn, Shauna. I wish you would have warned me with that one. That was a good one. Who gets crabs these days? I thought the critters were extinct. Corey had to be digging into the dirtiest and oldest poon- poon to catch that," Phoenix said, still laughing.

This caused Vivian and Serena to giggle too.

"You might as well be talking to the wall, Phoenix, because Dawn ain't hearing you. She's not going to be satisfied until she catches a disease she can't get rid of. But I wish you the best of luck with that, sis," I said coldly, putting my hand on my forehead and saluting her. "Now, go on with your fake-ass wedding, but don't expect me to support you in ruining your life."

"So you saying you're not coming to my wedding?" Dawn asked.

"That's exactly what I'm saying," I answered, getting up from the table and walking over to the island, needing to get away from her.

"Do all y'all feel like that?" Dawn addressed our other sisters, looking at each of them.

Vivian was the only one at the table with Dawn, but the other two were standing at the stove and sink while I glared at her from the center island.

"I'm just saying Shauna has a point. No matter how you try to make shit smell like roses, it's still going to be shit," Phoenix said.

Dawn giggled agitatedly and said, "Y'all jealous."

"We jealous?" Phoenix asked.

Dawn held her hand up for her to shut up as she stood to her feet.

"You see. She hasn't heard anything we said. That's why I can't talk to her," I said, turning away.

Dawn looked at me first and said, "Shauna, you mad because you with a woman-beater who damn near killed your behind. But why should we be surprised when most of the times you pick men who don't do anything for you anyway?

They have no job, no money, and not a pot to piss in, but you run to them like something stupid."

I turned to face her with my eyes stretched, but before I could say anything pertaining to what she said, Dawn turned her anger to Vivian.

"Vivian, you mad because you don't have a man. You have booty calls, or I should shorten it to *a* booty call. You think you are the rock of this family, but you really not. If you were so strong, you wouldn't let your ex-man use you when he's good and ready to. But keep doing what you doing, because you might get a man one day."

Dawn then turned her attention toward Serena and said, "You have a man, but you were dumb enough to have a child with him out of wedlock. Get used to playing wifey because as long as you are with him, his son, and his baby mama, you and Nevaeh will always be second best."

"Dawn has lost her ever-lovin' mind," Serena replied.

"And now to my baby sister, Phoenix. You're nothing but a high-class whore. You walk around all the time dressed to kill, with money all in your pockets and living a lifestyle none of us understand, but we know you pimping yourself out. Ass for cash, right?" Dawn said, taking away that smirk Phoenix had had on her face most of the night. It was now replaced with a scowl.

Dawn continued to say to her, "No man wants to turn a whore into a housewife, so I understand why you have chosen to never marry. No man with common sense would want to marry a common whore."

"Okay, that's it. I'm going to kick her ass," I said, snapping as I dropped the towel I was wrapping around my hand to relieve the anger bursting to release, but that was it. I was so done with Dawn's mouth. I sprinted across the room so fast she didn't see me coming. Vivian jumped up and stepped in my path to stop me as Dawn stepped back, knowing I was about to snatch her up.

"You want to talk truth? Here's the truth," I yelled.

"No, Shauna, don't do this," Vivian urged, but I ignored her as she continued to hold me back from putting my hands on Dawn.

"You settling just like our dad did when he chose to sleep with your mother and leave our mom for her. You're calling Phoenix a whore. What was your mother?"

Silence fell upon the room as each of my sisters looked around at one another. Viv was the one breaking the awkward silence by yelling, "Shauna, that's enough!"

But I was ticked off. Dawn wanted to take it there and hurt people's feelings. She was about to get a dose of her own medicine.

"After all we have done for you. After our mom took you in as her own daughter when your mother committed suicide because she couldn't handle the fact that our daddy wanted to come back home to us. She was too weak to want to live for you. You want to throw around jealousy."

"Shauna, no!" Serena screamed with tears forming in her eyes.

"You are jealous of us. You can't accept the fact our dad chose our mother and tossed yours to the side. You can't turn a whore into a housewife; isn't that what you said? She was a side whore who settled and would rather die than live for you, and now you are doing the same thing: settling. I guess you are going to die for this punk, too."

"Stop it, Shauna," Viv said, trying to cover my mouth, but my rage was stronger as I removed her hand and kept spewing the anger that had built up for years.

"We always treated you like you came from our mother, but you have always thought you were better than us, somehow, which I can't understand, because you are the result of adultery.

You sitting here talking about Serena's baby being born out of wedlock. What about you? At least we were created in love and not lust."

"Please, can somebody shut her up?" Serena begged.

Vivian tried to push me out of the room but couldn't. She then tried to put her hand over my mouth again, but I moved her hand and continued my rant.

"You thought we were the enemy, but it was our father," I said, moving my arms in a circular motion to include all of us, "and your mother," I said, pointing at Dawn, "who tore this family apart. And, who was the rock that held us together and looked beyond blood to be the bigger person? Our mom. Who took you in? Our mom," I said, beating my chest. "Who loved you regardless of how you were created? We have. And who has been there for you despite the bad circumstance? We have."

Tears began to stream down Dawn's face. I knew my words were cutting her deep as I hoped they would. The truth had been dormant for way too long. We all went on like things were great, never speaking of this, but today I was letting Dawn know how it really was. She needed to be reminded so she could get knocked down off that self-righteous pedestal of hers and see things the way they really were.

Serena, along with Vivian, was wiping tears now also.

“So that’s how y’all have felt about me?” Dawn asked glumly.

“No, Dawn,” Vivian answered.

Dawn was trying to hear what anybody had to say now. She reached down to pick up her purse, which was hanging off the back of the dining room chair she was sitting in. She wiped tears away as she pulled out her car keys, saying, “I don’t need none of y’all to show up to my wedding. As far as I’m concerned, our sisterly bond has officially been severed,” she said shamelessly as she exited the kitchen and stormed out of Vivian’s home.

Chapter 16

Shauna

Once I calmed down, I immediately regretted what I had said to Dawn. My sisters were looking at me like I'd done the worst thing imaginable. Vivian was so livid she didn't say anything to me. She started clearing the table and putting things up like we weren't in her house. In our commotion, little Nevaeh had woken up, so Serena was tending to her. She was sitting at the island on the barstool feeding her, and Phoenix was leaned against the wall, gaping at me.

"Y'all, I'm sorry," I said sincerely.

"I can't believe you, Shauna," Vivian spat. "How could you do that to her?"

"She made me mad and I lost it."

"You more than lost it. You destroyed Dawn in the process, and possibly this entire family. You know we have promised ourselves we would never speak on those events, especially in anger," Phoenix reminded me.

"I know, and I can't say enough that I'm sorry," I pleaded.

"The person you need to be saying sorry to is Dawn," Vivian urged.

"Do you think she's going to want to hear anything I have to say after what I just did?" I asked.

"Hell naw," Phoenix said. "But you are still going to have to apologize. Call her now and see if you can get her. You shouldn't go to sleep with this lingering in the air among us."

I took Phoenix's advice and pulled out my cell phone to call Dawn. Pulling her number up, I dialed it. The call was sent straight to voicemail. I tried again, only for the same thing to happen.

"She's not accepting my calls," I said dejectedly.

"Well, can you blame her?" Viv asked, putting the leftover pot of gumbo into the refrigerator and pulling out a bottle of Moscato. "Now she's thinking this is how all of us feel, and it's not that way at all."

"Honestly, I've thought about telling Dawn the exact thing Shauna did," Serena confessed, looking down at little Nevaeh drinking her bottle of milk.

"So you agree with how Shauna let Dawn know?" Vivian asked, looking in a drawer for the bottle opener.

"Yes," Serena said, looking up and speaking matter-of-factly. "Dawn hit below the belt first, and Shauna returned the blows."

"I can't believe what you are saying right now," Vivian retorted, finally finding the contraption that would get her closer to easing her stress with a glass of wine.

"For years I've had an issue with Dawn, but I embraced her because it wasn't her fault she was brought into a situation of adultery, just like it wasn't our fault our daddy created another sibling outside his relationship with our mother. It wasn't Dawn's fault her mom gave up on life. At the same time, we were supposed to go on like this happy little family, letting her come into the fold like everything was sunshine and rainbows. I've never understood that. Did anyone ever think how it would affect us?" Serena asked.

"Exactly," I agreed, nodding to what Serena just said.

"Mom wanted it that way," Phoenix reminded us.

"Did she, or did she feel sorry for a child who didn't deserve the hand that was dealt to her?" Serena asked.

"Mama was good for helping people," I agreed. "So why not help the very child her man created?

She had already taken him back. What was she supposed to do, tell him, 'I don't want that child in my house' after hearing Dawn's mother blew her brains out?"

"Regardless of how things played out in our past, what happened tonight never should have happened. We have all come a long way," Vivian argued.

"Dawn always starts stuff by running that mouth of hers, and she can't ever take it when she's on the losing end of the situation. Case in point, Paige. And let us not forget what she did to our dad."

The room fell silent then.

"Our dad is in jail because of her," Serena said, picking up Nevaeh and laying her over her lap to burp her as she bounced her leg gently. "Have you all forgiven her for putting him there? Because I haven't. I love Dawn, don't get me wrong, but it's been difficult for me to pretend I don't have a problem with her."

"You've done an awesome job hiding your feelings," Phoenix said.

"I didn't have a choice. I didn't want to be the one rocking the boat on us getting along," Serena revealed.

"Don't put this on us. You could have said something or brought it up before now," Phoenix said.

"And then what, have y'all mad at me and talking to me about how I need to forgive and forget? Y'all know y'all would have done that," Serena replied.

"You're right," Vivian agreed.

"Look, I went ballistic tonight. It brought things out that should have been brought to the forefront years ago. Now it's time to deal with them," I said.

"I'm not ready to deal," Vivian countered, surprising us all.

"Why? You are always the one who wants to work things out," I said.

"Things are not always what they appear to be," Vivian responded.

"What does that mean?" Serena asked.

"Look, I'm done talking about this tonight. I'm ready to go to bed," Vivian said, clicking off the light over the sink.

"I guess that's our cue to leave," Phoenix said, walking over to the table and grabbing her purse. "We Johnson sisters never fail to entertain, regardless of the outcome."

"You ain't never lied," Serena agreed, picking up a now sleeping Nevaeh and hopping down off the stool carefully. She walked over to the carrier and placed little Nevaeh in it, strapping her down for the trip home.

"One day these issues are going to have to be dealt with for us to move on. We can't keep pretending like they don't exist. That's all I'm saying," I said, looking at Vivian, who was still holding her unopened bottle of Moscato. I guessed she was waiting to open it after we left, probably fearing we would want some, which I would. I wasn't going to push it. She was ready for us to be gone, and I was ready to go home.

"Tonight doesn't have to be the night to resolve our issues, so let's sleep on it and figure out what to do later," Vivian said, practically pushing us out of the door.

Yes, I had opened a can of worms, which had been created a long time ago, and now I was the one who turned the can over, making a mess of things. This was our elephant in the room that we had been ignoring for quite some time. We didn't realize how the actions of our father would affect us in the long run. Tonight seemed to be filled with skeletons rolling out of the closet, and I couldn't help but wonder what other remains were going to appear before all of this was over.

Chapter 17

Vivian

As much as I loved these dinners with my sisters, I was always glad when they were over, especially tonight. Like always, there was an argument and disagreements. Who knew tonight Dawn's soon-to-be marriage would be the beginning of a squabble that caused issues from the past to spill out like red wine on white carpet? These issues were the tarnish we couldn't get rid of. For Dawn to go off on us like she did was so uncalled for, but the response Shauna delivered was way worse than anything Dawn said. I wondered if our relationship could withstand some of the things that came out of her mouth tonight. I didn't think so, and I wished things would have been left alone. As deep as the wounds were dug, I wasn't sure this time was the right time to heal them.

Even in all of that commotion, I'm not going to lie, a part of me was a bit jealous of Dawn announcing her soon-to-be wedding. I was the oldest, so I felt like I should have been the first to get married. At the same time, how could I be jealous when I didn't even have a man to tie the knot with? She was right about that. My career was my man. I was making money and buying my home and car and basically living a lucrative life, but all of this was done with no one to share it with.

As together as it seemed like I had it, no one knew the turmoil that brewed beneath my exterior. My hair stayed done, nails done, everything done. I sauntered like I owned the world. I looked like I had it together, but deep down inside I didn't. I think the toll of trying to be this perfectionist was finally catching up to me. Around people I could fake it better than anybody, but once I was alone, the reality of everything always hit me like a ton of bricks. My mind became the devil's playground, and some of the things he'd been telling me to do scared me.

After work, all I looked forward to was coming home, slipping out of my clothes, and crawling into bed. There had been days when I didn't get up until the next morning without so much as a morsel of food consumed. My bed was my haven.

One of the things that seemed to take my mind off my own issues was watching other peoples' lives unfold on reality TV. I would watch it until sleep took over. This was when I was my happiest, in slumber land without having to do a thing but rest. It was the only time when my mind was in a state of peace.

Crawling into my refuge with my Tinker Bell sleepwear on, I turned on the TV, jumping quickly back into my routine. It was a little after 10:30 p.m. and I was surprised, after all the drama tonight, that I wasn't sleepy. I guessed Dawn's engagement and Shauna's mudslinging were more than I could handle. I wished I could be happy for Dawn, but I couldn't. How could I, when I felt like my life was somewhat over at the ripe age of thirty-four? I had become a hermit. The only drive I had was with my job. When it came to quality time with me, I shafted myself.

The bottle of wine I gripped earlier was sitting on my nightstand in a bucket of ice. I was waiting for my sisters to leave so I wouldn't have to share any of it with them. Tonight, the entire bottle was mine. I reached over and grabbed it, along with the corkscrew to open it. Twisting it into the cork, I had the bottle opened in seconds. The popping sound was like music to my ears as a small cloud escaped the bottle. I reached over and put the corkscrew down and grabbed my wine glass. I was almost tempted to drink out of the bottle but thought a glass would be better.

Filling the glass halfway, I gulped down the cold, delicious liquid. I moaned with delight as the cool liquid made its way down my esophagus. I poured another glass, filling it to the rim. This time I sipped. I put the bottle with the remaining Moscato back in the bucket of ice on my nightstand and got cozy. Leaning back on my pillows, I was going to sip until I felt the wine do its magic and relax me.

My cell phone rang, breaking my tranquil moment. I reached over to my nightstand and answered it. "Hello."

"Yo, open the door. I'm pulling up now."

"What happened to your key, Sheldon?"

"Oh, I forgot you gave me one. I can't get used to having it," he said, giggling with the music blaring in the background. I was surprised he could hear me at all with the way his music was blaring in my ear and I wasn't even in the car.

"Just come in. I'm in the bedroom."

"Are you watching TV or reading a book?" he asked.

"I'm watching TV. There's nothing else better to do."

"I'll be in there in a minute to perk you up."

"Okay, and make sure you lock the door back when you come in. You are good for leaving it unlocked," I told him.

"Like somebody is fool enough to come in there while I'm here."

"A gun doesn't know anybody, so lock it please. You can't play hero if you're dead."

Sheldon laughed and hung up.

All my sisters thought I was a fool to not be with Sheldon. He was fine as hell, but I loved the six-year friendship we had developed, and I didn't want to do anything to jeopardize it. We'd never had sex or even kissed one another. I mean, we kissed each other, but it was on the cheek with a hug. Nothing more than that. He was the fun part of my life, and a lot of times I lived through him. He did bring me joy. I honestly didn't know if I could make it without him.

About five minutes later, Sheldon was walking in my bedroom. "I swear you need to find something else to do other than cuddle in your bed all the time," Sheldon said, coming in. Then he saw me holding a glass. "And you are drinking. You didn't tell me that."

"I didn't think it was important."

"Of course it is when I might want some."

"Sorry. This bottle is all mine. If you want one of your own, you can get it out the fridge," I told him.

"Not even a sip?" Sheldon asked, walking over and picking up the bottle of wine from the bucket.

"Here, boy," I said, handing him my glass. "And only a sip. I know how you do. You will gulp that—"

Before I could get those words out of my mouth, Sheldon downed the wine, leaving my glass empty once again. I frowned at him like, "Really?"

"Sorry, Viv. I needed it after the night I've had," he said, handing me the empty glass.

"Trust me. I've had the same type of night," I retorted. "Well, you look nice," I complimented him, looking at him wearing a pair of dark denim jeans, a black shirt, a black leather jacket, and black Timberlands.

"Thank you," he said, kicking off his boots. He took his jacket off, tossing it on my bench at the foot of my bed. "You know I had to come over here and tell you about my date," Sheldon said, coming over to the bed and climbing in.

"Boy, are you clean? I don't want no other woman's remnants in my bed," I told him.

"Viv, I'm good. You know I know better than that," he said, crawling next to me.

"Okay. I'm just checking. You know you have before," I said, pouring me another glass of wine.

"That was so long ago," he said, smiling.

I looked at him like, "Boy, please."

"So why is your date over so soon?" I asked. "I thought you would be taking her home and hanging out like you do."

"Viv, it was the *Nightmare on Elm Street* reincarnated through this woman," he said jokingly. "I'm never going on a blind date again."

"What? Did she look like Freddie Krueger or something?"

"No, this woman wasn't bad looking at all."

"So what was the problem?" I asked.

He sighed, tilting his head like he didn't want to say, and just his hesitation made me burst into laughter. I said to him, "Sheldon, it couldn't have been that bad."

"Yes, it was. Like I said, this woman was cute and had a nice little shape on her, but her mouth . . ."

"What about her mouth?" I asked.

"I thought Phoenix and Shauna cursed a lot, but this chick had 'motherfuck this' and 'fuck that' flying out of her mouth to the point I was embarrassed to be around her. And I curse," Sheldon said.

I laughed.

"Not only did she curse a lot, Viv, but she revealed to me she had eight kids," he said, holding up eight fingers.

"Eight?" I asked, frowning.

"Yes, eight with seven different baby daddies."

"She told you this?"

"Yes," he yelled like he still couldn't believe it. "Who admits something like that on the first date?"

"Didn't she know that was a date killer?"

"Right," he agreed. "And, Viv, she was only twenty-nine. All night I kept thinking how in the hell do you have eight kids by thirty? You know I love kids, but eight?" Sheldon said, causing me to giggle. "I thought one of her kids was going to interrupt our dinner, singing the song, 'One, two, my daddy's coming for you. Three, four, gonna lock the door. Five, six, trying to get your chips.'"

I burst into laughter again, happy that Sheldon had taken me out of my dreadful mood. He always knew how to do this, even if it sometimes came at the expense of his horrible dates.

"I was looking for a little girl wearing that same dress that kid wore in *Nightmare on Elm Street* for real, Viv. I was scared."

"Boy, you weren't scared."

"Like hell I wasn't," he said seriously.

"Where did y'all go to eat?" I asked.

"Cheddars. You know I love their croissants."

"And you didn't bring me any?"

"Damn. I did. I brought nine. I left them in the car. I'll get them in a minute."

"I'm not going to eat nine croissants," I said.

"I got them for the both of us. Did you make that gumbo like you said you were?"

"Yes, it's some left. I made sure to save you some."

"That's what I'm talking about," he said, rubbing his hands together. "Thanks for looking out, because I know Phoenix would have taken all them leftovers home with her," Sheldon said.

"Oh, believe me, she tried, but I hid some before they all got here. It eliminates one less issue between us."

"So tonight was crazy?" he asked. "I can tell by your mood and your bottle of bubbly."

"Was it? Why did Dawn tell us she's getting married?"

"To who?" he asked in astonishment.

"Corey of all people," I revealed.

"Cheater cheater pussy-eater."

"Sheldon!"

"Well, that's what he's known for in the streets. Dude dives down more than a SCUBA instructor giving diving lessons. Why you think he gets so many women? They're trying to see what the tongue feels like."

"You didn't have to say it like that. You can't say coochie or poon-poon?" I joked.

"Viv, what I look like saying *coochie*? I'm a man for goodness' sake, and I say pussy," he retorted.

"I forgot who I was talking to," I replied, taking a sip of my wine.

"Evidently you did. Now, did you tell Dawn she lost her damn mind?" Sheldon asked, lying down on his left side to face me, propping himself up on the pillows.

"Of course. I think the only one who didn't really argue tonight was Phoenix."

"Tell me you're lying."

"I'm serious. She made her little comments, but me, Shauna, and Serena had it out with Dawn."

"Phoenix always got something smart to say," Sheldon said.

"I know, but tonight she was too busy spitting gumbo all over my kitchen."

"Okay. That explains it. She was busy laughing her ass off, huh?"

"Basically. Shauna was the one who lost it tonight. She got so mad at Dawn she told her she's not going to have anything to do with the wedding," I told him.

"Daaaaamn. Y'all really went at it."

"That wasn't even the half. Dawn decided to tell us about ourselves and ended up throwing all of us under the bus."

"How?" Sheldon asked.

"Well, I'm being used by men. Serena was stupid for having her baby by a man who already has a kid out of wedlock. Shauna's dumb enough to be with a woman- beater. And Phoenix is a whore who's never going to be good enough to be any man's wife," I recapped.

"Daaaamn. Dawn took it there for real. I wish I was here to play referee. It would have been better than my nightmare of a date."

"It gets worse," I said.

"Viv, I don't think it can get worse than that."

"Believe you me it did. Shauna lost it. I mean, she blacked the hell out. She brought back so much stuff I wanted buried from our past that I think only Jesus Himself needs to come down here and be the intermediary between them two now. I feel like this will cause a major rift between us sisters."

"Please tell me she didn't mention anything about Dawn's mother?" Sheldon asked.

I nodded, saying, "She took it there. And now I don't know how to fix it."

"First off, Viv, you can't fix it. It's not up to you to fix everything. All you can do is be the big sister you are. You are putting too much pressure on yourself. Pray about it and let God handle it."

Sheldon was right. I always wanted things perfect, even though I knew this wasn't a perfect world we lived in. It did feel good talking to him about it. Sheldon knew everything about how we grew up. I told him about Daddy cheating on Mom and having a child outside his relationship. I told Sheldon everything. Well, almost everything.

"Enough about my night. What did you do? Because I know you did something. Did you leave her sitting at the table? Because you're good for ditching a woman," I said, looking at *Family Guy* on Cartoon Network.

"I was a gentleman this time. I stayed as long as I could stand her, and then I was honest and told her I had somewhere else to be. She didn't seem happy and made it known."

"How?" I asked.

"Viv, she went off on me in the middle of this restaurant, talking about I was leaving her to go sleep with some other woman."

"Shut up," I said, putting my hand to my mouth.

"She said she felt disrespected because she was really feeling me and was hoping our relationship was going to go to another level."

"Damn, she was getting ready to make you baby daddy number eight," I said, laughing.

"I felt like that too. I only knew this chick for a couple of hours and she acted like we had been dating for years. You know I hate confrontation because of my temper, Viv. I told you on several occasions I need anger management."

"Boy, do I know," I said sarcastically. "So what did you do?"

"I tried to be nice," Sheldon explained.

"What did you do?" I asked again.

"I called her out her name and told her she didn't know me like that."

"And?" I said, knowing there was more.

"And I told her she was a whore and needed to learn how to keep her legs closed and I wouldn't sleep with her if her pussy spit out hundred-dollar bills."

"Sheldon!" I yelled, hitting him on the arm.

"She deserved it. She screamed on me until I exited the restaurant. I don't know if I can ever show my face there again."

"Take me next time," I said jokingly.

"They might turn me away at the door once they see me coming with another female," he said, causing me to laugh.

"Well, I'm glad you escaped without any charges being filed."

Sheldon was so nice and sweet, but don't let his laidback demeanor fool you. He really did need anger management. I think he liked confrontation. His frame alone was intimidating, since he lifted weights a few times a week. He wasn't real big, not like those weightlifters looked with veins popping out of their necks. Sheldon had a nice build, but his size was threatening to some people.

One time Sheldon and I went to the grocery store to get items to have a hot dog night, so we could chill and watch movies. While we were in the bread aisle looking for some hot dog buns, this middle-aged Caucasian man came walking up and stopped right in front of us, blocking our view. Sheldon looked at me, pointing at the dude like, "What the hell?"

"It's okay," I said, upset by this man's ill manners also, although I couldn't show this because I knew how Sheldon was. He wasn't racist, but as an African American man, he felt like he was always been targeted. I do believe this has been the case sometimes. So when it came to some races, he felt like he needed to be on guard, and for this man to blatantly stop dead in front of us like we were a nonfactor ticked both of us off. One disrespectful person doesn't define an entire race in my book, and Sheldon believed this too, but when things like this happened, his judgment sometimes got clouded.

"Yo, my man. You didn't see us standing here looking for bread too?"

The man turned and looked at Sheldon but didn't say a word. Then he turned back around like Sheldon didn't say anything. I knew it was going to be on now. Here was the nonfactor situation that this man put us in, and Sheldon was about to let him know the true facts about the type of man he was.

Sheldon stepped around the dude, getting all up in the man's face. "Did you hear me talking to you, man?" he asked furiously as the man backed up fearfully now. "Where are your damn manners?"

"Don't make me call the cops," the man said.

"You see, Viv, this is the type of shit I'm talking about. The man sees I'm black and immediately thinks the cops need to be involved," Sheldon addressed me.

"Sheldon, it's okay. Let him get his bread and go."

Sheldon turned his attention back to the middle-aged man and asked "How are you going to dial the cops with broken fingers and the ability to not say nothing once I knock all your damn teeth out your mouth?" Sheldon threatened.

"I just came here for some bread."

"So did we, before you rudely stood in front of us. Now, I would advise you to get the hell out of here, but not before apologizing to this young woman." Sheldon gestured toward me.

The man ended up saying he was sorry. He looked at me when he said it, because Sheldon was still up in his face. I nodded it was okay, but I did that because I wanted this to be over. I didn't want Sheldon to get in trouble.

"Sheldon, he said he was sorry. Step back and let the man get his bread," I told him.

Sheldon listened, and the man left without any bread. I was waiting for management or security to come and escort Sheldon out of the store, but no one ever came, thank goodness.

Then there was the night we went out to a bar for drinks and this dude wasted a drink on Sheldon's back. Instead of apologizing, the guy started laughing like it was funny. Sheldon punched the guy in the face, breaking his nose. Sheldon ended up with an assault charge, having to pay the man's medical bills. So yes, he did need to get some help for his anger.

"Viv, I'm going outside to get the bread. Can you heat up some gumbo and we can have a little pajama party?" he asked.

"You don't have any pajamas."

"I came prepared. I packed a bag just in case to come over here. So I brought some."

"Well, aren't you the one who plans ahead?" I said.

"I knew it in my gut that this date wasn't going to work, and I was right. I should have stayed here and ate dinner with y'all."

"We can eat now. Go get my bread and I'll heat us up some gumbo," I said, pulling the covers back to get up and go into the kitchen. I drank the last bit of wine that was in my glass.

Sheldon jumped up too, sliding on his boots to go get the bread. My night had turned around quickly, and I was happy for the diversion. Thanks to Sheldon, my evening was turning out to be a good one after all.

Chapter 18

Dawn

Just when I didn't think my night could get any worse, I was being pulled over by the police. I merged over to the shoulder of the road, with the police car doing the same. I did not need this right now. I wiped at the tears that were steadily falling from my eyes. More tears trickled down my face as I watched the officer walk up to my window and tap on it.

"Good evening, ma'am," the African American officer said, with his left hand holding a flash-light and the other hand on his gun.

"Yes," I said angrily, looking up at him. His skin was dark like chocolate. I scanned his body, which looked like he worked out. The uniform was tight across his chest, and the silver shield identified him as Officer Winn.

He shined the light around my car to see if anyone else was with me, which there wasn't.

"Can I see your driver's license and registration please?" he asked.

I reached into my glove compartment, retrieving my registration. I then pulled my license out of my wallet and handed both to the officer.

He shined the light down on it and then asked, "Do you know why I pulled you over, ma'am?"

"No, sir, I don't." I shrugged, answering him through tears, which were still trickling from my eyes.

"Are you okay, ma'am?" he asked, bending down a bit to get a better look at me.

"No, not really. I've had a really bad night," I explained.

"I'm sorry to hear that. And I'm pretty sure this isn't making it any better," he said kindly.

"You would be correct."

"I'm just doing my job. I pulled you over because you were doing forty-two in a twenty-five mile an hour zone."

"Okay," was all I could say. I was so defeated at this point I didn't care. I was hurting. I was sad. I was angry. He stood there like he expected me to say something else or talk my way out of this, but I didn't have any fight left in me. I wasn't Phoenix, who would probably show some cleavage or pull out her breast to get a warning, or Shauna, who would probably cuss the officer out and get arrested. I was Dawn, the Dawn who had no fight left.

The officer must have caught the hint and said, "Ma'am, I'm going to run your information. I'll be right back." He walked to his car and got in.

I saw there was another officer with him and a camera on the dashboard, recording this violation. I lowered my head, willing the tears to stop falling, but they wouldn't. As hard as I tried, the stress of my evening won and broke me down. I didn't want to look up, because I didn't want the people riding by, as their speed slowed after seeing the flashing lights, to see who it was who got pulled over. Just like I had done in the past, they were probably counting their lucky stars it wasn't them.

Minutes later, the officer was back at my car with a slip of paper, letting me know he went through with giving me the ticket. *Great,* I thought. *Like I should expect anything less with the type of night I'm having. Let's just add more things to my already terrible evening.*

"Sign here, ma'am. This is stating I stopped you for doing forty-two in a twenty-five mile an hour zone. Your court date is here if you want to dispute this. And here is the address you can mail your money to if you decide not to dispute it. There is a number here if you have any questions. Do you understand what I have told you tonight?"

"Yes," I said dejectedly.

"Honestly, I would have let you off with a warning, but my superior officer is with me, and I had to do it," he said kindly.

I nodded as I agreed and signed the paper. I didn't care. I took the ticket, rolled my window up, and tried my best not to squeal tires as I pulled off.

When I walked into the house, I walked to the den to see Corey lying on the couch, watching a football game. I was so happy to see him.

"Hey, baby. How was dinner?" he asked.

"Horrible," I said, dropping everything in my hands to the floor.

"Baby, what's wrong?" he asked, sitting up. "Come over here," he said, patting the spot next to him.

I did what he asked and fell into his open arms.

"I guess you told them about us getting married."

"I thought regardless of how they felt about you, Corey, they would be happy for me, but they jumped on me, saying you are a dog and a cheater," I said through tears.

"Wow. Strong opinions coming from people who mean nothing to me in my life," he said.

"But they mean something to me. Rather, they did," I said glumly.

"You can't help who your siblings are, but you can control your own happiness. I hope being with me will make you happy," he said, kissing me on the cheek.

"You do make me happy, baby," I said, wrapping my arms around him.

"I know I've made mistakes, and I hoped they wouldn't hold those mistakes against me, but I guess I was wrong. I have changed. I hope you can see that. They haven't changed your mind about us getting married, have they?" he asked.

I looked up at him, saying, "No. I want to be your wife."

"Even if it costs you your sisters?" Corey asked.

I paused, thinking about it for a minute. I knew I hadn't told Corey the full story about what happened tonight, but he didn't know everything that pertained to my past either, and I wanted to keep it that way. I was pretty sure there were things I didn't know about his also, so why tell him how my life had turned out? All he knew was my real mother passed away. He didn't know which mother I was referring to, because as far as he knew, my sisters and I had the same mother and father. He knew my dad was in jail, but he didn't know the real reason why. I told him it was for embezzlement and fraud. Of course, that was a lie. I knew going into our marriage with a bunch of lies was wrong, but what else was I supposed to do? My business was my business, with the exception of my sisters knowing the huge aspects that made up my dysfunctional life.

Until tonight, I didn't know the things that happened had affected them like they did. Shauna's words hurt more than anything I'd felt in my life. It began to make me wonder how they all really felt about me. I felt like the black sheep, and in a way I was, due to the fact that our dad and my real mom caused all this drama in our lives. Why did we, as the children, have to pay for the sins of our parents? As mad as I was, I had to look at all sides, which was something I was not ready to do at this time. My antagonism prompted the floodgates to release devastation on us. I could have heard what each of them had to say and kept it moving, but I had to push back like I always did. This time it backfired, leaving me brokenhearted and my spirit destroyed. I had to figure out how I was going to put the pieces of this situation back together.

My sisters were my world, but Corey was going to be my husband and my life. He should come first before them. After what went down tonight, it made it that much easier choosing him over them.

I looked up at Corey and said, "Even if it costs me my relationship with my sisters, I'm going to be with you forever."

"I love you," he said, kissing me again and wiping away my tears. "I can't wait to make you my wife. I want a big wedding. I want everybody to know how much we love one another. So . . ."

"So, what?" I asked, smiling.

"You ready to make some money for this extravagant wedding we are going to have?" he asked devilishly.

"You want to do that tonight? We did it last night."

"I know. We said a couple of times a week, but the more money we can make, the better. Did you see the last amount of money we made?" Corey asked.

"Yes," I said, remembering my excitement when I had seen four figures.

"Then let's make this money, baby," he said, chuckling.

"Okay. Give me fifteen minutes to freshen up and get ready. You go set everything up," I told him, removing myself from his arms and rising from the sofa.

"It's already done. All I need is my leading lady," he said, causing me to blush.

Corey smacked my behind, causing me to giggle. Even though my night had turned out horrible, I was going to make sure the ending was fantastic.

Chapter 19

Serena

I got a crazy baby mama in my life. I'm not talking about her getting on my nerves every now and then. I'm saying she's literally crazy. The elevator don't go all the way to the top crazy. It gets stuck in the damn basement where darkness lies crazy. I'd never been a person who was scared of anybody, but this demented chick had me reconsidering.

"Is you and your baby dead yet?" she asked, calling my house for the seventeenth time that day. "Your baby too ugly to be living. Maybe you should drop her from the second floor of your house."

"Trick, I told you to stop calling my damn house," I yelled.

"Or what? What are you going to do?"

"Keep calling and you will find out."

"I been calling you, bitch, and you ain't done a damn thing. You ain't nobody, and neither is that ugly baby of yours," she yelled.

"Oh, okay. I know what this is about. You mad because Tyree is with me and I gave him the daughter he's always wanted and you couldn't," I taunted.

"I'm pregnant now with his child, bitch," she revealed.

"In your dreams," I tried to say back with confidence, hoping she didn't hear the uncertainty in my voice from her revelation. I can't lie; her saying that was like a gut punch, but then again, everything she said to me was gut punches. Still, a small part of me wondered, was she telling me the truth?

"No, bitch, in my reality. You think you have Tyree all to yourself. Please. He comes over here all the time, and it's not only to see his son. He keeps coming back to get some of my good pussy."

I didn't believe Juanita. After all the hell she took Tyree through, the sliced tires, the bleached clothes, getting him fired, and even cheating on him, he would be a damn fool to go back and screw her.

"If you call my house one more time, I'm going to call and have a restraining order put on you for harassment," I threatened.

"Well, get ready to dial, because I'm going to call as many times as I damn well—"

I hung up on her. I didn't have time to argue with this trick. As soon as I walked away from the phone, it rang again. I looked at the caller ID to see it was Juanita again. I clicked the line on, but immediately clicked it right back off, hanging up on her again.

Tyree walked into the kitchen, yawning and wiping the sleep out of his eyes, asking, "Who keeps calling?"

"Juanita, that's who," I said furiously. "You better check her, Tyree, or I'm going to hurt her, and I mean it," I warned.

"Baby, calm down," he said nonchalantly.

"Don't tell me to calm down. She calling here asking me if our baby is dead yet and how I should drop her from the second-floor window. I mean, who does that?"

"Juanita," Tyree said, walking over to the coffee pot on the counter and pouring himself a cup of coffee like this was a normal day for him.

"Tyree, I'm tired of this. It was bad enough she had the nerve to call me in the hospital while trying to deliver Nevaeh, wishing we both died during childbirth. Now she's calling our home."

The phone rang again, and I picked up the receiver to see it was her again. I held the phone up to show Tyree, and he held his hand out to take the phone.

"Naw. Let the voicemail pick it up. The more threatening messages she leaves, the more evidence I'll have against her to file harassment charges and put a restraining order against her," I said, slamming the phone down on the counter.

"You don't have to do all that," he said, walking over to the kitchen table to sit down.

"You suggested I do that at the hospital. Then you talked me out of it for your son's sake. She's taking this thing too far. I listened to you and left it alone, but look where that has gotten me," I said with outstretched hands.

"She's not worth it. She's mad because I chose you, babe," Tyree said convincingly.

"Are you sure you chose me? Because she told me you two are still sleeping together and she's pregnant with your baby."

Tyree took a gulp, forgetting he was drinking hot coffee. He yelped as the hot liquid burned his mouth. He ran over to the sink and ran cold water into his hand, cupping it as he brought the liquid to his mouth to help cool it.

I stood there with my arms crossed. Was that a sign of guilt or what? He was that damn nervous to forget what he was drinking. "So you are sleeping with her," I said suspiciously, hoping his further behavior wouldn't make the hairs on the back of my neck stand up more than they already were.

"No," he said, standing and turning to me. "You know I don't want her."

"Then why burn yourself?"

"You caught me off-guard. There is no way in the world I would ever go back to her. I regret the day I ever met her."

I gave him a skeptical look.

"Come on, Serena. I wouldn't do that to you or my daughter. For goodness' sake, she's threatening my child. I couldn't be with anybody like that."

The phone rang again, and again it was Juanita. He dropped his head in defeat as I held the phone up again for him to see it was her. I waited for the phone to stop ringing and decided to listen to the voicemail messages to see what else this trick had to say. I put the phone on speaker so Tyree could hear what his baby mama was saying.

"You have five new messages. First message . . ."

"Bitch, I know you still at home. Don't make me come over there and check you and that ugly baby of yours. Will y'all please die already? It would make this world so much better. Two ugly bitches gone for good. So kill your baby first, and then kill yourself."

I saved that message and went to the next, looking at Tyree like, "You see what I'm saying?"

Second message: "Trick, pick up the phone. I need to speak to my man for a minute. His son would like to speak with him. Pick up, trick. I know you there."

I saved that message also, still looking at Tyree, fuming with each message that played.

Third message: "Say, 'Die, bitch,' . . . Die, bitch."

Tyree stood straight up then. Juanita had the nerve to have their son on the phone repeating what she was telling him to say.

I looked at him and tilted my head at him like, "Now what?"

"Say, 'Your baby ugly.' . . . Your baby ugly.

"Say, 'I hate you.' . . . I hate you.

"Say, 'bitch.' . . . Bitch.

"Say, 'bitch' again. . . . Bitch.

"Say, 'Kill yourself, bitch." . . . Kill self, bitch."

"That's enough!" Tyree yelled.

I saved that message too. I started to listen to the next one knowing it was from her, but I decided to click the phone off. I placed the phone down on the counter and looked at him. "But you don't want me to file charges."

"I can't believe she's got my three-year-old son saying that," Tyree said in disbelief.

"Believe it. If she can do that, Tyree, what else is she capable of? I'm trying to protect our daughter here. You might not take Juanita seriously, but I do. I remember the stories you told me she did to you when y'all were together, and it was enough to make me leave you; but I didn't because I loved you too much. I'm here now, with your daughter, in our house, trying to make this work, but, Tyree, I can't deal with Juanita. Something has to give," I pleaded.

Tyree walked up to me. He wrapped his arms around me and pulled me close to him. "Babe, I'm sorry. You are right. You don't deserve what she's doing. If you want to call the cops, I'm behind you."

Tyree backed away a bit to look down at me. I looked up and our eyes met.

"I love you, Serena. I love our daughter. Do whatever you got to do, okay?"

I nodded and leaned in to kiss him as the phone rang once again.

Chapter 20

Vivian

I didn't know who to talk to, but the first person who popped in my mind was Renee. Man, I missed her for times like this. I really needed her shoulder right now. Then I thought about Dawn, but she wasn't speaking to me, so she was not an option. Shauna was at work, and Phoenix didn't answer her phone, so that left Serena. I called her, and she told me to come right over, which I was happy about.

Serena and I didn't talk much without the others around. It wasn't like I didn't love her. I was used to turning to Renee before she passed. Now that she was gone, I turned to Dawn with my issues, and I saw where that had gotten me. She used my situation against me. I called Dawn to apologize about what happened, but she kept sending my calls to voicemail. She had yet to return my call. Why I was apologizing was beyond me, but I felt like somebody needed to step up and try to start mending things between us. I was willing to do that to get back our sisterly bond, but nothing was working. Dawn was stubborn, but I was persistent and wouldn't stop bugging her until she spoke to me. But today that wasn't going to happen. I was going over to Serena's home to talk to her about some things going on with me.

I walked into my niece's nursery to see Serena changing little Nevaeh's Pampers. My niece was not happy about it either. She was screaming at the top of her little lungs and had the nerve for some tears to run down the sides of her little face.

"Aw, what's wrong, sweetie?" I asked, leaning down and rubbing her head, but she kept squalling.

"She's mad because I'm changing her butt. Some days she's good, and other days she squeals like this. I think this time she's hungry, but I didn't want to feed her without getting that poop off her first," Serena said, snapping her pink onesie and then picking Nevaeh up. "You can stop crying now, Miss Thang. I'm going to feed you," Serena told her as Nevaeh whimpered. She even had the nerve to stick out her bottom lip before she burst into tears again.

"Can I feed her?" I asked, putting my purse on the first shelf of the changing table.

"Sure," Serena said, handing my niece to me.

She was still crying. I placed her on my shoulder and bounced with her for a bit, but it wasn't working. Serena picked up her bottle out of the warmer and put it to her cheek. She then squirted some of the milk on her wrist, checking the temperature, making sure it was perfect.

I sat down in the reddish brown swivel chair trimmed in pink contour lines and the matching ottoman, which was positioned next to the window. I didn't know the cushiony chair glided until I sat in it. "I like these chairs," I said, looking at an identical one on the other side of me. A pink table sat between the two chairs positioned right under the window.

"They were a gift from Tyree. He wanted us to have two so one of us wouldn't feel left out on nights we could sit in here together."

"Aw, that's sweet. Have you guys sat in here together yet?" I asked.

"We sit in here a lot. I think it's the tranquil innocence of the space. This room definitely calms me," Serena said, looking around the nursery.

I put Nevaeh in the crook of my left arm, covering her with her pink receiving blanket.

Serena handed me the bottle, and I placed it in my niece's little mouth. As soon as she felt the nipple, she began sucking the warm liquid down.

"You see. She eats all the time," Serena said, gathering the dirty Pampers up and placing it into the Diaper Genie. "Would you like something to drink? I got water, juice, and soda."

"I'll take some water," I said, gliding back and forth.

Serena left the nursery. I looked around at how my sister had decorated the space. Light pink was on the walls. Nevaeh's name in white letters was over the espresso-colored crib. Pink-and-brown bedding adorned the crib with ruffles and soft blankets. The closet was open to reveal the tiniest of clothes hanging up. And it was full. This room was beautiful and serene. I leaned my head back, continuing to rock back and forth in the rocker. I looked down at my niece. She had her little fist balled up around her face as she looked up at me.

"You are so precious," I said to her. I knew she couldn't understand what I was saying, but she had to feel my words were said in love.

Serena came back into the room, putting the water down on a coaster she placed on the pink table. She then sat down in the glider across from me and began drinking the bottle of water she brought for herself.

"Serena, you have done a beautiful job in this nursery."

"Thank you," she said, looking around at her work.

"I know you were surprised to hear from me," I said.

"It has been a while since you wanted to talk to me. You usually talk to Dawn. I guess she's not an option now," Serena said.

"You're right. She's not speaking to me right now."

"Nevertheless, I know whatever you have to say has to be big for you to come over here and see me," she said, taking another sip of her water.

"I hope you don't mind me wanting to talk to you?" I asked, looking down at Nevaeh, who was still looking up at me.

"Girl, I don't mind. I'm here for you always. So what's going on?" Serena asked, getting more comfortable as she brought one of her knees to her chest, with the other tucked beneath her. My sister looked comfortable in a pair of gray drawstring pants and a white tee with a gray feather print on the front.

"Before we get started on me, what's wrong with you?" I asked.

"Nothing. Why are you asking?"

"Come on, Serena. I can tell something is going on with you. I know we don't talk often, one on one, but you are still my sister. I can tell when something is up with you."

She sighed and paused, taking another sip of her water. She looked at me and said, "You didn't come over here to hear my problems, Viv."

"Just like you just told me and, yes, I'm going to give your own words back to you. I'm here for you always."

Serena smiled and got up off the chair, walking out of the room. For a minute I thought I had offended her, but I couldn't see how. It wasn't long before Serena came back into the room. She plopped down in the chair with an envelope in her hand. When she held it up for me to read, my mouth fell open.

"What in the hell is that?" I asked.

"It's what it says it is," she explained.

"But medical facilities aren't supposed to print up envelopes like that. That's an invasion of someone's rights to privacy. Hell, I know about the HIPAA laws."

"This was in my mailbox today," she said glumly.

"Stop lying," I said.

"Vivian, I wish I were."

I was looking at a stamped envelope addressed to Tyree Coleman. In big, bold capital letters across the front for everybody handling this piece of mail to see, it said HERPES TEST RESULTS INSIDE.

"Did you open it?" I asked.

"You damn right I did. Sis, I was so mad I forgot about any federal offense laws and the possibility of me being arrested for opening his mail. I didn't care. I had to see what was inside."

"And?" I asked curiously.

Serena reached in the envelope, pulling out the piece of paper. She opened it and began reading it to me:

"Get checked, Tyree, because you may have herpes. And since you have been sleeping with me, I thought you should know you need to get checked. Sorry for any inconvenience, sweetie. Love, Juanita."

"You have got to be kidding me," I said in astonishment.

"This woman is certifiable. I mean, who does this? She sent this through the postal service on purpose, stamped, delivery confirmation and all. Look where it came from," Serena said, pointing to the postal stamp.

"New York," I said.

"Exactly. This bitch just left New York, taking her son to visit with some of her family. She sent the letter from there with this official-looking envelope," Serena explained.

"I'm sorry, sis. My problem is nothing compared to what you are dealing with right now. Does Tyree know?"

"Yeah, I showed it to him and he was pissed."

"I hope he hasn't left to go over and confront her," I said.

"He said he wasn't, but who knows. As mad as he was, he might have. Really, I don't care at this point. This is too much for me to deal with. I was so happy when you called me this morning wanting to come over."

"I feel bad now."

"Please don't. As you can see, I needed you as much as you need me. Now let's stop talking about me. What's your deal?" Serena asked.

"I did something that I think I might regret," I began to reveal.

"And what's that?" She looked at me suspiciously.

"I slept with Sheldon," I said, flinching like what I said hurt.

"For real?" she asked excitedly. "When?" Serena damn near jumped up and down on the chair.

"The night of our disaster dinner. He came over after his hell date, and we chilled out like we always do."

"I know it was good. He looks like he can lay some good pipe—and real long pipe," she said.

"Serena," I said, giggling.

"I'm sorry, but that man is fine, Viv. I know it was good, wasn't it? I want to know. Give me all the juicy details," she said eagerly as she propped her elbow on the arm of the glider and leaned in to listen.

I paused before saying, "It was real good. I mean, it was so good he had me *gon* good. G-o-n, gon. No man—and I mean no man—has ever made my body feel like Sheldon did."

"Damn, Viv. He put it down on you like that?"

"It was so good, Serena, that when we got up the next morning, we did it again, and it was just as good, if not better, than the hours before. I was sore as hell, but I didn't care. To have that man's body next to mine felt right," I said, looking down at little Nevaeh's eyes beginning to close.

"So, what now?"

"That's just it. I don't know. Sheldon and I are best friends."

"A fine best friend at that," Serena said.

"Now that we've crossed this line, I wonder how is this going to affect our friendship. This man knows more about me than y'all do. He knows my favorite ice cream and has seen me looking my worst without makeup. He knows my bad habits and deals with my attitudes no matter what. He knows about all the men I've slept with and vice versa. We are so close that if I get a pimple, this man will pop it. We pass gas around each other. As crazy as all this sounds, Serena, I love him for that. He is my comfort zone."

"Wow. He sounds like the perfect man for you, Viv," Serena said in a suggestive tone.

"But he's my perfect friend. I never thought of him as my man."

"Never?" she questioned.

"Never," I said.

"Y'all didn't talk about what happened that morning?"

"When we finished, we both fell back to sleep. When I woke up, he was gone."

"You haven't called him?" Serena asked.

"And say what? 'Hey, how's it going? By the way, let's talk about the sex we had the other night'?"

"Yes," Serena blurted, chuckling.

"I can't do that."

"Why are you scared?" my sister asked.

"I just am. I can't explain it."

"You have known Sheldon forever. Talk to him. You will be okay. Just like you said, this man knows everything about you, so regardless if you talk to him now or later, when you do see him, he's going to know something is up by your demeanor."

My sister was right. I never looked at it like that. This man could read me like a book.

"I don't want this to ruin our friendship. Sheldon is the best thing that's happened to me in a very long time. I could confide in him about anything, Serena. If sex changes this between us, I'm going to be devastated."

I removed the bottle from Nevaeh's mouth and picked her up, placing her on my shoulder, patting her back to burp her. She was sound asleep and looked so beautiful. I could feel her little breaths on my cheek, which caused me to smile.

Serena said, "Viv, you can't pretend like this never happened. You never know; you might get around him again and your hormones might start to rage. You know you are going to jump his bones again."

"It can't happen again," I disagreed.

"If you say so, but I know it is. If it's as good as you say it is, and for that man to come back for seconds the following morning, it's going to happen again. You two need to talk this over if you don't want it to ruin you all's friendship for real."

Serena was right. As much as I wanted to pretend like nothing happened, my body let me know it did. I could still feel the residual effects of what his manhood brought to my body. Thinking of Sheldon used to make me happy. Now the thought of him made me horny. I loved him as my friend, but I loved him even more as my lover. I didn't want to fall in love with him, but in a weird sort of way, I already had. The sex took it to the level I'd been fighting a long time. I didn't want to feel this way if he didn't feel the same about me. I knew that was what my hesitation in this entire situation was about: him not feeling anything for me after our night together.

I hoped Dawn wasn't right. I hoped Sheldon wouldn't be another man who would use me for what he could get out of me. But why should I think this way? This was my best friend. He would never use me. I did know him better than that. What I didn't know, and feared most, was if this would break our bond. The thought that I could lose him saddened me.

Chapter 21

Vivian

I took Serena's advice and decided to call Sheldon, who agreed to come by and see me that afternoon. I was so nervous. I had never been nervous about him coming over. This man could walk in my house without knocking and it hadn't bothered me one bit, but now I was pacing the floor like a stranger was about to walk through my door.

Every time I heard a car drive by my house, I peeped out the window to see if it was him. I was disappointed at least ten times, until I looked out and saw Sheldon's gray SUV pull up in my driveway. Just like Sheldon to have this music blasting when he arrived.

I wrung my hands together, hoping it would help decrease the uneasy energy rocketing throughout my body, but it wasn't working. I then went over to my love seat to sit down like things were cool. I had to look normal. I had to act like what happened between us didn't affect me one bit.

My front door swung open and Sheldon walked in, saying, "What up, Viv?"

He was in a great mood, which helped a bit with my own anxious mood. I smiled and said, "Hey, Sheldon."

"I see you chilling. And you not in the bed," he said, tossing his keys on the coffee table. "That's good to see."

When he said I wasn't in the bed, I got more rigid, because I kept envisioning the two of us having sex.

Sheldon sat down beside me on the chair, and I pushed back a bit, sitting with my legs beneath me. As usual, this man looked sexy as ever. He smelled even better as I caught a whiff of his cologne. Black and gray were Sheldon's favorite colors, so it was surprising to see him in dark blue denim jeans and a bright green collared polo shirt and white sneakers. Of course, his clothes fit his body like a glove. Just looking at him brought out sensations in me that I knew I had to restrain, the main awareness being the sudden throbbing between my thighs.

"Man, I'm tired," he said, slouching down and leaning his head back on my sofa.

"You had a rough day?" I asked as casually as I possibly could.

"It was a'ight," he said, pushing his dreads from his face. He didn't have them tied back today. He was letting them hang freely around his chiseled face. He had a midnight shadow effect going on, as his beard had grown in slightly. It looked sexy on him. I liked when he let a little stubble grow.

Sheldon continued to say, "I washed my ride, did a little bit of grocery shopping, and then washed some of my clothes. You know, the small stuff you let go until you really need to do it."

"I know. I need to wash clothes myself," I admitted, trying to sound normal, but I guess I didn't.

Frowning, Sheldon tilted his head and asked, "Is everything okay with you?"

"Everything is good," I lied. "Why do you ask?"

"Are you sure? Because earlier you sounded like something was wrong. Now you're looking like you about to cry or something. Did something happen?"

"No," I said.

"Please tell me it's not Eric or your sisters again," he said, reaching over and putting his hand on my knee. Just that touch caused me to become tense, but the smell of him caused me to drip.

Trying to urge the sexy thoughts of Sheldon out of my head, I said, "I'm done with Eric. As for my sisters, nothing has changed really between us. The only one I've talked to since the altercation is Serena."

"Okay, so what's going on with you?" he asked, staring back at me as he got more comfortable with the cushions of my love seat.

Sighing, I said, "I called you over here to talk about what happened between us the other night."

"Okay. I was wondering when we were going to get around to talking about that."

"So what happened, Sheldon?"

"You don't know?" he said jokingly with a smirk on his handsome face.

"Boy, I know, but you know what I'm saying. How did it happen? We are friends. Best friends at that," I said, sincerely happy that the conversation was underway.

"You talking like what happened between us was a bad thing," he said apprehensively.

"No. I'm not saying that. I don't want what happened to affect the friendship we have," I said.

"And how will it do that?" he questioned, clasping his fingers together as he positioned them across his broad chest. I felt like this was some type of defense mode, but I kept talking.

"You know once sex gets involved things change," I said.

"Nothing has changed for me. Are you trying to say it has for you?" he asked.

"I don't know," I said with uncertainty. "I don't want what happened to change our friendship, that's all. I love what we have."

Sheldon nodded as his full lips thinned from bringing them together. This let me know he really wasn't feeling what I was saying. Then he stood, saying, "Okay. I understand. Look, I got to go. I got some things to handle."

Standing, I said, "Sheldon, what's wrong?"

"Nothing's wrong, Viv. I got what you saying."

"So why do you seem upset?" I asked worriedly.

"I'm not. I just got things to handle," he said, opening the door. "I'll talk to you later." And out the door Sheldon went, leaving abruptly.

And there it was: the changing dynamic of our friendship that I feared would happen. I didn't know how to take his reaction. The awkwardness crept in. I was wondering, should I have said anything at all? He came in fine but left distressed. Maybe I should have kept my mouth shut and pretended like nothing happened; but something did happen, and no matter how many times I tried to erase the moment we had with one another, it crept back like raging waters during a flash flood. I'd thought about our moment at least a hundred times.

That night we had ended up falling asleep after eating in bed and watching a mini marathon of *Family Guy,* which was one of our favorite shows. The next thing I knew, Sheldon was cuddled up behind me, asleep. We were in the spooning position. His arm was around my waist. I had to admit I loved when he did this. We did this quite often, and at times I did wonder if that was what friends did. Nevertheless, I felt like this was how it was supposed to be.

I tried to fall back to sleep, but it was difficult with Sheldon's hardness against my behind. Feeling it up against me did cause emotions within me to stir, but I knew I couldn't react to them. I also couldn't figure out why, of all the times we'd done this, I was now turned on by this man's body being pressed up against me like this. Had he always been erect like this and I never paid attention? No, as big as he felt, I knew I would have remembered this feeling.

I closed my eyes and tried to fall back to sleep. Sheldon shifted a bit. It seemed like he moved closer to me, pushing his stiffness into me. I think I sucked in breath when he did this. I must have, because the next sound I heard was Sheldon asking me a question.

"You okay?" he muttered.

Hearing his voice startled me. I thought he was asleep. I replied by saying, "I'm good."

"Why you jump?" he asked in his deep baritone voice.

"I didn't."

"Yes, you did."

"Boy, go back to sleep. You talking crazy," I said, trying to play it off as his hardness continued to stimulate me.

"I know why you jumped, Viv," he said, moving his hand to my hips. He began rubbing me soothingly, sending tingles through me.

"Why?" I asked naively.

He pushed himself closer to me, causing me to feel his full erection even better, saying, "This is why."

I couldn't say one word. His manhood stole my voice. Sheldon continued to stroke my hips. With each stroke the heat between my thighs intensified. As much as I liked it, I didn't move. I didn't know what to do. He was my best friend, and things like this weren't supposed to happen.

He nestled closer to me, his chin resting in the crook of my neck. I could feel his warm breath on the nape of my neck. I knew my heart was pounding at this point, and I hoped he didn't hear it or feel it. Sheldon then kissed the nape of my neck gently. It was a seductive kiss, the kind of kiss where I felt the warmth from his mouth and the softness of his lips, which made my body quiver.

My mind was spinning and my womanhood was throbbing. The more he stroked and laid kisses on me, the more turned on I became.

Sheldon tugged on my shoulder, turning me to my back. He wanted to take this further, which made my heart thump even more. I didn't think it could pound any harder. I didn't want to push him away and say this couldn't happen, but I didn't know if I wanted this to stop. Was it the wine? Was it feeling his hardness against me, or was this inevitable? Either way, I was going to go with the flow.

Sheldon propped himself up on his elbow and gazed down at me. I wouldn't allow myself to look at him. Not yet. I peered up, looking at the ceiling. He gripped my chin, gently tugging for me to face him. Our eyes met. He didn't say anything, but the expression on his face told me everything I needed to know. He wanted me. Sheldon leaned in and kissed me tenderly. Just our lips converged, soft sensual pecks done leisurely and seductively. I didn't kiss him back. I closed my eyes, relishing the fact that this was happening but wondering what we were doing.

It wasn't seconds before my lips perked up to gently kiss him back.

What started out as a sensual kiss soon became animalistic. Sheldon began to kiss me deeply. I recklessly responded as I threw myself into him. His hand roamed my body, becoming familiar with it for the first time ever in this erotic way. As much as I was enjoying this, I was still uncomfortable, because I wasn't happy with my body.

I released our kiss and tried to pull away from him, thinking this was going way further than I thought it should, but Sheldon wouldn't let me. He begged, "Please don't pull away from me."

The way he said this mesmerized me into a trance to obey. He kissed me again, this time letting his hand maneuver its way to my womanhood to explore regions that had been off-limits during the duration of our friendship. Sliding his hand beneath the material of my PJs, Sheldon found my opening. One of his fingers parted my lips as another made its way inside me. Gently plunging as far as he could push his fingers into me, he skillfully pleasured my womanhood, making it drip with bliss. I was in heaven.

Sheldon removed his hand from me after I reached an orgasm. He smirked at my quivering body and climbed out of the bed. He pulled the covers back and then proceeded to get on his knees. He began to remove my bottoms, exposing the body I was unhappy with. I wanted to pull the covers back over me to hide myself, but I got comfortable with the fact that the darkness helped in him not seeing me fully. Once my clothes were removed, I could hear him scuffling around. I knew Sheldon was removing his shorts also. My heart was thrashing so fast I thought it was going to come up through my throat and suffocate me. What in the hell were we doing?

Before my mind had a chance to register an answer, Sheldon climbed on top of me, pulling the cover around his waist. Like magic, my legs opened wide, welcoming him to cross into my threshold. On one elbow, he reached down and angled his manhood to my opening. The tip touched my lips, but he didn't push himself into me immediately. He brought his hand back up and began kissing me again. The tip teased but never entered me completely as his tongue engulfed me. Just the anticipation of him thrusting forward was enough to make me want to have a panic attack. It was the not knowing when he would enter me that was driving me crazy. Each time I thought this was the stroke as he continued to tease me with his head, he didn't thrust his way in. I wanted to lose it. I wanted to say, “Stick it in already,” because I couldn’t take his hesitancy.

I finally got my wish. Sheldon propelled forward with all of his depth, penetrating me like no man had ever done before. My nails dug into his masculine back as he submerged his girth in my wet walls. In and out of me, he plunged into shallow waters as the rock hardness of his manhood quickly took me to unfathomable depths. Everything about him felt good: the weight of his body, the muscles flexing in his arms with each stroke, his scent, his sweat, and his taste. I loved it all. It didn’t take me long before I was erupting all over his manhood, raining down a tsunami of pleasurable waves. A slight smirk crept across his handsome face as he watched my seismic quake tentatively. With shortened breaths, I asked, “Why are you looking at me like that?”

With that same smirk, he said, “I love the reaction you are giving me.”

I didn’t know whether to smile or be embarrassed at him watching. I wasn’t used to a man looking at me the way he was taking me in. It felt uncomfortable, but I had to quickly think that these were my own insecurities. So I smiled and decided to say, “I love the way you make me feel.”

Before this interaction of sexual desire, I wanted to go to sleep, afraid of this very thing happening. Now I was going to sleep because the sex we had put me to sleep. And for us to wake the next morning doing it again hadn't bothered me. I was motivated by the sure excitement of what I knew his body could bring to mine. I wanted him so bad, and for once I didn't care if he saw me. The sex was better the second go-round. This time I was in the "ass up, face down" position, one of my favorites, I might add. Sheldon worked me over like a damn champion. Back-to-back explosions ripped through me, which slipped me right back into slumber land.

It wasn't until I woke up to see him gone that I began to have regrets. And from the way things had gone down today, our relationship was heading down a road I never wanted to travel with him. I wanted him as my friend, but it felt even better to have him as my lover. One wasn't an option in my opinion, so now what? Where were we going to go from here?

Chapter 22

Shauna

I was at the end of my shift and was having a great day so far. I had made $247 in tips, which made this day even better. I was tired though. I worked hard for every dime of that money. I had a couple of large groups to serve, but it paid off. Twenty more minutes to go and I would be going home.

One of my coworkers came back saying someone was sitting in my section, and I thought, *Damn*. It would be my last table. Didn't it always happen like this? As soon as I was getting ready to leave, I had to start serving another table.

When I approached the customer I said, "Hi, my name is Shauna and I'm going to be your server today." I got tired of saying this sometimes. I hated being fake. It was too much like kissing ass to me; but this time I didn't know I would have an asshole sitting at the table.

As soon as I saw it was him, I turned to walk away, but he grabbed me by my arm to stop me. "Wait a minute, Shauna," Cal said.

"Let me go," I said, jerking away from him. This sudden movement caused a couple sitting behind me to glance in our direction to see what was going on. I turned to look at them and smiled even though I didn't feel like it.

I hadn't seen this man since the night he put his hands on me. My bruises were just starting to go away, and here he was sitting in my section like I was supposed to be cool talking with him.

"I'm going to get someone else to serve you," I said, still with this fake grin plastered on my face. I didn't want to cause a scene and give the patrons around me a reason to be worried; but when Cal grabbed my arm again it was hard not to have this look like some type of altercation was going to break out.

"Please wait. I need to talk to you," he said, gripping my wrist.

"I don't want to talk to you," I said, trying to pull away, but this time he had my wrist gripped extra tight so I couldn't jerk away. I didn't want to cause a scene on my job, but the way he was holding my wrist was pissing me off. I knew I was seconds away from going off on him.

"Look. Calm down, please, and I will let you go," he said, looking around nervously. He had a black-and-orange San Francisco Giants snapback on his head with a matching shirt. Cal had the snapback pulled down so far over his eyes that it looked like he was trying to hide. He probably was, since my cousin Big Ray and them was still looking for him. He must not have cared much if he showed his face here.

I told him again, "Let me go, Cal."

"I will when you calm down," he said through clenched teeth.

"Oh, you are going to let me go whether it's with a scream, with force, or with the cops coming to arrest you for assault," I said sternly.

"Okay, Shauna," he said, releasing my wrist, "but please give me two minutes. Can you please do that for me?"

"What would you like to drink?" I asked him, hoping this would clue him in that he had two minutes.

"I didn't mean to come by your job, but you wouldn't take any of my calls."

"Tick, tick, tick," I said, looking at my watch.

"I'm sorry for what happened. I didn't mean to hurt you. You know I love you."

"Love doesn't require you abusing me like you did. You damn near killed me," I snapped.

"I don't know what happened. I lost it."

"And your losing it caused me many bruises physically and psychologically, Cal. No man has ever put his hands on me, not even my father, and I'll be damned if I'll be with a man who thinks he can," I said angrily.

He dropped his head, clenching his hands in front of him on the table. When he looked up, he had tears streaming down his face.

Wow, he really wanted his apology to look genuine. What pathetic depths did he have to dig down and pull from in order to produce these fake-ass tears? They didn't mean a damn thing to me. This punk cried all the damn time anyway. I think if we watched the childhood movie *Charlotte's Web* this man would cry like a baby. I truly believed he could will his tears to come when he wanted them to. It was his "I'm a sensitive man" thing, where in the past women swooned over men like him. At one time, I was one of those women, but never again. I wasn't a fool who fell for the same trick twice, and no matter how many tears he shed, I was never going back to him again.

Isn't that like abusers? The first ones to smack you upside your head, and then they drop tears later, feeling sorry for what they did. This may work on the Lifetime Network, but here today it meant absolutely nothing to me.

"Babe, I'm really sorry," he said, getting choked up and grabbing his face like he was trying to hold his sobs back.

I looked at him like, "Whatever."

"For real I am. I love you too much to ever hurt you like that again. I want you to know that. I want you to give us another chance. We are great together," he begged.

"Apology noted. Now, what can I get you to drink? Your time is almost up," I said, holding the pad to take his order.

"Shauna, I love you, babe. Please give us another chance."

"I'm not ever getting back with you, Cal. You can cry buckets of tears and it still will never make me take you back. So if you didn't get it before, hear me now. We are done. Your time is up. I will send another waitress to serve you," I said, attempting to walk away, but this fool jumped up from his table.

I looked at him, wondering what his sudden movement was about. I knew he wasn't stupid enough to put his hands on me in here. If he did, I had plenty of eyewitnesses to help put his behind in jail.

"You can't do this, Shauna," he said loudly, causing others to look at us even more.

No, he wasn't doing this here and now. Not at my job. Not when I was fifteen minutes away from leaving for the day. Hell, I would have preferred he confront me in the parking lot. Yes, it was less safe, but at least it wasn't in front of a roomful of people where I made my money.

"You are causing a scene," I tried to mumble as I looked around to see who was watching.

"Is it someone else? Are you fucking another man?" he asked.

"What?" I questioned him like I didn't hear him the first time; and I wished I hadn't, because he repeated himself, but louder this time.

"Are you fucking another man? Is that why you are not taking me back?" Cal yelled.

"Please leave," I said, walking away. I didn't have to stand here and be the target of his craziness.

"All you had to do was tell me. You don't have to be a bitch about this, Shauna. Be a woman and tell me if you are fucking another man," he said, following me.

"Is everything okay?" my manager asked, coming up to me, placing a comforting hand on my shoulder. My manager looked around me to Cal and then back down at me. I knew Cal would take this wrong because that was the type of guy he was. It didn't help that my manager was very attractive. Standing six feet two inches, about 220 pounds, with a clean-shaven face, close-cut hair, and almond-shaped eyes, my manager, Grayson, was hot to trot.

"Oh, is this the guy you fucking?" Cal asked heatedly.

"No, everything is not okay," I answered my manager. "This is my ex, and I told him to leave, but he keeps harassing me," I explained.

"Sir, we are going to have to ask you to leave," my manager told Cal.

This infuriated him even more.

"Is this your loverboy?" Cal asked, ignoring Grayson. I refused to answer him.

"Leave," I told Cal.

Cal began to come toward me, but my manager stepped in front of me. "Sir, please leave," Grayson demanded.

"I'm not going no damn where," Cal said, stepping so close to Grayson that they were practically nose to nose.

Without flinching or stepping back, Grayson calmly replied, "Then we are going to call the police and have them remove you."

"Call them. I don't give a damn. By the time they get here, I will have beaten your ass anyway for sleeping with my woman," Cal threatened.

"We don't want any problems here," Grayson said, voice still as calm as could be.

I stood back watching, hoping Cal wouldn't be stupid enough to try to fight my manager; but this was Cal we were talking about. He was always trying to play the big man who didn't take any shit. I didn't know when he was going to learn there were plenty of people who could always teach him a lesson.

Cal said, "I have a problem with you butting your nose in me and my girl's relationship."

"There is no relationship," I said, stepping to the side so I could look Cal in his face.

"We are over when I say we are over," Cal retorted.

"Shauna said it's over, then it's over," Grayson responded.

"Move out of my way," Cal said, trying to push past Grayson.

Grayson held his hand up to stop him as I stepped back to get away from Cal, and that's when Cal swung on Grayson. I screamed when I saw this. I couldn't believe this was happening.

"Stop it, Cal!" I screamed.

Before I knew it, Cal was lying on the floor. Grayson blocked his punch and threw Cal down. Cal got up again to try to rush Grayson, but Grayson caught him again and threw him to the floor. It was as if Cal was a puppet to Grayson.

He was hardly moving as he tossed Cal around like he was nothing.

When Cal got up again, he reached over to one of the tables and grabbed a steak knife, but before he had a chance to swing the blade, Grayson took it from him. He then grabbed Cal by the wrist and twisted his arm around, bending Cal's arm behind him, causing him to scream in pain. Grayson had him locked down. The more Cal tried to move, the more he screamed in pain.

"Let me go!" Cal yelled.

"Not until the police get here."

Chapter 23

Shauna

Cal was taken away in handcuffs by the police. My drama-filled love life had played out over baked potatoes and iced tea. My fifteen minutes of work turned into over an hour being here in this restaurant, and the sad part about it was this was not overtime.

After questioning me, the police were taking statements from several people about what happened, and I was embarrassed beyond belief. After everything calmed down, I had to meet with my manager in his office. I knew this would be my very last day working there. I couldn't blame him for firing me. What went on in my life outside of this place jeopardized the safety of the patrons who attended this establishment, and that wasn't cool.

"Come in," Grayson said as I tapped at the open door. "Can you shut the door behind you?"

he asked, writing something down. I did as he asked. "Have a seat."

I did that, too. I was a person moving as if someone was sending signals of action. I kept quiet, waiting for him to ream me out about what happened between me and Cal. I looked around his office, and the tan walls were bare. There was nothing hanging up, not even a clock or painting. The room felt cold and intimidated the hell out of me. A window behind Grayson held mini blinds that were open. The sun beaming in was the only refreshing thing about the space.

Grayson wrote for a couple more minutes before he gave me his undivided attention. I had to wonder if this was another intimidating tactic he used to make people like me nervous.

"You do know why I called you into my office?" Grayson asked.

"Yes."

"We can't have what happened here today ever happen again, Shauna. This is a place of business."

"I know, and I'm sorry for everything that happened. I tried to make him leave, but he kept coming at me," I said sadly.

"I know. I watched the entire thing."

"You did?" I asked, surprised. His once-stern face softened, causing my shoulders to relax a bit.

"Shauna, as much as you think I don't pay attention, I do. Just like when you tried to cover up your bruises with makeup," he said, causing me to drop my head in shame. "I'm not saying this to embarrass you. I'm saying this because you could have come to me."

I looked up, taken aback by what he was saying.

"I know most people don't want other people in their business, and I get that, but I thought you felt comfortable enough to come and talk to me about what was going on," Grayson explained.

"I don't like telling anybody about my life. I told my sisters, and things escalated before I knew it. You are my boss. What do I look like coming to you saying my boyfriend tried to kill me?"

"It would look like you telling a friend. I know I'm your boss, but we were friends first, Shauna. I've known you since high school."

"But things change, and so do people."

"I haven't changed," he said sweetly. "I might have some authority here, but I'm still the same Grayson from back in the day. I got a bit bigger and matured a lot, but nothing else about me has changed. You could have come to me."

"This is embarrassing for me to talk about. I haven't been able to register what has happened myself. Nothing like this has ever happened to me before."

"I know that," he said.

"How?" I asked curiously.

"Because I know you. I remember you fighting in school and not taking junk from nobody. Not even a dude. You didn't play, nor did you back down from anything. So why would I think you allowed this to happen? No woman allows abuse to happen to her."

I nodded and said, "He caught me off-guard."

"Exactly. Even the best fall sometimes. As much as you think you can fight like a man, there is always a man stronger than you. That punk had no right to put his hands on you."

"Well, you made him fall pretty good," I said, smiling.

"I wanted to punch him in his nose and break both of his arms, but I couldn't," he said.

"I wish you would have."

"My hands are deadly weapons. One punch from me and I could have killed that dude," Grayson admitted.

"Your hands are deadly?" I asked, frowning a bit.

"I have a black belt in martial arts," he boasted. "Not many people know that. Only my mom and my two brothers know this."

"Impressive. No wonder you could throw him around like he was nothing," I retorted.

"So now you know why I didn't swing. It wasn't a fair fight."

"Still, you should have hurt him. He tried to stab you with a steak knife."

"As long as no one was hurt, I'm good. He's in a better place now."

"I plan on pressing charges and getting a restraining order against that fool," I said.

"I hope so. I hope you know after today you can come to me about anything," Grayson offered.

"So you are not firing me?" I asked.

"No," he said, frowning like he couldn't believe I'd said that. "You tried to resolve the issue. You couldn't help that it escalated like it did. Your ex has been banned from this establishment for good, but just in case he manages to get back in here and approaches you, come find me. Yell, even. You have to take care of yourself regardless of your setting, especially with someone as unstable as he is."

I smiled and told him, "Thank you, Grayson. I appreciate this."

"You are so welcome."

"I'm going to have to make you dinner or something as a thank-you, but you are my boss, so I'm not trying to overstep any boundaries between employee and employer," I joked.

"What people don't know won't hurt them," he said with a look that made me wonder if Grayson wanted more than friendship from me.

"So dinner tomorrow night at seven?" I asked, throwing the hook out to see if he would bite.

"Tomorrow at seven sounds great," he agreed, smiling, and just like that I went from sad to delighted.

Chapter 24

Shauna

Boy, was I tired. I thought the day would never end. It was so hard pretending like I loved my job when I hated dealing with people. Only my dumb self would get a job that required dealing with people all damn day. Still, the day ended well despite how Cal tried to ruin it. I was off for the next two days, so I was looking forward to relaxing a bit, and also my dinner with Grayson tomorrow.

I walked into my home and plopped down on my sofa, wishing my shower was already taken. I took one before I went to work, but I always needed to take another to wash off the stench of the restaurant, which to me smelled like grease and onions. I sat up and unbuttoned the burgundy collared shirt and took it off because I was tired of smelling it. I needed a few minutes before I willed myself to the bathroom to wash this aroma off of me.

Picking up the mail I'd just gotten out of my mailbox, I saw that all of the envelopes were bills. *Can once, just once, somebody send me a damn check? I'll even take a credit for overpayment on something; anything that would require money coming in instead of always going out.* I tossed the pile of envelopes back on my coffee table. When I did that, Dawn's invitation fell to the floor.

"If that ain't a damn sign," I mumbled to myself. I leaned down to pick it up. I read the black-and-white invitation again.

Dawn Cherie Johnson and Corey
Raquon Lewis
Request the honor of your presence
at their wedding
On Saturday, the ninth of January two
thousand and sixteen
At five o'clock in the evening
At the Mount Zion Baptist Church.

Who in the hell gets married two weeks after Christmas? They must call themselves starting the year off right. How wrong was she? She was marrying a man who was no damn good for her, and she was too stupid to see it, yet she was mad at us. *She puts us down for trying to help her stupid behind, but raises this punk up like he's a saint.*

Every time I read this and thought about Dawn and how she went off on us over a month ago, I got pissed off all over again. The nerve of her, taking my ordeal with Cal to make her own situation look better. It was so wrong to me. What happened to me was a one-time thing, like I told her. If a man puts his hands on me, it's a done deal. Hell, if he cheats on me, his behind could get to steppin' then, too. I was not going to put up with any type of bullshit from nobody, and that included my impolite sister.

I hadn't tried to call Dawn, and she hadn't bothered to call me either. I guessed she was busy planning her nuptials. I was surprised she sent me an invitation at all, but maybe she did this to rub her wedding in our faces, and maybe it was just to let us know she was still going through with it.

The only one who really knew what was going on was Vivian. Even after all the stuff Dawn said to her, Vivian took it upon herself to try to resolve things. It took her a while to get through to her, but at least now they were talking. I didn't know why Viv tried to resolve things with Dawn. We weren't wrong. How Dawn treated us was uncalled for, and she just got dealt some of her own medicine.

Vivian kept us in the loop on what was going on with our sister. Things got so good between them two that Vivian was now a bridesmaid in her wedding. The last I heard from her was that she was trying to get Serena and Phoenix to come around also, just like she tried to do with me, but I wasn't having it.

"Come on, Shauna. Dawn is our sister," Vivian said.

"And?"

"And we need to work this out. You have to be there. How can you not come?"

"It's easy, Viv. I don't agree with it, and I damn sure don't appreciate what she said to us," I argued.

"A lot of things were said that night that were wrong. Now we need to come back together and let all of that go. One day you don't want to look back and regret not being there for her."

"Then I'll deal with that day when it comes, but for now, I don't give a rat's ass about Dawn or her bogus wedding."

"If she apologizes, will you come to her wedding?" Vivian asked.

"Like she's going to do that. Dawn is more stubborn than I am. You know damn well she's not going to let the words 'I'm sorry' pass through her lips."

"But what if she does?" Vivian asked.

"I don't know, Viv."

"We are going to fix this. This has gone on for too long."

I hadn't heard anything from Dawn yet, but I didn't expect to hear from her. She was standing her ground and I was too. Dawn getting married to Corey was a big mistake. As her sister, I had a right to say so. You can't force anything in life to work, especially a relationship doomed for disaster.

Look at me. I didn't try to work it out with Cal after he beat me. Before our confrontation today, he was texting me over and over again, talking about how sorry he was and how he would never do it again if I gave him another chance.

> Baby plse txt me bck.
>
> I'm sorry baby. U no I luv u. It will never happen again.
>
> What can I do 2 make us wrk?
>
> I'm miserable w/o u.
>
> U no u made me do it.
>
> I'm sorry. I need you baby.

Nothing but a bunch of lies. I may not be the smartest person in the world, but I knew never to take an abusive man back for him to do it again. That next time could possibly kill me. I wasn't the one, and I wouldn't be the one for Cal. I thought the only reason he really wanted to come back to me was because he needed a place to stay. He didn't want to go back and live with his mother, her man, his sister, and her four kids in a three-bedroom apartment, which was exactly where he had to go unless he wanted to live in the park. As far as I was concerned, Cal could continue to kick rocks, because I was done with him. Hell, I was done with stupid people. If you didn't get it and didn't want help, you could get out my face. It was simple as that. I have this one life to live, and I wasn't about to waste my time on people who only cared about themselves.

I finally managed to get up to go take my shower when there was a knock at the door. Instantly I became panic-stricken. I wasn't expecting anyone, so who was knocking at my door? Was it Cal coming back to exact more revenge after what happened today? I tiptoed to the door to check the peephole first to see who was standing on the other side before I opened it. If it was Cal, he wasn't getting in here to try to hurt me again. I would immediately call the cops, because he would be violating the restraining order I filed against him before I got home.

Peeping through the hole, I saw it wasn't Cal, but the person standing there shocked me. Picking up my shirt, I put it back on, attempting to button it back up. I swung the door open.

"Hey, Grayson," I said, smiling sheepishly.

"I hope you don't mind me dropping by like this."

"No, not at all. Come in." I gestured, stepping back for him to walk in, and he did.

I shut the door, making sure to lock it just in case Cal managed to get out of jail and was somewhere scoping out my place. As crazy as he acted earlier, I wouldn't put it past him. I hoped he was still in jail, but I knew his mom had probably already bailed him out.

"I'm sorry to show up like this, but I'm here making sure you made it home okay," Grayson said with his hands in his pockets.

"Aw, that's sweet," I said. "You can sit down if you like," I suggested, and he did so nervously. "You know you could have called me to see if I made it okay, Grayson." I smirked.

"I know, but seeing you for myself is better than hearing it from your lips," he said.

I stretched my eyes at how he said that, and instantly got turned on. I guessed he noticed the surprised look on my face, because he backpedaled and tried to find a better way of saying it.

"I meant I wanted to see for myself," he corrected.

"Well, here I am, and as you can see, I'm okay."

"I'm glad, but I'm seeing more than you probably want me to," Grayson said, nodding toward me.

I looked down to see one of my buttons was undone, revealing my black lace bra.

"Oh, I'm sorry," I said, embarrassed as I buttoned my shirt. "I was getting ready to get out of these clothes and take my shower when you knocked."

He giggled, saying, "You know I didn't mind."

Again with his slick remarks, I thought. After making sure none of my body parts were showing, I looked back up at Grayson.

"You know, I don't think Cal would be dumb enough to try anything stupid." I lied because I didn't know what he was capable of, but the one thing I did know was I wasn't scared. Well, maybe a little bit, but I was prepared for him now. The gun I kept in my top drawer now made me feel more secure, and I wouldn't hesitate using it on him if need be.

"You can't put anything past someone like him," Grayson said.

"You are right, but I'm going to be okay," I said, feeling like I was trying to find something to talk about with him. I felt like there was something else he wanted to talk to me about, but I couldn't put my finger on it, so I asked.

"Did you come over for something else, Grayson?" I asked, not beating around the bush. I wasn't at work now, so I could talk like I wanted to.

He dropped his head as he smiled. "You got me," he said, clasping his hands together.

"So what's this visit really about?"

Chapter 25

Serena

It was not even seven in the morning when I heard a horn blaring outside. It woke me out of my sleep. At first I thought I was dreaming, but when I opened my eyes and still heard the high-pitched horn, I realized I wasn't. Whoever it was wasn't just beeping the horn. They were laying on the horn for a long time. I was so aggravated because Nevaeh had finally done well sleeping last night, and the one morning I was able to sleep in, a car blowing its horn wakes me up.

I sighed with much frustration and crawled out of bed to look out of the window to see who it was disturbing the entire neighborhood this early in the morning. To my dismay, it was Juanita. I recognized that bright red coupe anywhere. She was parked in front of our house in the wrong direction, making a spectacle of herself. Something was on the side of her car, but I couldn't quite make it out.

I snatched my robe off my chair and went over to Tyree's side of the bed, shaking him.

"Hum," he said, making me mad because he was able to sleep through all of this commotion. This man could sleep through a category-five hurricane, which could rip our house to shreds, and he would still be snoozing like nothing was happening.

I shook him again but made sure to do it harder this time. If I couldn't sleep, he wasn't going to sleep either.

"What?" he muttered.

"Get up, Tyree. Juanita is outside."

"What?" he asked again, disoriented.

"Get up!" I yelled. "Juanita is outside waking the neighborhood with her horn blowing. You need to get her out of here."

Tyree was lying on his stomach and positioned himself up on his elbows. His head was down in his hands, and then he rubbed his eyes. Juanita blew her horn again, and Tyree shook his head. I stood over him with my arms crossed, waiting for him to get up. He slowly rose. He sat up on the side of the bed, stretching and yawning; all the while Juanita was still blaring her horn like a maniac.

"Hurry up and come on. This is embarrassing, Tyree. Get her out of her," I said, pulling on him.

"I'm coming," he said, rising to his feet. His morning erection was saluting me. He reached down and grabbed it as he walked to our master bathroom.

We made our way downstairs. Tyree opened the front door to an even louder horn being blown, since we didn't have the walls of our home to block out some of the sound now. What I saw shocked the hell out of me. This woman had the nerve to have a banner with Tyree's picture on it plastered to the sides of her car, reading: TYREE WANTED FOR CHILD SUPPORT. HE IS A DEADBEAT DAD.

When Juanita saw us standing in our doorway, she laid on the horn even harder. By now some neighbors were coming outside or peeping out of their windows to see what was going on.

She rolled her window down and began yelling, "Deadbeat dad. Deadbeat dad," over and over again.

"Juanita, what in the hell do you think you are doing?" Tyree yelled, trying to scream over her blowing the horn.

"What does it look like I'm doing? I'm protesting your sorry ass because you a deadbeat father to our son," she screamed and then laid on the horn again.

Tyree ran over to the car. Juanita let the window up before he could get to her. He tried to open the door, but she had them locked. She was looking at him with evil intent, still blaring her horn like somebody crazy.

"You got my son with you," Tyree said, looking in the back seat to see Zamir. "Where's his car seat? Open the door, Juanita, and give me my son," Tyree yelled, banging on her window.

I could tell Tyree was getting mad. I ran over to him and grabbed him by the arm to stop him before he did something stupid. "Come on, Tyree. Let's call the cops. This is what she wants," I told him.

"But she has my son," he said, looking at Zamir, who was looking at us crying. Tears were streaming down his little cheeks. "Give me my son," Tyree demanded again, banging on the window, but Juanita ignored him, still pushing down on her horn.

I tugged at Tyree, but it was no use. He was not budging. He kept jerking his arm away from me, which was ticking me off. I finally gave up and ran into the house. Picking up the phone off the console table in our living room, I called the police. The dispatcher let me know a call had already been made about a disturbance in the neighborhood, and a unit was on its way. I was happy to hear that, but I needed them here now before Tyree did something that could land him in some trouble.

When I went outside, I saw it was too late. Tyree had put his fist through the driver's side window of Juanita's car. This was the only time she let go of that damn horn. She was screaming like somebody was trying to kill her. Tyree was reaching in, trying to unlock the door, and Juanita was fighting him and screaming for someone to help her.

He wasn't even touching her, but Juanita was screaming, "He's attacking me!"

"Tyree, stop!" I yelled to him, but he didn't.

He managed to get the door open. Juanita went wild, swinging and punching at him while he struggled to reach on the door to unlock all the doors, giving him access to open the back driver's side door. Once he did that, Tyree went to the back door to open it.

Juanita hopped out, punching him in the back. I had to hand it to Tyree; he didn't swing on her. As a man he knew he couldn't, but I could. I went over and jerked Juanita by her left arm, causing her to now turn her rage to me. I didn't care, because this allowed Tyree to reach into the back seat and retrieve his son.

Juanita swung on me and landed a nice right hook to my jaw, which caused me to stumble back. I lost my balance and fell to the ground. Juanita resumed inflicting her rage on Tyree. She didn't care that he was holding their son, who was screaming his little heart out.

Tyree held his arm out like he was trying to push her back from landing any blows to his son. The next thing I know, Juanita was throwing herself to the ground. I turned to see the cops arriving at the worst moment possible. I wasn't sure how much they'd witnessed, but as they came to a stop, the two officers jumped out of the squad car and drew their weapons on Tyree.

"Get down on the ground!" one of the officers demanded.

"He beat me," Juanita lied.

"Ain't nobody beat you," Tyree yelled, bouncing his son, who seemed to have calmed down.

The officer yelled his demand again. "Sir, get down on the ground now!"

Tyree stood there disobeying the officers. "Are you serious? You want me to get down on the ground holding my son?" he asked angrily.

"Tyree," I said, now on my feet. I began to approach him.

"Ma'am, get back," the other officer said, pointing his weapon at me to halt as I threw my hands in the air.

"Why?" I asked. "I'm just going to get Zamir from him. His son doesn't need to see your guns being drawn on his father," I said.

"Just do as we asked," the officer said.

I didn't move, but I said, "Tyree, listen to the officers. Please get down before they shoot you and your son."

Tyree gaped at me as I gave him an assuring look. He then dropped to his knees, still holding his son.

"Put your hands on your head," the officer demanded.

"Now you have gone too far. Explain to me how that is feasible," Tyree exclaimed, looking at his son. The officer caught the hint. He really did need to think before he spoke.

"Ma'am, you can get the little boy," he told me. I approached Tyree and took Zamir from his arms.

"Just do what they want, babe. This will be resolved, okay?" I said softly.

Tyree looked at me with skepticism, and I couldn't blame him. Two Caucasian officers had their weapons drawn on him when he didn't do anything wrong. We didn't need another black man getting slain because a police officer got trigger-happy.

"Now step away from him, ma'am," the officer yelled.

Tyree proceeded to put his hands behind his head like he was familiar with the procedure. The officer who told him to get down kept his weapon drawn on Tyree, while the other officer approached him from behind and began to handcuff his hands behind his back.

"You are under arrest," the officer who was putting his handcuffs on him told him.

"For what?" Tyree questioned.

"Assault and battery," the officer answered.

"Assault? I haven't assaulted anybody."

"He hurt me. He tried to kill me!" Juanita screamed, lying on the ground and holding her face like Tyree had hit her. "He broke my window and then hit me, Officers. I'm pregnant with his child," she yelled.

"Like hell you are. I didn't do anything to you," Tyree retorted, still on his knees as the officer holding the gun went over to check on Juanita like she was the victim here.

I ran over to the officer who was putting the handcuffs on Tyree to explain, but he got all nervous, putting one hand on his gun and holding the other hand up to stop me.

"Ma'am, get back. I'm not going to tell you again."

"But he didn't do anything. She's the one who's causing the disturbance. Just ask them," I said, pointing at the people who were watching this spectacle happen. "She's the one you need to be arresting. Plus, I have a restraining order against her. She's not even supposed to be here," I tried to explain.

"I was dropping off my son, Officer. It's Tyree's weekend to have his son, and out of nowhere he attacked me," she lied.

"No, he didn't," I yelled.

"Look at my car. Look at how he punched the window out, which our son was in. What kind of father does that?" Juanita was putting on the performance of her life. She then gripped her stomach, saying, "I'm hurting. I hoping I'm not miscarrying our child."

One of the officers spoke into his shoulder walkie-talkie, saying they needed an ambulance dispatched.

"But she's not pregnant," I yelled.

"Yes, I am. How many times do I need to tell you that? Here, if you don't believe me, look at this," Juanita said, reaching in her jacket pocket and pulling out a white stick. She threw it at me, and I jumped back so it wouldn't hit me.

Like it was meant to happen, the white stick she threw to me landed face up. I saw this stick was indeed a pregnancy test, which showed two pink lines. Juanita was pregnant.

I was dumbfounded. *Pregnant?* I looked at her as she acted like she was in pain, holding her stomach and everything. In my heart I still didn't believe her. She could have gotten somebody who was pregnant to pee on this stick for her, just so she could make me upset. Still, I wasn't sure. This crazy woman was about to get away with her lies. Or was she lying? Either way she had no business outside my house this early in the morning, making a scene like she was doing.

Snapping back to the reality Tyree was about to be arrested, I said, "Officer, please let him go. He didn't do anything."

"Ma'am, we saw him throw this woman to the ground."

"She threw herself to the ground. She was swinging on him while Tyree was holding their son. Why aren't you arresting her for assault and battery, trespassing, disturbing the peace, and driving without a license for that matter?" I said, looking at Juanita angrily.

The police officer's eyes fell on her too. She looked back and forth between the both of us like I had burst her little bubble.

"Why don't you check that? Run her name and you will see the suspended license and the restraining order I have against her," I said as little Zamir laid his head on my shoulder. I could tell Juanita didn't like this, but I didn't care. Her son probably knew his mother was crazy too.

"I was bringing my son to his father," Juanita repeated through clenched teeth.

"We're supposed to pick Zamir up at your mother's house, Juanita. That was what the court order said. You know you're not supposed to be over here. And still that had nothing to do with you blaring your horn so early in the morning, waking the neighborhood."

As if what I was saying was lies, Juanita said, "I knocked on the door and no one would answer. I called and you all ignored my call, so I blew my horn a couple of times."

"Officer, she laid on her horn for a good fifteen minutes. She woke me out my sleep. Ask the neighbors," I said, pointing again to the ones who were still standing on their lawns to witness this nonsense. "When I called the police, a call had already been made by one of my neighbors, complaining about her. She's lying to you. I will go get my and Tyree's phone to show you she didn't call," I said, peering at Juanita. "I got voicemail evidence of her continued harassment, but we were trying to be nice by not having her arrested for going against the order; but, as you can see, she does what she wants to do, regardless of what the law says," I said strongly.

If she thought she was going to play us, she had another think coming. I would do everything in my power to have this trick get exactly what she deserved.

"Ma'am, we will take their statements and verify your information, but we still have to take this man downtown until we verify everything," the police officer said.

"I want to press charges. What do I have to do?" Juanita asked.

"Just lie here until the ambulance gets here, and someone will take your statement," the officer told her.

"I would like to press charges on her also. She hit me. Ask the neighbors, because some of them witnessed this," I said, glaring at Juanita.

I could tell by her expression she was surprised I'd said this. For too long I'd let things ride for the sake of Tyree and Zamir, but I was done giving in to this tramp. If she wanted to play games, then I was going to show her how the game was really played.

One of the officers lifted Tyree from the ground and escorted him to the police car. Juanita smirked at me as she looked at Tyree being put in the car. It wasn't long after that the ambulance arrived to take Juanita to the hospital. She was still lying on the ground, playing her poor, defenseless role, while I stood to the side, watching and holding their son. Juanita was placed into the ambulance, and I heard her call one of the officers over to her. He walked up to the ambulance where she was. I couldn't hear what she was saying, but when he looked at me, I knew whatever he was being told was not going to be good. He spoke something into his walkie-talkie on his shoulder as he stared at me.

I looked over to Tyree sitting in the patrol car. He was looking at me with so much anger on his face. I smiled and he tried to return it. I knew how hard this was on him, and I had to wonder, in moments like this, did he regret ever getting involved with someone like Juanita?

It wasn't long before I found out what Juanita was talking to the officer about. He approached me to inform me that social services was on their way to get little Zamir from me. When I questioned him about this, he informed me Zamir couldn't stay with me because I wasn't a family member. I asked him what that had to do with anything, since I was with Zamir's father. He went on to explain Juanita didn't want him around me because she felt I was mistreating her son. I told the officer this was another fabrication on the part of a crazy, jealous, spiteful woman, but he told me he still had to let Zamir go with this social worker until everything got resolved.

To see little Zamir grasping at my clothing as the social worker peeled him from my arms broke my heart. Tears streamed down my cheeks as I watched the woman walk a screaming Zamir to her car and strap him into the car seat she had centered in her back seat.

I was furious. Juanita was so hell bent on making me and Tyree pay that she couldn't see she was making her son pay in the process also. She would rather have him go into the system than see him safe with us, and that was trifling. Did she think about what could happen to her child once social services got involved? They could take him away from both of them and place that little boy into a foster home until they decided it was fit to put him back into either of our homes. Did she realize what people did to children once they got them? A lot of individuals taking in foster children weren't in it because they loved these children. Most of them were in it for their own selfish reasons, and the main one was money. It really sickened me when I considered what the next one was. Children were sexually abused all the time in the system; yet Juanita didn't care. She was willing to take that risk, which went to show what type of unfit mother she was. And she had the nerve to be having another one, so she said.

I stood in my yard a minute, watching as all the vehicles left the scene. I had not had a cup of coffee yet, and I had already dealt with guns drawn on us, the arrest of my man, a fight with Tyree's baby mama, a pregnancy test thrown at me, and social services taking Zamir away. This was too much to be dealing with this early in the morning. Now I had to get dressed, go downtown, and see what I needed to do in order to get Tyree released. But before all of that, I needed to go in the house and check on Nevaeh to make sure she was okay. I was worried about Zamir when I needed to be worried about my own daughter.

Chapter 26

Serena

Once the officers took statements from our neighbors and ran Juanita's name in their database to see the restraining order I had against her, they let Tyree go. There were too many witnesses who corroborated our story on what went down. As hard as Juanita had tried to press charges against Tyree, it didn't work. Now the so-called victim was found to be the perpetrator of this entire event, and the cops knew this. She was now facing multiple charges, including her assault on me. I would have given anything to see the look on her face once she found out Tyree was freed and she was the one who was having charges filed against her. That would teach her not to mess with us.

One thing Tyree was charged with was failure to pay child support. He had to go to court to appear in front of a judge in a month to handle the issues with that. Still, that was nothing to us, since the charges he would have been facing were more serious to the point he would have had to pull some jail time. I knew not paying child support also could land him in jail, but after Tyree showed the receipts and other documentation showing what he had contributed to Juanita, we were pretty sure the judge would throw the case out, finding that Juanita was a spiteful baby mama looking to cash in.

Needless to say, when we got home we were exhausted. Tyree was still in his basketball shorts, wife beater, and slides when we walked into the house. On our way home, I attempted to pick Nevaeh up from Vivian's home. I had asked Viv if she minded watching her while I went to get Tyree out of police custody. My sister jumped at the chance, excited that she could do this for me. She acted like she didn't want to give her up when I came by to pick her up. When she offered to keep Nevaeh while we rested, I didn't look that gift horse in the mouth. I took her up on her offer. Now it was just me and Tyree, alone in our home, and I couldn't wait to get back in my bed and take a nap.

"I'm so glad this is over," I said, plopping down on my sofa.

"Me too, and I'm glad I filed for custody of Zamir. He doesn't need to be with her."

"I'm happy you did, too, but you do know it's going to be hard for a judge to take a child away from his mother and give the child to the father. That rarely happens," I said.

"I know, but I have to try. We have—or rather, you have—collected evidence of how she's taunted us. The judge has to see it our way."

Tyree went to the fridge and pulled out some turkey, cheese, lettuce, and tomato to make himself a sandwich. "I'm so hungry. I haven't eaten anything all day."

"They didn't feed you there?" I asked.

"I didn't want that food," Tyree said, frowning.

"I bet you would have eaten it if they kept you for a few days," I said.

"Probably so, but lucky for me I didn't have to go through all of that."

"If you would have listened to me, Tyree, things might have turned out differently."

"I know. I should have. I was so mad though. Seeing my son crying like that pissed me off," Tyree said, taking out the bread and pulling out two slices and placing it on a plate.

"That's all Juanita wanted was for you to act a fool, and you fell right into her trap," I said, kicking off my shoes to bring my feet up on the couch.

"I know that now," he said, spreading mayonnaise and mustard onto his bread.

"Juanita is good at trapping you, Tyree."

He looked over at me, saying, "Why you say it like that?"

"She tossed me a pregnancy test showing me she was expecting."

There was a slight pause, which I didn't like at all. It was one of those moments when the hairs on the back of your neck stand up and you know things aren't right.

"And you believed it?" Tyree finally asked. "You know Juanita ain't right. She probably rummaged through somebody's garbage until she found it. Or maybe she got one of her chickenhead friends to pee on it for her."

"That may be true, but my gut is telling me she's not lying," I said, crossing my arms, waiting to see how Tyree would react. I watched him, paid attention to his mannerisms to see how he reacted to my line of questioning, and I didn't like what I was seeing. He kept looking down like he was concentrating that hard on making that damn sandwich. He would glance my way but never looked into my face fully, like he was trying to avoid eye contact. But I wasn't going to get mad. Not now anyway.

Tyree looked up to see me still staring at him. He paused long enough to say, "Honey, come on. It ain't true. You know you can't believe anything she has to say."

"Tyree, you know I love you, right?"

"I know this, babe. I love you too," he told me.

"If you slept with Juanita, I hope you would be man enough to tell me, because if I find out some other way, things aren't going to go well for us," I threatened.

He sliced the completed turkey sandwich in half and then grabbed the bag of sour cream and onion chips out of the cabinet.

"You did hear what I said, didn't you? Or are you trying to ignore me?" I asked.

Tyree paused, leaning against the counter like he wanted to say something.

"Tell me the truth," I told him.

He looked over at me, and it was an expression I hadn't seen from him before. The look was enough for me to feel an ache in the pit of my stomach. I crossed my arms tighter to squeeze the pain away as I stared him down. I was waiting for him to come clean. As much as I wanted to know the truth, I didn't really want to know, because that meant what we had had been a lie.

Tyree came over and sat next to me with his turkey sandwich, potato chips, and a glass of

Kool-Aid in hand. He set his drink down on the coffee table along with the chips, but held on to his sandwich. He glared at me for a moment too long to deny his innocence, and I knew then that he had indeed slept with her.

I closed my eyes in anguish.

"Serena, it was one time," he said as his words cut me like a hot knife through butter.

"When?" I managed to mumble.

"A few months ago. I went to see my son, and things just happened," he said regretfully.

I nodded slowly, tongue to cheek. He placed his hand on my knee and said, "Baby, I'm sorry. I didn't mean for any of this to happen."

"This explains why Juanita has been acting nuttier than ever. She thinks you two still have a thing."

"But we don't."

"But you do. As soon as you slept with her, Tyree, you let her know she still has a chance. All that taunting she's been doing to me and our baby, yet I'm the one looking like the damn fool in the end."

"Baby."

"How do you think that makes me feel? I believed you, and you made me look stupid. I was giving birth to your daughter and this crazy bitch was wishing death upon us. Hell, she still is. Got your son calling us bitches. The phone calls, the herpes letter in the mail, and now this," I said, beginning to cry.

"Serena, please don't cry."

"All of this happening wasn't enough to make you not want to fall into her bed?" I asked.

Tyree set his sandwich down on the coffee table. He attempted to move closer to me on the sofa, but I held my hand up for him to remain where he was. He didn't know how hard I was trying to control my anger right now, because all I wanted to do was get up off this sofa and beat the living hell out of him.

Taking a deep breath, I managed to ask, "Do I need to get checked? Was the herpes test a lie, or was there some truth to it?"

"No, baby, it was fake."

"Juanita is crazy enough to spread disease, Tyree. Especially if she thinks it's going to affect us in any way. She'll do anything to get back at you and me."

"Serena, no. It was forged. I don't have anything," he said assuredly.

"How do you know?" I asked. "Did you get checked?"

Tyree couldn't answer.

"Exactly. You don't know for sure." I turned away from him and got up off the sofa, saying, "I need some time to think."

"Where are you going?" he asked.

"I don't know. Somewhere quiet. Somewhere away from you," I said, picking up my purse and keys from the counter, and then I was out the door.

Chapter 27

Vivian

I didn't know how I managed it, but I did it. I got my sisters together for dinner again. We hadn't eaten together since that night things exploded between us over five weeks ago. For us not to all be together for that amount of time didn't seem customary. We'd always been close. As crazy as we were, as much drama as had happened, we still never went more than a week without speaking to one another.

I made the decision to have dinner at a restaurant this time. I hoped this would alleviate some craziness with us being in public; but just in case, I asked to be seated in a room in the back. We were a boisterous bunch. We all spoke our minds, and I knew even this restaurant might not keep us from exploding on one another.

The waiter sat me down at a round table covered in white linen. "Can I get you something to drink?" the brunette man asked.

"Just water for everyone now, thanks," I said, and the guy left me to myself.

I was so happy tonight was not a busy night. The room we were seated in was empty. I had to wonder if that was a sign. Did something happen here and that was the reason the restaurant didn't have many patrons? I hadn't heard anything about it. At the same time, I didn't watch the news much or read the paper to find out. That's usually where you hear about places not being up to code. It wasn't like it was Friday or Saturday, which seemed to be the busiest for most places; still, I wondered if everything was okay here. I had had one too many bad experiences with restaurants. To this day the thought of this one place I used to eat at frequently made my stomach churn in disgust.

It was about two years ago. I used to order Chinese food from this place. I had to admit it was really good; that was, until I saw them on the six o'clock news. The crew was shooting footage of the back door of the kitchen open and the cooks having the meat sitting in a large metal bowl near the door on the floor. Like that wasn't bad enough, they showed a damn dog come up and start licking the meat in the pan. One of the workers tried to catch the dog, but the dog scampered away. The man then picked up the pan of tainted meat and took it back in the restaurant to cook. I mean really. He didn't rinse it or nothing, not that water running over the meat would have mattered much. He threw some of the meat on the grill like it was nothing. Who does that? That couldn't have been the first time they did that. Then it was suspected the meat they cooked was cats and dogs. That's why they had the pan of meat sitting by the open door to lure the animals so they could catch them, kill them, and serve them up like some General Tso's chicken. I was sick for days after that footage.

And don't you know they didn't shut this restaurant down. I mean, they did for a few days, until they got things up to code, but they were back open within a week, and people actually still showed up to eat. Don't get me wrong; I know different cultures eat different things, but let me be the chooser of what goes in my mouth.

More power to them. I knew I was a customer they lost for life. It's one thing to not know what they do to the food in the kitchen of these restaurants, but it was another to find out the meat you were eating could be someone's pet dog Rover. To this day I couldn't eat Chinese food for fear it was man's best friend.

I took a sip of the water the waiter put before me, wondering where my sisters were. I looked at my watch and realized I did arrive early. Twenty minutes early, to be exact. For some reason I was nervous. I didn't feel like any arguing tonight. I wasn't in the mood, but my love for my sisters pushed me to go through with this.

"Hey, sis," Serena said, walking in with Phoenix.

"What the . . . ?" I said in shock.

"I know. I'm on time," Phoenix said. "You can thank Serena here," she said, leaning down to give me a quick hug.

She looked cute in a pair of dark denim jeans, caramel-colored riding boots, a white tee, tan jacket, and orange scarf. Serena had on jeans also, with a white tank, gray jacket, with a pink scarf and gray boots.

"Don't y'all look cute," I complimented them.

"Thanks," Serena said. "I think Phoenix was looking through my window when I got dressed."

"Girl, please. You're biting my style. We all know I'm the fashionista of all of you guys, so don't act like you don't know," Phoenix retorted, looking Serena up and down.

"You wish," Serena joked, knowing if she kept pushing the issue, this would get Phoenix started.

"Boo boo, look at me. You better recognize. I know you biting. Just admit it and sit your little tail down," Phoenix countered.

"Please sit down," I said, giggling. "Phoenix is the cutest sister. You happy now?" I said, looking at her.

"I know that. I don't need you telling me that, but I appreciate the love." She grinned. "So who's sitting where?" Phoenix asked, looking at the four empty chairs.

"I think you should sit beside Vivian, and we will sit Shauna beside you. That way you and Shauna will not have to sit by Dawn," Serena suggested.

"I think that is a good idea," Phoenix said, pulling out the chair beside me and sitting down. "I'm going to tell y'all like this: I'm not in the mood for Dawn's BS this evening."

"Please don't start," Serena said, sitting down and leaving an empty chair between her and Phoenix.

"I'm just saying. Y'all know how I am. If she decides to diss us like she did the last time we were together, I'm going to shut her mouth with my fist," Phoenix said.

"There is not going to be any fighting here tonight," I said.

"That's why you had us meet here, isn't it?" Phoenix asked.

"Exactly. We all know if this had been at any of our houses, things would have turned left real quick. I'm hoping being in public will make us rethink our actions," I said.

"True," Phoenix agreed.

"We are sisters. We shouldn't be taking it to the point of hand-to-hand combat anyway," I said.

"I'm just saying if Dawn wants to bring it, then I'm going to get to swinging," Phoenix said, rolling her eyes as she picked up a straw the waiter placed on the table and put it into her water to take a sip.

"Dang, I don't know who's more upset, you or Shauna," Serena quipped.

"Does it matter?" Phoenix retorted, positioning her diva sunglasses on the top of her head. "I got a headache and I'm not for the bull tonight."

"Why didn't you take something for your headache?" I asked.

"I wanted to, but I'd be 'sleep right now," Phoenix said.

"What are you taking that's going to have you 'sleep?" Serena asked. "I know Motrin don't put you to sleep."

"My doctor prescribed me muscle relaxers because it helps with my tension headaches. I was this close to not coming," Phoenix said, holding her pointing finger and thumb an inch from each other. "Y'all better be glad I love y'all."

"We love you too. Hopefully this won't take long. Then you can go home and pop you a pill to go to sleep," I said.

As hard as Serena was trying to look happy, I could tell she wasn't. Something wasn't right with her either, and I had to wonder if it had to do with the crazy baby mama she talked to me about the other day. When she picked up Nevaeh, she was obviously upset, but she refused to talk about what was wrong, so I left the situation alone.

"Serena, are you okay?" I asked, looking at her sincerely.

"Yes, I'm okay."

"You see. Even Vivian noticed something is wrong." Phoenix turned to me and said, "I've been trying to get whatever is bothering her out. On our car ride here she was quiet as a church mouse, and when have you ever known Serena to be quiet?"

"Serena, come on, sis. You can talk to us. Remember, I'm here for you no matter what,"

I said, looking at her with a smile. "You were there for me, so let me return the favor and be here for you."

Serena managed to smile even though it was a bleak one. She put her elbows on the table, bringing her hands together and leaning her face against them. Water began to form in her eyes.

"Oh, hell no," Phoenix said. "Who do we got to beat down this time?" she asked indignantly. "Say the word and it's done."

"Phoenix, why does it always have to end in violence with you?" I asked.

"Because most times that's the way it is. Individuals never get it when you trying to be nice. You always have to act a damn fool in order for them to understand the picture. If someone is bringing my sister to tears, they need to get dealt with," Phoenix explained, getting as ghetto as she could.

"You guys, I'm okay," Serena struggled to say.

"No, you not," Phoenix yelled. "You're messing up your makeup and everything. You are not all right."

"Really, Phoenix. You had to go to her makeup?" I asked.

Phoenix pointed to Serena and said, "She's starting to look like a raccoon. Her eyeliner and mascara is running all over the place."

Serena giggled through her tears as she picked up a napkin, which surrounded the silverware, and unrolled the utensils from it. She placed the silverware down on the table and dabbed at her tearstained face.

"Make her feel better why don't you," I said.

"I'm just saying," Phoenix shot back.

"We can talk about this another time if you like," I told Serena.

"No, it's fine. We can discuss it now," she said, sniffling.

Both Phoenix and I looked at her while she got herself together enough to tell us what was wrong with her.

Our sister looked up at us dejectedly and said, "Tyree told me he cheated on me with Juanita a few months ago."

"What?" Phoenix said, hitting the table with her fist hard enough for the silverware Serena placed on the table to clank.

Serena nodded and continued to say, "And it gets worse."

"Worse?" Phoenix bellowed.

"She might be pregnant with his child."

"Hold up," Phoenix said, raising her right hand. "Tyree cheated with nutcase Juanita."

Serena nodded. "There was an altercation in front of our house. Tyree bust her window out.

Me and Juanita got into a fight. The cops came. Social services came to take Zamir. Tyree went to jail, and—"

"Whoa, slow down, Serena," Phoenix said. "When did all of this happen?"

"A few days ago. To make a long story short, this trick had the nerve to toss a pregnancy test to me, showing me that she was knocked up supposedly with Tyree's child," Serena continued to explain.

"Wait, wait, wait, wait, wait," Phoenix repeated. "Let's back this thing up. How in the hell did she toss a test to you in the first place?"

Serena went on to explain about the incident. Here I was thinking today was going to be about resolving our sister-issues, and it looked like all of us had our own personal ones to deal with. So far this was not turning out like I expected; but at the same time, I should have expected this, because this was what always seemed to happen with us. The great thing was that Serena was getting it out and letting us know what had been going on instead of holding all of that in.

"I can't believe we are just hearing about this now."

"Phoenix, I haven't had time to register this information myself. This is hard for me," Serena said, starting to cry again. "I love him so much, and we've been through a lot with this crazy-ass woman. For him to do this after everything we've had to deal with regarding her, I don't know if staying with him is worth it at this point, especially when I can't trust that he won't do it again."

"Leave his ass. That's what you need to do," Phoenix blurted.

"Phoenix," I called out to calm her.

"What? You know I'm right. I'm so sick of all these dogs thinking it's okay to go from one bitch to another. He was dead wrong. What he needs to do is apologize and then pack his belongings and leave. You did kick him out, right?" Phoenix asked, looking at Serena like, "You better have." I could see her hesitating.

"No, I didn't kick him out yet," she said.

"Yet! Do you need me to help you dispose of his possessions?"

"No, Phoenix," Serena said, giggling.

"'Cause I can do that for you. Call me Sister Kick a Negro Out, 'cause I can make that happen."

I couldn't help but laugh at Phoenix's antics. My sister never held any punches. As many difficulties as Serena was having I did believe Phoenix's foolishness brought some happiness to her today. I hoped she would make the right decision for her and Nevaeh. Tyree was a good guy. He made a bad decision, but sometimes you have to make difficult decisions based on what is going to be in your best interest. I wished I could take my own advice.

Chapter 28

Vivian

"Where's the waiter? I need a drink," Phoenix said sardonically.

"You can't drink if you are going to take that medication when you get home. Are you trying to kill yourself?" Serena asked.

"Hell naw. I love myself too much to hurt me."

"Then it's either drinking or relaxers later. Pick one," Serena said, finally getting herself together.

"I choose drinks, please. I'm going to need it to get through this dinner," Phoenix admitted as she turned to find the waiter.

I wondered where he was also. It wasn't like this place was packed.

"Waiter," Phoenix yelled, holding her hand up for him to come over.

I hit Phoenix on her arm to stop her from yelling across the room, but she looked at me with a frown and kept waving her hand frantically until she got his attention to come over.

"Yes, ma'am. Can I help you?" the waiter asked.

"Yes. I would like a glass of Moscato, please. Better yet, if you have a bottle, I would prefer that in a bucket of ice. I'm going to need it," Phoenix told him.

"Yes, I can get that for you. Can I get you ladies anything else?" he asked. "Are you ready to order?"

"Yes, can we get the menus please?" I said.

"Yes, ma'am. I'm sorry about that. I will bring everything to you in a few minutes," he said, walking away.

"Hey," Shauna said, walking up to the table, surprising us.

We didn't see her approaching since we were too busy trying to get Phoenix's wine and our menus so we could order.

"It's about time, Ms. Thang," Phoenix said.

"Look who's talking, the one who's always late," Shauna said, giggling.

"I'm not late today. I beat you here."

"All because of me," Serena murmured.

Shauna walked around and gave each of us a hug, which was unusual for her, because Shauna didn't give hugs. "Sorry I'm late. I just got off of work and I had to run home and get those stinky clothes off of me."

"You're fine," I said. "Phoenix just ordered some wine and we are still waiting for Dawn to arrive."

"If she arrives," Shauna mumbled.

"She said she was coming," I countered.

"I'll believe it when I see it," Phoenix retorted.

The waiter brought over the menus and the wine Phoenix requested. She and Shauna didn't waste any time pouring themselves a glass and downing their Moscato like it was the last one they were ever going to have.

Serena and I eyed one another knowing this was not good. Yes, things were going okay for the moment, but once alcohol was introduced into any situation, especially ours, it tended to change the mood of things. I knew if my two sisters kept downing that wine like they were, their lips would become loose and things were going to come out in the crudest ways.

"Okay, y'all. We are going to get along tonight. This tiff we've had going on for the past few weeks has to end. We are sisters," Serena blurted. "I want to enjoy our evening. I need this."

"Me too. We might not always agree, but we still have to love one another," I said.

"Are y'all done with the 'can't we all just get along' speech? I'm hungry and I'm ready to order," Phoenix said.

"Don't you think we should wait until Dawn gets here?" I asked.

"No." She looked at me with a scowl. "Because I don't think she's going to show. She's already late."

"She's only twenty minutes late."

"Come on, Viv. We are talking about Dawn here. You know, the one who never likes to be late to anything. If she wanted to be here, she would have been here already," Phoenix countered.

She had a point. Punctuality should be Dawn's middle name.

"So I'm getting ready to order my food," Phoenix said, picking up her menu. "And if she does show up, then we can get down to business."

Just then my cell phone rang. My sisters looked at me. Shauna gave me the look like, "That's her." When I looked down at my cell, Dawn's face was on the screen and my stomach sank.

"Hello."

"Hey, Vivian," Dawn spoke.

"Hey, girl. Where are you? The gang's all here and we are waiting on you to show up."

"Aw. I'm sorry, Vivian, but I'm not going to be able to make it," Dawn said.

My sisters stared in my face, knowing exactly what she was telling me.

"Why?" I asked pitifully.

Phoenix threw her hands in the air like, "I told you so." I frowned for her to quit it.

"I forgot about a dinner date Corey set up for us tonight. If it weren't for that, I would be there," she said.

I felt like she was making excuses, but I continued to be as nice as I could. "Okay, I understand."

"But we will get up, I promise," she said cheerfully. "And I promise I will double check my schedule to make sure, okay," Dawn said.

"Okay."

We both hung up. My sisters were still staring at me.

Phoenix said, "Told you."

"But she told me she was coming," I said with disappointment. "I didn't want to believe she would bail on us."

"I can believe it. I mean, come on, Viv, the last time we got together, it was damn near a knockdown, drag-out fight. Dawn is not ready to face us after everything that went down," Serena said.

"What was her excuse?" Phoenix asked.

"She said she had a previous engagement with Corey," I revealed hesitantly, knowing what my sisters' reactions would be.

"You know that's a bunch of bull, right?" Phoenix asked. "She could have cancelled being with Corey to be with us. Dag, she's getting ready to spend the rest of her life with him. What's one night for a couple of hours with us?"

"I want this fixed. She's getting married soon. I think we should be there to support her marriage," I said.

"I told you how I felt about it," Shauna said.

"You can't swallow your pride and give in just this once? This is our sister's first marriage."

"I bet you it won't be her last," Phoenix joked.

"Regardless, we should support her," I urged.

"Okay, Viv. You have finally talked me into it. I will support Dawn and go to her wedding," Shauna said, shocking me.

I knew she was going to be the hardest one to convince about going, so it did stun me that she agreed so easily now. I thought I would be trying to convince her all the way up to the day of the wedding.

"You will?" I said, excited. "And what about you guys?" I asked.

"I'm willing to go," Serena said.

"Phoenix," I called her.

"I don't know."

"If Shauna can come, so can you," Serena said.

Phoenix looked at Shauna, who was staring her down. She said, "Okay, I will go."

I clapped my hands with excitement. "That's great. I'm so glad you guys are going to do this."

"I'm not going to be happy about it. I still don't like Corey," Shauna admitted.

"Can we not talk about them since they are not here? Can we talk about something I'm going through right now?" Phoenix asked.

"Sure, anything for the almighty Phoenix," Serena said teasingly.

"Thanks, sis. Let me tell y'all about what the hell is going on with me. I got a man living with me."

"You finally snagged Tyson Beckford?" Shauna said, causing laughter around the table.

Phoenix had always said there wasn't a man on earth who could ever move in with her, unless he was Tyson Beckford. I didn't think Phoenix met that hunk of a man yet. If she had, I was going home with her just to gawk at that delectable piece of chocolate.

"I wish. More like Tyson Weakford. I knew I shouldn't have slept with this man. My poon-poon was too good for him to handle, and now he's lost his damn mind in the wonders of me and won't leave my house."

"What do you mean he won't leave your house? It's your house, right?" Shauna asked.

"Hell yeah," Phoenix answered with an attitude, and I could tell the headache was subsiding and the Moscato was taking effect.

"Did you call the cops?" Shauna asked.

"I did. But don't you know they couldn't make him leave my house."

We all frowned. It was her house, so how could the cops not make this man leave? Things weren't making sense to me, but Phoenix went on explaining her dilemma.

"This man convinced them he had been living with me and they couldn't remove him because he had tenant rights."

"Now that's a hot mess," Serena said, taking a sip of her water.

"I know, right? I had to go down to the courthouse and file an eviction notice, which means this man can be in my house from three to six months until this thing is resolved."

"Wow!" Shauna said in amazement.

"I've done everything possible to get him to leave. I've asked him nicely. I've cussed his ass out. I've ignored him. I've had other men over to flaunt in his face. I've even slept with other men, screaming like it's so good to me just so he can hear me, and he still hasn't budged," Phoenix explained with frustration. She picked up her glass and took another sip of her wine.

"What did he say about your passionate screams?" I asked, smirking.

"He told me he wanted to be next."

We burst into laughter, and for once it felt like old times.

"Hearing me moaning and groaning only made him horny for me. He had the audacity to tell me he has jerked off a couple of times listening to me having sex."

"What did you say to that?" Shauna asked.

"I cussed him out. He just stood there grinning and had the nerve to get a hard on right there in front of me while I was screaming on his ass."

"Did you give him some?" Shauna asked teasingly.

Laughter exuded from the table again.

"Hell naw," Phoenix said loudly. "Something is wrong with him. I ignore him and the man makes me a five-course dinner. I scream louder and the man buys me gifts, along with jerking off in my spare bedroom. The more I do to him, the more he seems to want me."

"Well, have you thought about giving in?" I asked, knowing the answer. "Maybe he's the one for you."

"What's wrong with you, Vivian? I mean really. Have I ever committed myself to one man?" she asked.

"It was—" Shauna started to say, but Phoenix held up one finger to shush her.

"We must never discuss him. He's my past, and I'm talking about my present life. Since the name that shall remain dead among us, have I committed to a relationship?"

"No," I said along with Shauna and Serena shaking their heads.

"Now then, y'all know me. He's going to know me too if he don't get the hell up out of my house."

"He sounds like somebody crazy," Shauna said.

"Damn right. What rock did you find him under?" Serena asked.

"No rocks. I don't deal with men coming from under rocks. He owns his own business," Phoenix explained.

"Was he at least good in bed when you slept with him?" Shauna asked noisily.

"I'm not going to lie," Phoenix said, holding up both her hands in the air. "He may be a dork and get on my nerves, but the man can lay some pipe. Looking at him you can't tell he has anything, but get him excited and that man has dick for days," Phoenix described.

"I don't see the problem. He lets you do what you want. He buys you what you want. The man is packing and he has money."

"Not the type of money I need to take care of me for life," I returned.

"He has money," Shauna repeated, "and his own businessm and he has good dick. Isn't that what you've always wanted in a man?"

"Shauna is right. No one has had those traits since . . ."

Phoenix glared at me with warning to not say her past lover's name.

"Why can't we say Noah? What's the big deal?" Shauna said, being defiant like I knew she would.

"Because," Phoenix finally spoke, but hearing his name caused her to get choked up.

"Because what?" Shauna asked.

"Look, y'all don't know what I've been through with that man," she said with hurt feelings.

"We know he hurt you," I said.

"No!" she said, pointing at me. "He did more than hurt me. Look, I told you all I don't want to hear his name, and I damn sure don't want to talk about my past."

Seeing Phoenix's mood change so drastically did make me wonder what else could have happened. I saw she was more like me than I thought. We were good at putting up a front, but beneath the surface lay a lot of pain. I knew Phoenix acted like she did to cover up something, but I never knew what that something was.

The skeletons beneath our surfaces were more than I could imagine, and I wondered, would I and my sisters ever get to a place of dealing with all of the demons that were slowly creeping their way into our lives?

Chapter 29

Phoenix

My head was still pounding when I got home. It was dark outside and I still wore my shades to shield my eyes from the light that intensified the hammering in my head. I thought the couple of bottles of Moscato I drank with Shauna would ease the throbbing at my temples, but it did nothing. The pain had moved down to between my eyes, which meant this was only going to get worse.

When I walked into the house, I heard Tobias in the kitchen doing something. At this point, I didn't care. I was going upstairs to my bedroom, closing my door, and getting in my bed to call it a night. I knew I promised my sisters I wouldn't take my muscle relaxers just so I could drink wine, but I had to. The pain was too much to bear right now.

The reason why I probably had this migraine at all was from the stress of dealing with Tobias in my house. I wanted him gone, and the more I thought about him walking around here like he owned the place, the more ticked off I got about it. Talk about making my life miserable. I knew as soon as he left my migraine would leave too. I hadn't had one of these headaches in over a year, and then it was when I was ending my relationship with Noah.

The thought of him made my temples throb even more. I stripped out of my clothes, dropping them to the floor until I had nothing on. My curtains were already pulled closed, and the only light I had on in the room was from the lamp on my nightstand. I couldn't wait to turn that off. I needed darkness as soon as possible, but I needed to take my pill first.

Reaching in the third drawer of my dresser, I pulled out the relaxers. Pouring two into my hand, I paused, thinking it may not be a good idea to take two since I was taking these after drinking. I put one back, put the top back on the bottle, and walked to my bathroom. I turned the light on without thinking, and the illumination caused pain to radiate through my head. I quickly turned it back off. Tossing the pill into my mouth, I turned the faucet on and cupped my hand under the cold water. I bent down and sucked the water into my mouth. I knew I should have used a cup, but I didn't have one in there and I wasn't about to go downstairs to my kitchen to get one. This would have to do. Swallowing the pill and water, I cut the water off. I dried my hands and made my way to my bed.

Clicking the light off, I climbed under my sheets and comforter, turning to my right side to lie down. It felt so good to be in the dark. I couldn't wait for the pill to take effect.

As soon as I could feel myself drift off, I heard a slight tap at my door. I ignored it. There was another knock, along with my door being opened. I knew this because my dark room was now lit by the light coming from the hallway.

"What!" I yelled, reaching for the pillow on the other side of my bed and putting it over my head for darkness to return.

"Are you okay, Phoenix?" Tobias asked.

"No!"

"Do you need me to do anything for you?"

"Yes. I need you to get out my house and stop stressing me out to the point of me getting migraines again," I told him through the pillow.

I heard the door shut and came from under the pillow, breathing a lot better. I never opened my eyes. I began to think about how my life had turned so drastically wrong. Then Noah came to my mind, and the thought of him caused water to well up in my eyes.

Noah was my fiancé, who I was with for six years. I knew this man was the one for me. I ate, drank, and slept me some Noah. I truly did love this man with everything in me and thought he loved me the same. That was until he came home one day to tell me he was moving to Italy.

Now, mind you, when he said he was moving, I was hearing *we* were moving to Italy. I was jumping up and down happy that my baby got another promotion that allowed him to move to a different location to work. He was one of the top marketing representatives in his firm, and his bank account proved it.

Please know that when I was with Noah, I wasn't this money-hungry woman I was today. I came from a background of humble beginnings. I knew I wanted better than how I came up, but I never imagined meeting someone like Noah and living the life his hard work provided.

We lived in this two-story brick colonial with five bedrooms, three-car garage, large kitchen with granite countertops and island. Our bedroom was huge, with a separate sitting area for reading and two walk-in closets and an immaculate master bath. He drove a Hummer and I drove a black Range Rover. When he asked me to marry him, he got down on one knee in front of all my family, sliding a four-carat diamond ring on my finger. I had the life and the perfect man, or so I thought. We were engaged for seven months with me planning this extravagant wedding. Even though Noah was the main breadwinner, I had a job, too, bringing in more money. My money wasn't what he was making, but I was a woman who liked to share in the finances also.

My imaginary world came crashing down when Noah revealed to me that we weren't moving. He was going to Italy without me.

"So you are going to go set up and send for me?" I had asked stupidly with his hands in mine.

"No, Phoenix. I mean, I'm going alone."

"You are coming back for the wedding, right?"

He paused, looking down.

"Right, Noah?" I asked with the smile on my face now disappearing.

"I'm not coming back at all, which means we are not having a wedding."

I let go of his hands like they were on fire, saying, "What do you mean there isn't going to be a wedding?"

"Phoenix, I've met someone else."

"What? What do you mean you met someone else?"

"I've fallen in love with someone else," he admitted to me boldly.

"How can you fall for someone else when you are with me? We are supposed to get married in a couple of months, Noah."

"I'm sorry you had to find out like this. No time would have been the right time to tell you. When I got this job offer, I knew this was the right time."

"So is she going with you?" I asked, distraught.

"Yes."

"Are you serious right now?" I yelled. "You are leaving me for someone else after you asked me to marry you, and you're moving her with you to Italy?"

"I'm so sorry about this."

"When are you leaving?" I asked him.

"I leave in two weeks."

"How can you leave me for her, first of all? And how are you going to leave me here to have to explain to everyone the wedding is off?"

"I've already told my family," he admitted. "My family knows exactly what's been going on and what my plans are."

"They know?" I asked vehemently.

"Yes. You were the only one left I needed to tell."

Putting my hands on my hips, I was in shock at his audacity. Not only was he standing here telling me he was moving to the other side of the world with another trick, but he'd already told his family our wedding was off. I was the last to know.

"I already have someone who's willing to buy this house and my car. You can keep yours," he told me.

"Oh. Is that my consolation prize for giving you over six years of my life?"

"If you want to look at it like that, then that's fine."

The look on his face was so callous, yet it still felt like he was not telling me something. I knew Noah like the back of my hand, but then I guess I didn't if I hadn't seen this coming. I thought he was happy with me. Maybe I was too caught up in planning our wedding to pay attention and see this man was cheating on me.

"What aren't you telling me?" I asked him through squinted eyes.

He sighed.

"Tell me, Noah."

"Emma is pregnant with my son."

I dropped to my knees right there where I stood. It felt like he had punched me in my stomach with that news. "A boy. Pregnant," I said, trying to process the information.

"Yes," he said softly.

"Emma. So that's her name. Forget that. It doesn't even matter. What matters is you're bringing her up like she's important."

"She is to me," he admitted.

"You say her name so freely, like that's supposed to sit well with me."

"What else am I supposed to call her?"

"How about bitch? Whore? Slut, even? She did break up this relationship."

"I broke this up. This was my choice, so don't blame her. If you want to blame anyone, blame me only, but leave her out of this."

I couldn't believe him. Now he was taking up for her. I shook my head in disgust. "How do you know it's a boy? How far along is she?"

"She's six and a half months."

I dropped my head in grief. Was he kidding me right now?

"Ever since I found out you couldn't have kids . . ."

I looked up at him and shot daggers his way, causing him to pause. "I can't have kids because you wanted me to get an abortion!" I screamed with tears running down my face. "You begged me to do that for you because you weren't ready for children. I told you we could make it work, but you kept on insisting we wait. So I listened and did what you asked."

"How was I supposed to know there were going to be complications from the procedure?"

"You never should have asked me to do something like that. I was killing my child for you," I yelled through tears. "Now you want to backpedal and leave me because of the complications, which ruined our chances of ever having children?" I spat.

"I eventually wanted kids, Phoenix. You knew this," he said coldly.

"And now that I can't give you what you want, you move on to the next trick," I said. "I guess the timing was perfect this time. You asked me to kill my child because it wasn't the right time, but Emma is getting ready to give birth, and now it's the right time."

"Phoenix, I told you I'm sorry."

"Do you really think an apology is going to lessen my ache and humiliation, Noah? You are standing here telling me you are leaving me for your pregnant girlfriend when just one year ago I got rid of our child for you. It's like you are punishing me because I did what you asked me to do and now I can't have kids."

"I'm sorry if it's coming off that way."

"Why did you ask me to marry you?" I asked angrily.

"Because at the time I did want to marry you. I wasn't planning on meeting Emma, but when I did and she got pregnant, I realized I had a second chance."

"A second chance. You had a second chance. What about my second chance, Noah? You took that away from me," I said, pointing at him.

"You made the final choice, Phoenix. I couldn't make you do anything you didn't want to do yourself," he retorted.

I jumped up from my knees and lunged for him. I punched, scratched, and even bit into Noah's flesh. I didn't know what else to do. Any way I could get this anger out of me, I was willing to do it. I knew if I had a gun in my hands, I would have shot him dead without even blinking an eye.

That man hurt me more than anyone knew. As far as my sisters knew, Noah called off the wedding and moved away for his job. They knew nothing about this other woman who was pregnant with his child, and they didn't know about me having an abortion and not being able to have children of my own. I played the role, acting like I never wanted kids, but if they only knew the truth. I did want children. I wanted at least three, and I thought those children would be by Noah. That's what I got for having faith in a man. I should have known from my own father's past that men couldn't be trusted.

Every day of my life I felt like I was being punished for taking a life. This was God's punishment for me not going with the order of things and interfering with what God set forth for me. But Noah got to go on with life, with a new woman and a baby who should have been ours. Was I bitter? Hell yes. Was I hurt? More than you could ever imagine.

So now I was the scornful Phoenix who used men like Noah used me. He left me with a vehicle and some money, but that was nothing compared to the scar he left on my heart and my womb. Ever since he did that to me, I promised myself I would never love another man again.

Chapter 30

Dawn

I wished I could say I regretted not going to the dinner tonight with my sisters, but I didn't. Not after how they treated me the last time we were together. Vivian had been the only one who reached out to me. In the beginning she was annoying the hell out of me, but the more she called and talked with me, the more I came around. I knew she loved me, but it was difficult to see this when I was still trying to get over how I ever came to exist.

I know that sounds crazy when they had nothing to do with our dad and my mom coming together to create me; still, I felt like our dad chose them over me. It took my mother taking her life for any of them to have anything to do with me. I knew I should be grateful, but at the same time, I felt like the charity case they were forced to take on, and hearing Shauna say I wasn't created in love hurt me to the core, because it was already a residual feeling I had about myself.

Shauna laying everything out on the table made me have to relive the moment I came home to find my mother dead. She decided to eat the end of a pistol. Just like any other day when I was eight years old, I got off the bus and let myself in the house with the key my mom put on a long necklace for me to keep around my neck. I always kept it hidden under my clothes so no one would see it. I let myself in the house like I always did. I knew when I got home, I was supposed to take my school clothes off first and change into my around-the-house clothes. Then I would go to the living room couch to do my homework. Mama told me to do it at the kitchen table, but I figured what she didn't know wouldn't hurt her, especially since I was getting my homework done anyway. Once my homework was done, I would get a snack, which usually consisted of some fruit and chips, and then I would relax back on the couch until Mama got home to fix dinner.

But this day was different. None of those things would happen, because on a Thursday afternoon twenty years ago, I found my mother's car still in the driveway. This time when I walked into the house, I called out to her, but she didn't answer. Entering the living room, I proceeded to go to the kitchen, thinking maybe she was there getting ready to prepare dinner. But she wasn't. I called out to her again, and still there was nothing.

I walked down the hallway to see Mama's bedroom door closed. Usually this meant she had somebody in there with her, but there was not another car outside indicating she had company. I knocked on the door gently. Nothing. I called out to her again and still nothing. I knocked harder the next time, hoping she would hear me this time, but still nothing. I was starting to get scared. This was not like my mother.

I remember putting my little hand on the knob and turning it. The door wasn't locked. What I saw next would change the person I was originally supposed to be. There, lying on her back, propped up on pillows, was my mother. It looked as though she was sleeping peacefully, but the blood spewing from her mouth and brain matter splattered on the wall behind her let me know my mother was not sleeping. She was gone.

I remember standing there staring at her for the longest. I don't know how long I stood there looking at my mother's lifeless body, the color red being singed into my consciousness to the point that for years the color made me cringe.

To this day I don't remember calling the paramedics. All I remember is the police arriving and trying to get me to leave the room where my mother's body was. They pronounced her dead at the scene. It didn't take a rocket scientist to see that. Even if my mother had been alive after such a wound, there was no way she would be normal, so death had to be the better of the two options. The option that should have been chosen was her wanting to live for me.

The social services worker showed up to take me into custody, and it was then when they asked me who my father was. I told them Edward Johnson. From the day he came to get me, things would always be weird and uncomfortable for me. In a matter of days, I went from having a mother who I thought loved me to living with my real father, a stepmother, and five half sisters. My dad and his wife welcomed me, along with Vivian and Renee, but it took Phoenix, Shauna, and Serena a bit longer to accept that I was going to be a part of their family. Eventually they did come around, or so I thought.

I thought they got past what happened, but I guessed if I couldn't, how could I expect them to? I knew they loved me, but I also knew I would never have a close sister-bond like the five of them had. And losing Renee like we did didn't help matters when it came to our relationship.

When I got home after running a quick errand, it was close to eight-thirty. I knew Corey wanted the lights, camera, action to go down around nine, so that only left me thirty minutes to get myself together.

"Honey, I'm home," I yelled.

"I'm in the kitchen getting a bottle of wine. Go get ready and I'll be right up," Corey yelled back.

When I walked in my bedroom, it was dimly lit with candles all around the room. Corey took it upon himself to change the black satin comforter to a champagne-colored one, which he must have purchased that day. I loved it.

I scurried into our master bathroom and took a quick shower. Once out, I dried off and wrapped the towel around me to get my hair looking good, which didn't take much since I had just had it done two days ago. I went into my walk-in closet and opened a drawer, pulling out a pink lingerie set. It was lace, and I liked the way you could see my nipples through the mesh material. Slipping it on, I oiled my body down and sprayed on some Victoria's Secret body spray to enhance the senses. Now I was ready.

Corey was lying down on top of the shimmery fabric with his hand behind his head, leaning against the headboard when I walked back into our bedroom. All he had on was a pair of red boxer briefs.

"Nice, baby. I like what you did," I told him, slowly making my way to him, trying my best to look sexy.

"I hoped you would," he said. "I figured our bodies would illuminate off this shiny material. You know, putting more of a spotlight on our love."

"Well, you did a good job picking it out. Too bad we are about to get it dirty," I said seductively.

"I'm ready to get it dirty," he said with his eyes stretched. The closer I got, the more I could see the hardness of his dick.

"Ready or not, here I come," I told him, crawling over to him and kissing him on the lips.

"Ummm. You are going to make me get all up in you without our viewing audience."

"It's not like we can't do a second take," I teased.

Corey kissed me again before sitting up to get off the bed. He went over to the camera and turned it on. Once the light was on, he came back over and resumed his position next to me.

"We are back, people, to give you what you love to watch, which is us," Corey said. "We appreciate your support and hope you enjoy the show."

If you haven't figured it out, Corey and I did amateur porn. Don't judge. It's a job, and one that paid well enough for me to quit my job. The more we performed, the more money we made. The kinkier we were, the more supporters paid to watch us. I had the looks, I had the body, and I was doing it with the man I loved in the confines of our bedroom. What could be better?

I have to admit at first I was against this. The day Corey came up with this idea made me furious. I wasn't a whore or a porn star. The thought of it made me feel grimy, but Corey convinced me to try it one time. With hesitation, I did it, and when I saw the money we made from that one act of love, I was sold.

Corey leaned over and began to kiss me deeply as his hands explored my body. "Damn, baby, you got me so hard," Corey said.

"You haven't seen anything yet," I told him, getting up from beside him and standing up on our bed. I began to dance seductively, swaying my hips and rubbing on my breasts as I looked at Corey lovingly.

"Do that shit," he said.

I smiled and began to slowly remove my lacey garment. I popped out one breast at a time, licking each nipple once it became exposed.

"Do you like this?" I asked him.

"Oh, yeah, baby, I like that," Corey moaned.

I caressed and squeezed my breast and slowly moved one of my hands downward until it was tucked between my thighs. I leaned my head back as I began to finger myself while Corey watched, slowly stroking himself.

"Yes, baby, plunge those fingers deep inside your sweetness," he said.

I enjoyed the pleasure I was giving myself. I dipped in and out of my hub until my hands were sopping wet with my juices. It wasn't long before I was exploding all over my fingers. My legs trembled as my body erupted into a bliss that made me drop to me knees on the bed before him. Corey was still stroking his erect dick but hadn't climaxed himself. I knew he wouldn't, because he always loved to climax on me.

"I want to blindfold you," Corey told me. As good as I was feeling right now, I didn't care. I nodded, easily submitting to whatever he wanted me to do. He laid me down on my back. He leaned over and placed the blindfold over my eyes.

"Can you see me?" he asked.

"No, I can't," I said, feeling the wind from Corey's hand moving back and forth to check, but I really couldn't see him.

"Get ready, baby," he told me.

I felt his warm hands touch my body. It sent immediate quivers all over me. His hands moved beneath the lace material to enter my folds, and he proceeded to please my center once more. His hands sent me to new levels of ecstasy. I bucked and grinded with each stroke of his large fingers. The closer I got to releasing, the more I bucked and grinded on his hand, until I released my warm juices all over him.

Corey lifted my legs. I tried to regain my composure, but he was eager to make me feel even better. He positioned himself between my thighs. I was on my back in the L position, legs straight up in the air, with Corey's manhood tapping at the outer core of my bull's-eye. With the beating of his manhood hitting my pleasure spot, I jumped with each knock of his hard wood. I wanted to remove my blindfold, but there was something more sensual about not being able to see what was going to happen next. My sense of touch was elevated by the loss of sight.

Corey's tip opened me slowly, and he pushed his way deep inside me. Like always, the first thrust was breathtaking. My feet curled around his neck as he penetrated me deeper than ever before. He held my legs and pounded his way to the finish line.

Moments later, a new position would happen as Corey turned me over and wanted to get deep inside me from the back. He gripped my hips and pulled me into his force as the finish line he was trying to get close to was fast approaching with each eager stroke of his manhood. This felt so good. My moans let him know I enjoyed what he was doing to my body. The closer he got, the harder he pounded and the more I screamed with delight. And the more I screamed, the more money was increasing in our account.

Corey whipped his manhood out of me and slid his thickness between the crevices of my butt cheeks, shooting his ooh-wee goodness all over my behind. I collapsed downward with my behind still in the air. Corey slowly removed himself off of me, and I fell down completely, waiting for him to bring me something to clean myself up with.

After he cleaned me up, I turned to my back. I had to take a minute before removing my blindfold, but once I did, I wished I had left it on.

Chapter 31

Dawn

I was in shock. Utter shock. With mouth open, I was looking at Corey sitting in the chair, which had been moved beside the bed. He was sitting in it, with some woman on her knees, butt-ass naked, giving him a blow job. Corey reached out, wanting me to hold his hand, but I couldn't take my eyes off this woman who was slurping on my soon-to-be husband's manhood like her life depended on it, while he was looking at me with a damn smile plastered on his face. What in the hell was there to smile about?

And then it hit me. If he was getting his manhood sucked by her, then who in the hell was fucking me? I looked around the room and didn't see anybody. Was there some invisible man? Or had Corey done me and then sat down quickly to finish getting his babies drunk by this nasty-ass heifer savoring his flavor? And that's when I heard the toilet flush. I looked toward the bathroom doorway and wondered who in the hell was in there. I knew we didn't have one of those toilets that flushed on their own, which meant someone else was here. As much as I wanted it to be this imaginary apparition, I knew it wasn't.

I watched the door intensely to see who would cross over into what used to be a love den meant for only me and Corey. I took a second to see the woman still lapping her way to pleasing Corey as his damn head leaned back like his ass was enjoying it.

This was in our home, where only the two of us were supposed to indulge in one another. This wasn't okay with me at all. Corey had brought up the idea of bringing other people into our bedroom, but I was against it. He'd already taken me out of my comfort zone by doing this Internet porn. Bringing others into our bedroom was a definite no, and I had told him this, but here he was choosing for me. I felt dirty, like someone had taken advantage of me. I had to wonder how I had not known it was someone else doing me. Or did I know and was too caught up in the moment to care?

A voice snapped me out of my thoughts, causing me to look in the direction the sound came from. Standing in the doorway of my bathroom was this Adonis of a man with dark chocolate skin and neatly trimmed goatee, which connected to a close cut faded to perfection. His muscles rippled from every part of his body, which had this sheen that made him glow. He was fine as hell. The brother walked closer to my bed. I didn't know whether to look at his gorgeous face or his massive manhood swinging and tapping his leg when he approached. *Is that what was inside me?* I thought. Corey's manhood—or what I had thought was Corey's manhood—felt bigger, but damn, this man right here was nothing but the truth. He had to be taking it easy on me from the looks of his extension.

I looked at Corey, who sat up to attention now. He was looking at me, still with that whack-ass grin on his face, all the while homegirl was still lapping him up. Damn, what type of jaw power did she have to be sucking on his manhood this damn long? I pulled the pillow around me as if to hide my nakedness from this stranger who had just rocked my world. He'd already seen what I had to offer and sampled it very well, but now that I knew it was someone else having sex with me, it was so different.

I was angry, and yet I was oddly attracted to the man who stood before me. I could not deny that he turned me on. He looked better than Corey hands down. And from the looks of his body, he took very good care of himself. Then my eyes fell to his inches again. He was lengthier and had more girth than Corey. The more I examined this stranger, the more I loved the idea that it was him I'd had inside me. But I couldn't let it go down like this, not after Corey tricked me into doing this.

I turned to say something, but homegirl finally came up for air. Corey gripped her by the arm to help her stand to her feet. She, too, was very attractive. I could see what Corey saw in her. Where my hair was long, hers was cut into a cool Mohawk, colored blond, and the style fit her face well. She smiled at me like we were friends, but I didn't return the gesture. I was too busy taking in how beautiful she was. The woman didn't have one blemish on her olive-tinted body. Looking at her did spark some jealously within me. She couldn't have been more than 130 pounds with her stomach flat, nice-sized breasts, a tight ass, and flawless appeal.

Corey mouthed, "The cameras are still rolling. Big money, honey."

I guessed he said this to keep me from going off in front of hundreds, or even thousands, who could be watching us right now. Honestly, I forgot we were taping when I realized two other individuals were in our bedroom.

This female leaned down, bending over to the camera and me, and began to tongue Corey down right there in front of me. It was then I noticed that she had her tongue pierced. I guessed that was something used to assist in pleasing men. He was stroking his dick while kissing her, like he needed any help at all getting up. She must have felt the movement of him doing this, because her hand joined his. I wanted to scream.

I wanted to jump off the bed, grab her by the hair and drag her out of my home, but I didn't. I watched as the two of them became more intimate with one another.

I looked over at the stallion who was still standing patiently by the bed, and he was staring me down with a smirk on his face. He, too, was watching along with me, and was stroking himself back to life. To see his manhood expand and grow to its maximum capacity made me sigh with amazement. My eyes went from his manhood back to his handsome face, and our eyes locked with one another. The way he looked at me was enough to make me cream right there in front of all of them.

Out of the corner of my eye, I saw the woman stand back up. Corey was still sitting in the chair and admiring this woman's body. Corey then scooted down a bit before reaching out to her. She took his hand, and he guided this woman to sit on his manhood backward. From the looks of it, she had done this plenty of times before. Once she was down on it completely, homegirl began to move her hips slowly back and forth. She leaned all the way back onto Corey's naked chest, and he wrapped his arms around her naked body. The two of them kissed again as he proceeded to grind into her.

And then it hit me. Was Corey slowly molding me to fit this woman he wanted me to be? You know, the woman who would be okay with my man—scratch that, my husband—sleeping with other women? Was this form of making money giving him the green light to do whatever he wanted, since he also allowed me to sleep with another man? Going into this amateur porn thing, I never thought other people would enter our bedroom.

I snapped out of my thoughts when the guy who just finished doing me walked over to this woman, who was now bouncing like a champ up and down on Corey's manhood. He gripped her hips with pleasure. The other guy stood in front of her and held out his manhood for her to take into her mouth. Without hesitation, she did just that. This Adonis's head fell back with pleasure as she bounced and slurped, showing she was very good at multitasking. I knew my juices were still on this man, but she clearly didn't care. As she sucked him, she was giving me a look like she wanted to come over and do me next. I'd never been with a woman and didn't know if I wanted to tonight. Corey had already taken this thing further than I ever anticipated.

This woman had both Corey's and this Adonis's minds blown so bad that neither of them noticed I was still in the room. I didn't know what to do. I didn't know how to feel. Should I be happy the two of them wanted her? I wasn't. I felt like the lonely, lost puppy who wanted attention also. Then I was mad at myself for feeling this way when the main feeling I should have been having was one of disrespect. I had no say-so in any of this. Corey decided all of this for me and didn't consider how I would feel.

The Adonis held his hand out to me, welcoming me in on the threesome they were having. The woman released her lips from his fully extended member long enough to hold her hand out to me also. I glanced at both of them. Then Corey leaned up to see what my next move was going to be. Both the woman and the Adonis had smiles on their faces like they were hoping I would take their hands. This was decision time. This was my chance to walk away; but instead, I reached out and grabbed their hands as I got off the bed.

Standing, the Adonis pulled me into him and kissed me deeply. The woman was still holding my hand but used her other to caress my hips. Next thing I knew, her fingers were inside me. I hate to admit it, but it felt good. She was pleasing me better than any man had. And just like that, Corey pulled me deeper into his uninhibited world as this sexual adventure swiftly turned into a foursome.

Chapter 32

Vivian

I did something I'd never done before. I went to a bar by myself to get some drinks and relax a bit. I'd always wanted to do this but felt like I should never come without a man on my arm or at least one of my sisters. Tonight I didn't care. I needed a drink or two, or five at this point. I wasn't happy with the way things had turned out with my sisters tonight. The fact that Dawn didn't show up only made things worse in my eyes and made it look like she wasn't interested in trying to work things out with us. After all I did to make this happen, she betrayed me by not showing up and made me look stupid in front of my sisters. I was offended.

"What can I get for you?" the blond, blue-eyed bartender asked, snapping me out of my thoughts.

"I would like a Painkiller, please."

The bartender's eyebrows rose and he said, "You don't look like you should have any pain to kill."

Was he flirting with me? The smirk on his face made me think so. *How flattering,* I thought. He was cute, too. Probably too young for me, but I could look at his nice physique

I smiled and responded by saying, "You would be surprised."

"Too bad. A woman as attractive as you shouldn't have any pain to kill," the cutie pie said.

"Thank you."

"I will get that to you in just a bit, okay?"

I smiled back at him and watched as the cutie pie walked away to take other drink orders. I looked around to see the place was crowded. Everybody was talking and smiling, and some men were watching the basketball game that was on the televisions above the bar. I looked up to see who was playing, but as I did that, I felt a hand on my shoulder. I turned and rolled my eyes when I saw him. As if my night could get any worse, I was staring into the eyes of Eric.

"What are you doing here?" he asked with a grin.

"Minding my own business," I said coldly, pushing his hand off of me.

"Aren't we in a bad mood?"

I ignored him and looked up at the television to see two college basketball teams playing.

He pulled out the chair next to me and sat down, saying, "I hope you don't mind if I join you."

My eyes were slits as I said, "Don't do me any favors. I don't want you slumming tonight."

"Okay, I deserve that, but come on, Vivian. You can't still be mad at me."

"Oh, I'm not mad," I said, sitting back on the tall stool and crossing my arms.

"You see. You got your guard up already."

"When it comes to you, Eric, I have to. You never do anything unless it's going to benefit you, so what is it tonight? Do you think I'm going to fall for your whack-ass charm and jump into bed with you again?" I asked heatedly.

"No, Vivian. Look, I'm sorry for saying the things I said to you the last time I saw you. I was having a bad night," he tried to explain.

"So you decided since your night was bad, you would make mine bad also, just like you are doing right now," I said, watching the bartender set my drink in front of me.

"Are you good?" cutie pie asked me, giving Eric a look that wasn't really nice.

I started to say, "Hell no, can you please ask security to remove this man from me?" Instead I said, "I'm okay."

Cutie pie winked his eye and walked away.

"Dude better watch himself," Eric said.

I ignored him, picked up my drink, and took a sip. The drink was really strong. I wasn't expecting it to be, but it was still good.

"I'm celebrating tonight," he said, waiting on a response from me, which I wasn't about to give him. I took another sip of my drink.

"You are not going to ask me what I'm celebrating?"

"Nope," I said curtly.

"I know you don't care, but I got a promotion today," he said excitedly.

"Great," I said uncaringly, hoping he would leave. Again he was making this about himself, and I didn't need this.

"Do you want me to leave you alone?" he asked.

"I sure do."

"So you are not going to give me any conversation. Just short answers?"

"I just agreed with you that I want you to leave," I said, glaring at him.

"Viv."

"Don't call me that. Only people who love me call me that," I snapped, instantly thinking about Sheldon.

He held his hands up, saying, "Okay, Vivian."

"You know what, Eric? I would appreciate if you would leave me alone. We have nothing more to say to each other. We said our hellos, so now can you excuse yourself so I can say good-bye?"

"You don't mean that. Not to the man you love."

"*Loved*. Get it right."

"I love you. You have to know you still have some feelings for me too," he said, fishing for compliments.

"Disgust comes to mind when I think about you. Regret, loathing, selfish, heartless, and even hate comes to mind when I think about you. Yeah, I think I may hate you, too. But the love is gone. Now, go celebrate your little promotion with someone who cares," I said, using my hand to shoo him away like an aggravating fly.

I went to pick up my drink again, but Eric grabbed my wrist. I looked at him like he was crazy, but he was giving me the same expression back. It was the same look he had on his face the night I kicked him out of my place.

"Who are you to ignore me?" he asked furiously.

"Here's the Eric I'm familiar with," I said, not being afraid of his reaction.

"I'm trying to be nice to you and you are dissing me?" he asked like he couldn't believe it.

"Dissed and dismissed, as a matter of fact, so let me go," I demanded.

"You should be happy I'm even talking to you. I mean, look at you. No one wants a woman like you," he told me.

"If that's the case, then why are you upset, yet again? Hear you tell it, I'm not worthy. So why you mad?" I asked him inquisitively.

"You will not get away with disrespecting me in front of all these people like you are somebody, because you are nothing."

"Eric, I'm not going to tell you again. Let me go before I have security drag your sorry ass out of here," I said, trying to pull away from him, but he had too tight a grip on my wrist.

"Oh, you don't need security."

I looked back to see Sheldon standing behind me.

"I would be happy to do the honors of kicking this fool out of here for you, Viv."

Sheldon gave Eric a look that told him if he didn't get his hands off of me immediately, he wouldn't have hands to enjoy the promotion he just got. Eric let go of me and adjusted his blazer as he sat back in his stool.

"Just like I thought," Sheldon said in a threatening tone. "You okay, Viv?"

"I am now," I said, rubbing my wrist. I could tell Eric caught that Sheldon called me Viv. As he glared at me, I said, "Only the people I love." Eric was ticked but didn't dare say anything with Sheldon standing here.

"Is this seat taken?" Sheldon asked, pointing at the seat Eric was sitting in.

"It's available. He was just about to leave," I said, glowering at Eric.

Eric hesitated for a moment. I think he wanted Sheldon to remove him from the seat, but I guess his better judgment kicked in knowing Sheldon was the type of guy who would do just that if need be. He stepped down from the stool without saying anything. He grimaced at me and then Sheldon before walking away. Sheldon took his place next to me, looking at Eric making his way to the other side of the bar.

"Thanks for that," I said.

"Anytime. You know I'm here for you."

His words touched me. And they were true. Sheldon was always here for me.

"What are you doing here?" he asked.

"I'm trying to relax."

"Oh, really, with dude here with you?"

"He just showed up. He was the last person I expected to see here," I said, picking up my drink and taking a sip.

"It's weird seeing you here, Viv. This isn't you. You don't do this," he said, looking at my drink and the bartender, who was waiting on two women sitting three stools down from me. When I looked their way, I saw them checking Sheldon out.

"You have admirers," I told him.

He looked at the women and smiled but turned his attention back to me, saying, "Those skeezers. They are here all the time. Probably thinking those eyes are going to make me send them a free drink. That's not going to happen."

I laughed louder than I expected to. I put my hand over my mouth to contain the giggles, but I couldn't stop.

"How many of these have you had?" he asked, picking up my drink.

"This is my first, Sheldon."

"And it's your last one for tonight."

"Dag. Can a girl unwind?" I asked, frowning at him and pulling my drink back to me to take another sip.

"Not here and not by yourself," he said.

"I'm a grown woman, boy. My daddy is . . ." I paused.

Sheldon must have seen my sadness creep in. He tossed a twenty on the bar and stood. He held his hand out to take mine.

"What?"

"I'm taking you home."

"But I'm not ready to go. I haven't finished my drink."

"Let's go, Viv."

I hesitated. I picked up my drink and finished what I could. Sheldon smirked but still had his hand out for me to take. I really wasn't ready to go, but I knew he would drag me out of there kicking and screaming, so I reached out, took his hand into mine, and got down from the stool. As soon as I stood, I felt my legs tingle from the drink I had just consumed.

"You good?" he asked, grinning.

"I'm fine," I said convincingly.

Once we were in the parking lot, Sheldon tried to get me to give him my keys. He wanted to drive me home, but I wouldn't let him. I wasn't drunk, so I could drive myself. After arguing in the parking lot for a bit, Sheldon finally conceded and told me he was going to follow me closely and to not speed. He knew I had a heavy foot, and tonight was not the night to get a speeding ticket along with a DUI.

I made it home without any mishaps. Sheldon pulled in to the driveway beside me. He got out of his ride and came around to my driver's side door and opened it.

"I think I got it from here," I told him.

"I'm making sure you get in the house first before I leave."

Getting out of my car, I said, "I haven't heard from you in days, and you show up treating me like a kid. Who do you think you are?"

"I'm your friend," he countered.

"Are you? My friend used to check in every day if it was just to say hey. My friend would drop in sometimes just to chill. I haven't heard or seen that friend in quite a while. Not since he fucked me."

Sheldon's jaws tightened at my words. He took two steps back, looking at me.

"What? You can't say anything."

"Look, you are tipsy."

"I'm not tipsy off of one damn drink, Sheldon," I lied.

"Let me take you in the house so I can go."

"You can go now. You don't have to wait until I'm safe. I can get myself in the house just fine, thank you," I said, slamming my car door shut and walking down my sidewalk. As I put my keys into the lock to open the door, I heard Sheldon cranking his ride to leave. I opened the door and looked back to see him backing out of my driveway.

Shaking my head, I went into my house slamming the door with tears in my eyes, wishing he would have stayed with me. I knew I pushed him away, but it was easier than accepting the fact that our relationship might never be the same again.

Chapter 33

Serena

I wasn't ready to go home yet. I didn't feel like dealing with the issue of Tyree's cheating ass sleeping with his crazy baby mama. We had yet to talk about it since I walked out that day. Each time we were around each other, there was silence. The only one in our home who was making any noise was Nevaeh.

I drove up to a stoplight wondering where in the hell I could go, because I really couldn't afford to ride around like this since gas was so high. Nowadays when you put gas in your car, you only drive it when you have a destination to go to. Riding around was not an option. While I was waiting on the light to change, my cell phone rang. I saw it was Tyree calling me. As much as I didn't want to answer, I did, just in case it had something to do with Nevaeh.

"Hello."

"Babe, where are you?"

"I'm out. Why?"

"I need you to come home. It's important," he said urgently.

"Is Nevaeh okay? Did something happen?" I asked nervously.

"Nevaeh is fine."

"So what's so important?" I asked.

"I'd rather not discuss this over the phone, so can you please come home? You know I wouldn't have called you if it wasn't important, Serena."

"I hope you are not going to tell me some more bad news about you and Juanita," I said, hoping this was not the case. I didn't think my heart could take another blow right now.

"No. This has nothing to do with her. Baby, please, come home," he begged.

"Okay. I'll be there in a bit."

When I walked through the door, I saw Tyree sitting on the sofa watching television. To me it didn't look like anything crucial as he screamed at the television about some basketball player missing a three-point shot. When he saw me, he instantly cut the television off and stood to greet me.

"Hey, babe," he spoke, looking uneasy.

"So what's so important that you needed me to come home?" I asked nonchalantly.

"It's about your sister."

"Which one?" I asked, thinking maybe this had something to do with Shauna or even Phoenix.

"Dawn."

"Did something happen to her?" I asked apprehensively.

"Nothing bad. Well, you might think it's bad."

"Tyree, spit it out already, because you are starting to scare me," I said with a raised voice.

"Come here," he said, taking my hand and pulling me into the bedroom.

"What?" I asked irritably, hoping this wasn't his way of getting me to sleep with him, because I wouldn't. Not after finding out his dick was in nasty-ass Juanita.

Tyree led me to our bedroom and over to the computer, which was in the corner by our window. We had to put it in here since we didn't have an office. It used to be in Nevaeh's room, but once she was born, we had to make the office into a nursery for her.

"Sit down," Tyree told me, and I did. Standing behind me, he leaned over and moved the mouse around. He began clicking on some things. He brought up the video player, and instantly the images of an African American woman popped up on the screen. She was lying on the bed, playing with herself.

"It's not bad enough you cheated on me. Now I find out you have a porn addiction too."

"Serena, I don't have a porn addiction," he countered.

"So what is this?" I said, pointing at the screen.

"Please watch."

"I don't feel like watching porn right now, Tyree."

"Serena, will you be quiet and watch this," he said, raising his voice. He clicked on the button, and all of a sudden a bedroom showed up on the screen. In this bedroom were the bodies and faces of Dawn and her soon-to-be husband, Corey.

"What is this?" I asked, trying to figure out what was going on.

"One of my boys called me and told me he had something for me to check out, that I wouldn't believe who was performing in this new video he just burned. He dropped it by today and told me to watch it. When I put the CD in, this is what came up," he said, pointing at the computer screen.

"This looks like their bedroom," I said, figuring out the space was my sister's private sanctum.

"I figured that."

"I can't believe this. Why would Dawn do something like this?"

"I don't know. And it gets worse," Tyree said.

As much as I wanted to turn away, my nosiness got the best of me. I had to see how far this would go, but I wasn't prepared for what happened next.

"What the . . . ?" I said in shock as my hand covered my mouth.

"I know. Can you believe it?"

"When did this happen?"

"My boy didn't go into details. He just recorded it to this disc and brought it to me," Tyree explained.

"Who else has seen this?" I asked angrily. "Has he been showing all your friends?"

"Serena, I don't know. I guess he brought me a copy to let us know what was going on, since he knew Dawn was basically like a sister-in-law to me."

"He could have just told you. He didn't have to record it," I yelled.

"Do you think you would have believed him, or me for that matter, if I told you without proof?" Tyree said.

He was right. I wouldn't have believed him. Not after he lied to me about sleeping with Juanita. Plus, it was something degrading regarding my sister. This couldn't be the Dawn who fell out with us over her no-good man. Not Ms. Goody Two-shoes. Seeing this made me question her sanity.

"I can't believe this," was all I kept saying. "She's having sex with someone else and posting it on the Internet."

"But that's not it," he said, reaching over me to eject the disc of my sister and her sexual escapades. He placed another one in, and I watched as the disc booted up. I wasn't sure if I wanted to see anything else, not after seeing my sister butt-ass naked getting screwed by some strange guy, while good-for-nothing Corey watched in the background with some floozy sucking on his manhood.

An image came up on the screen, and it appeared to be someone else's bedroom that I was not familiar with. A woman walking backward to the bed came into view as she gave the come-here finger to someone else in the room. Then a man appeared, walking up to her and holding the woman in his arms. They kissed deeply.

"What is this, Tyree? This doesn't look like Dawn," I said.

"But pay attention to who the man is."

At first I didn't pay attention because the man's back was to the camera. The woman crawled up on the bed, again backward, scooting to the middle, and the man climbed on top of her. He kissed her again before making his way down her body until his face rested between her thighs. And then he looked at the camera with a smirk.

"You have got to be kidding me," I said.

"This CD has several different women on it, with Corey being the main actor on this disc."

"So Corey is a porn star. I don't even want to call him a star or actor, because this man isn't acting. He's doing what he loves."

"And it's one more thing, babe."

"You know I'm getting tired of you saying that," I said, not wanting to see another thing, but if Tyree was telling me this, then it had to be important.

He reached over me and clicked the mouse, going from chapter to chapter through the different women Corey was playing hide-the-salami with, until Tyree came to chapter eight.

"Prepare yourself," Tyree said, but what came up on the screen was nothing I could prepare myself for.

"What?" was all I could say as water filled my eyes. I turned to Tyree, who looked at me lovingly. "Is this real?"

"It has to be, babe," he said sincerely.

"Why would my sister do this?"

"I don't know."

"Turn it off," I spat. "Please turn it off," I said, getting up from the chair and walking to the other side of our bedroom to catch my breath. Tyree did as I asked, closing the video player down.

He then turned to me and asked, "Babe, are you okay?"

"No, I'm not okay. Would you be okay if you saw that?"

Tyree didn't say anything. He sat down in the office chair and ejected the disc from the computer tower. "I'm sorry, Serena," Tyree said genuinely. "I didn't want you to find out this way, but I felt like you needed to know."

"What is happening in my life?" I said, sitting down on the bed and beginning to cry. "What is she thinking?" I asked.

"I don't know, but you really need to talk to your sister. Something is definitely up with her."

"I appreciate you telling me this, or should I say showing me this," I said with a nervous giggle, even though nothing about this situation was funny.

"You know I love your sisters like they are my own. I have three sisters myself, and I hope if you heard or saw something like this you would tell me," he said honestly.

"You know I would," I said, loving this man even more, despite him betraying me.

Tyree put both discs in a plastic case and set them on the desk. He then came over to the bed and sat down beside me. "You sure you are okay?" he asked with concern, rubbing my back.

"It's too much going on. First it was Juanita threatening me and Nevaeh. Then it was my sisters falling out. Now you've told me you cheated on me and could have a child on the way, and now this. The problems keep stacking up."

"But our relationship does not have to be one of those problems."

"Your cheating on me is a problem," I yelled.

"I know I was wrong, but I swear I was only with her one time," he pleaded.

"How do I know that? Far as I knew, you weren't with her or anybody else. I trusted that you were faithful to me, and you broke that trust."

He nodded, saying, "Serena, on everything I love, my mother, my sisters, and my own daughter, I only cheated on you that one time. It was the biggest mistake I've ever made in my life."

"No, your biggest was ever getting involved with that woman."

"I can say that, but then I wouldn't have my son," he retorted, and I understood. "I hope this mistake doesn't cause me to lose you," he said compassionately. He got up and kneeled down in front of me, positioning himself between my thighs so we were face to face.

"Serena, I love you with everything in me. Baby, I don't want you to leave me. I promise as long as I live, I will never cheat on you again."

His words were gentle, loving, and felt genuine. Tears ran down my cheeks as I looked down, fiddling around with the hem of my orange sundress. As much as I wanted to believe him, I was afraid to. Tyree reached up and wiped my tears away, but more tears replaced them when he touched me. His hands were so warm.

"You really hurt me, Tyree," I said through tears.

"I know, baby, and I'm so sorry."

"I'm worried you will do this again."

"Look at me, Serena," he said with a comforting voice.

I looked into his sincere eyes.

"Don't leave me. Please don't leave me. Give us another chance. I'll do anything you want me to do to make this work."

"I wish you didn't have to deal with Juanita," I said. "But I know that will never happen since you two have a child together, and you may be having another one with her," I said overwhelmed by this realization.

Tyree dropped his head in defeat. He said, "I would never wish any ill will toward Juanita and this unborn child, but I do wish she weren't pregnant."

"Me too."

"This child didn't ask for the turmoil it will be born into. And you know if it is my child . . ."

"You have to take care of it," I said, finishing his sentence.

"And you best believe I'm going to find out whether this child is mine."

"Well, I hope it's not. It's bad enough you had one with that crazy woman," I said.

"True, but it did give me my beautiful son, who's my world along with Nevaeh."

"They are beautiful children, aren't they?" I said, smiling. "Despite the unstableness of Juanita, Zamir is a good boy."

Tyree nodded. There was a silence between us as we stared at one another.

I broke the silence by saying, "As much as I would love to leave you, I love you too much to do so."

Tyree leaned in and kissed me tenderly on the lips. Nothing lustful, just a kiss of admiration.

"Thank you," he said.

"Don't thank me yet, because I still haven't forgiven you."

"I understand."

"It's going to take some time for me to get over this, Tyree."

"I wouldn't expect any less," he said. "I'm glad we had this talk."

"And it was all due to my sister's sex acts," I said, giggling.

"Make sure you thank her for me," he said jokingly.

"I'm not sure I like the way you said that. I mean, you did just see my sister naked," I said, smiling.

"And it sickened me," he said, smirking.

"Sure," I said.

"I'm serious. I told you your sisters are my sisters. Who wants to see their sisters getting it on with any dude?"

"I get that," I said, looking down at my hands in his.

"I love you, Serena."

I looked into his loving eyes and leaned forward, wrapping my arms around Tyree, who returned the embrace. It felt good to have one problem resolved somewhat. Now I had to figure out how I was going to handle Dawn's situation. Would this be something else that would drive another wedge between us?

Chapter 34

Vivian

An emergency sister-meeting had been called by Serena, who rang my phone off the hook last night until I picked up to talk with her. She wanted to use my house as the location, but she wouldn't tell me what it was about. By the tone of her voice, I knew whatever she had to tell us couldn't have been good.

I really didn't need this right now after the night I had. I'd finished my bottle of wine after Sheldon dragged me from the bar and left me standing on my stoop to wallow in the grief of losing him. As soon as I entered my home, I called him, but he wouldn't answer his phone. He was sending me to his voicemail, which was something Sheldon never did. I was feeling so low about this situation.

The strength needed to maintain this demeanor of mine was wearing thin. And who could I tell,

Dawn? No, because she was planning her wedding. Serena? She had her problems with Tyree cheating. Phoenix was dealing with a squatter, and then there was Shauna, who would probably tell me to get a drink and let things roll off my back. The only one who would have been here regardless of anything going on in my life was my sister Renee, and she was no longer among us. The thought of her caused water to well up in my eyes. A tear ran down my right cheek.

"I miss you so much," I whispered, hoping her spirit heard me. I wished she could answer me.

"Why did you have to die?" I questioned. "Why, God? Why did you have to take her from me?" I asked, knowing God wasn't going to answer me. I hadn't had that moment yet where God spoke to me. I didn't know what that felt like. I always wanted it to happen to me, but I'd never experienced it. I knew there was a higher power, but I wondered why He never talked to me. What was wrong with me? What was the reason God didn't answer?

I dropped my head in sorrow, sitting on the side of my bed. It was close to eleven. That was the time my sisters were supposed to get here, and here I was still in my pajamas. I wasn't going to change. For what? I was at home. It was Saturday, my day to concentrate on me. If it were really up to me, I wouldn't have any of them over here. I would close the blinds, unplug the phone, and watch TV in darkness.

I knew I had to get it together before any of them arrived, even if it was just washing my face. I willed myself to get up, and when I did, my cell phone rang. I looked over at my nightstand, watching my cell phone ringing and buzzing as it moved around the wooden top. To my surprise, it was Sheldon's face smiling back at me. I quickly picked it up.

"Hello," I said with eagerness.

"Viv."

"Yeah, Sheldon, it's me."

"You okay?" he asked questionably. "You sound funny."

"I'm okay," I lied.

"No, you are not," he said, causing more tears to form.

"Sheldon, I never could lie to you. I'm not okay. I got a lot going on right now."

"I know some of what you are going through has to do with me," he said.

I paused for a moment before saying, "Yes. I miss you."

"I miss you too."

"So what's going on with us? Things have been different ever since that night we . . . we . . . you know."

"Slept together," he finished.

"Yes."

"Look, Viv. This is not anything I want to talk to you about over the phone. Can I come over so we can talk?"

"Me and my sisters are having an emergency meeting this morning, and they should be arriving any minute, but you can come over after that."

"What's going on now?" he asked.

"I don't know. Serena called the meeting, so I will find out when she gets here."

"Okay. Hit me up when your sisters leave, and I will swing through then. Is that okay?"

"That sounds good. You never know; depending on what Serena has to tell me, I might need your shoulder. You know how things go once all of us get together."

"I know, right."

There was a slight pause before either of us spoke again.

"Sheldon, thank you," I told him.

"For what?" he asked.

"For not giving up on me. I know I've overreacted and treated you bad after our episode, but I didn't mean to."

"I know."

"I'm serious. You calling me today has made me so happy, and I can't wait to see you," I admitted.

"I can't wait to see you either. So don't forget; call me when they leave, a'ight?"

"I will."

I hung up the phone.

Hearing Sheldon's voice was the boost I needed to get ready for whatever my sister Serena had to reveal to us. Now that I had a little bit of pep in my step, I went to my bathroom to at least wash my face. As I made my way, a small voice said, *I got you*. I halted and looked around to see who said it, and then this warm feeling came over me. I smiled, thinking God had heard me—and now He'd spoken to me.

Chapter 35

Shauna

With his black jacket tossed over his shoulder, Grayson caressed the side of my face as he kissed me. I hated to see this man go. Our night together was amazing, and I wished I could rewind time to do it all over again. I was still left pondering what it would be like to sleep with this man. Well, we slept together in the sense of lying beside one another all night long, but that was as far as things went with us. There was kissing. Boy, was there kissing. That man's tongue in my mouth only piqued my curiosity, wondering how it would be to have his manhood inside me. We touched and caressed and felt each other up through our clothes to the point that I wanted to rip his off and tell him to take me right then and there, but I didn't want to come off like a common whore. We'd gone out a few times, but not enough to warrant me giving up the goodies so quickly. That was a mistake I'd made with Cal.

I knew it was wrong to start any type of relationship with my boss, but I would quit my job to keep this man in my life. So far no one knew we had anything going on. We both kept the employer-employee relationship just that at work, not wanting to give anyone any reason to get all up in our business, which we'd done a great job at so far.

"I had a wonderful time with you, Grayson."

"I hope we can do this again real soon," he suggested.

"How about tonight?" I asked with a smile.

"Tonight sounds good to me," he said, smirking. He leaned in and kissed me again. "I'll see you later."

Grayson left my apartment and left me with a smile that would last until we saw each other again—that's if whatever Serena had to tell us didn't rip the smile off my face.

I started to go to my room to get ready to go to Vivian's house when there was a knock at the door.

I jogged over, opening it with a smile, saying, "Did you forget something?"

As those words slipped from my lips, my eyes landed on an angry Cal standing before me. I quickly tried to shut the door in his face, but he placed his foot in the door, prohibiting me from closing it. As hard as I struggled to shut the door, it was no use. Cal was too strong for me. Using his shoulder, he rammed the door, causing it to knock me backward, giving him just enough time to come into my home and slam the door shut. I quickly ran across the room to get away from him.

"Get out of my place, Cal," I told him, but the evil look in his eyes let me know he was not about to go anywhere. "Did you forget about the restraining order?"

Ignoring my question, he asked his own. "So you're cheating on me now?"

"How can I cheat on you when I'm not with you?" I asked sarcastically.

"You couldn't wait to get rid of me so you could sleep with someone else."

"You got rid of yourself when you put your hands on me," I told him.

"After all I've done for you. After everything I did to help you get where you are."

I looked at him with a scowl, puzzled because I didn't know what he was talking about. I asked, "What did you do for me?"

"I helped you get this place. I gave you money. I bought you things. I made a car payment for you."

"Ummmmm, Cal, you must be getting me mixed up with one of your other women, because you haven't done none of those things for me. If anything, I gave you money. I paid your mama rent where you were staying to help y'all, and I bought your non-dressing behind clothes. So before you come out your mouth all crazy, you better rethink the situation and the woman, because you got me mixed up with somebody else."

Cal looked off like he was pondering my statement. He knew he made a mistake just like I said he did. Now he stood there looking stupid. *He's going to come over here like he cares about me, but sticks his foot in his own mouth by getting me mixed up with his other women.* I had suspected he was doing a little something outside of me, but I could never prove it. Now he just did.

"It's all coming back to you now," I said, giggling. "That's what happens when you got too many women on your roster. But you know what? You can take me off permanently, because I'll be damned if I'm going to deal with any more of your bullshit."

"Are you sleeping with dude?" he asked, dismissing my statements.

"What do you think? I mean, he is leaving this morning, isn't he?" I said disdainfully. "That's the reason why you are asking, because you saw him leave, right?"

"I thought you loved me," he said pitifully.

"No. I never loved you. I had a strong like for you. Now Grayson, I could see myself loving that man."

"You just met him."

"But I've known him for quite some time. In just a few weeks, this man has shown me what it's supposed to feel like to have a good man next to me. I'm sad to say I never knew that until I met him."

"Well, you can end it because I want you back," Cal admitted.

"You can want me all you want. It's not going to happen, Cal. You think I'm supposed to fall into your arms after you bust your way into my place, coming up in here like you're Mr. Big Stuff. Like I'm supposed to be scared of you, but I'm not afraid."

"You should be," he threatened.

"Please, of what? What are you going to do, beat me again?"

"I told you I was sorry about that."

"And I'm supposed to forget the way you pounded my head into the floor screaming, 'I'm going to kill you, bitch'? I'm supposed to forget about all of that and say, 'Yes, Cal, I love you and I want you back'?"

"Yes," he said sternly.

"Then you're crazier than I thought. You need help. Go find some doctor to help you work on that mind of yours, because you have truly lost it," I said, crossing my arms across my chest.

"Shauna, you know you want me," he said, holding his hands out like he was some sort of male model. Little did he know he was far from it.

"Look at me and look at you. I don't need a lot of men to validate me. Ain't that why you got Laura and Janice and Cookie waiting for you to call them?"

Cal's arms fell dejectedly at the mention of their names. He rubbed his head as he pivoted from foot to foot. I knew he didn't like the way this conversation was going.

"That's right. I know about those women. Two of them called me, and another showed up at my job the other day, letting me know she's your woman and to stay away from you. Funny how things turn out, isn't it? All the while you trying to get me back, your women are going behind your back, letting me know they already have you. You better talk to them, because they blew up your spot. You are used to dealing with chickenheads who are willing to settle, but that's not me. You got the wrong one here if you think I'm going to take you back and deal with your cheating-ass, beating-on-women ways," I said coolly.

The more I talked, the madder he got. His rage seemed to increase when he realized I knew a lot more than he thought I did. He was probably cussing those women out in his mind.

"Get out of my place before I call the cops and have you locked up again, and this time it's going to be for violating your restraining order."

Cal didn't say anything. He stood scowling at me. I guessed he had a chance to think about what I was telling him.

I walked in his direction to the door to open it for him to leave. When I attempted to pass him, he grabbed me by the arm. "You really think it's going to be this easy to get rid of me?"

"Let me go, Cal," I warned.

"Or what? You don't have your little boss here to protect you now."

When Cal said that, he reared back and swung. His fist landed on my right cheek. The force from his punch caused me to fall back onto my sofa, releasing me from his grasp. Cal didn't halt one minute before he was on me, swinging and punching. I held my hands up to block his blows, but they were coming too fast. Too many were landing on my head. I think I was screaming. And then all of a sudden, he was off me.

I looked up to see Grayson throwing Cal to the floor. Cal quickly jumped up and swung at Grayson. He missed. Grayson retaliated by hitting him in his throat. That one move caused Cal to stumble back. He grabbed his neck, struggling to breathe. His eyes began to bulge like he couldn't catch his breath. Grayson grabbed him, wrapping his hand around Cal's throat.

"Don't do it, Grayson," I yelled to him.

The look he gave me asked, "Why not?"

I answered by saying, "He's not worth it. He's not worth you ruining your future."

I could see this registering within him. He looked back at Cal, who seemed like he didn't want any more. That one punch to his throat was enough to make Cal recoil like the coward he was. Grayson let go. Cal moaned while I ran and called the police.

The police arrived, taking Cal away in handcuffs. Once we told the police about the restraining order, Cal tried to say I called him over there. Then he tried his best to say Grayson was the one who attacked him, but it was two against one here. Plus, the bruises on my body were enough to let the police know Cal was the perpetrator.

Once the police were gone, Grayson came over to check on me again to see how I was doing. "Are you okay?" he asked for the twentieth time already.

"I'm fine, Grayson," I told him with a smile.

"I want to make sure. I wish I would have got here in time."

"How did you know to come when you did?" I asked curiously.

"I sat in the parking lot for a minute because the restaurant called me with an issue. After talking with my coworker for a bit, I pulled off and looked at my gas hand, seeing I needed to get some gas. Then it hit me. How could I pay for gas with no wallet?"

"You left your wallet on my dresser?" I asked in amazement.

"Yep. I turned around, and when I got to the door, I heard you screaming. That's when I burst in. I wish I would have shown up earlier than that."

"Grayson, it's okay. I'm glad you showed up when you did. You're my hero again," I said, reaching over and caressing his hand.

Grayson lifted his other hand to my bruised face. He gently rubbed it, saying, "We need to get some ice to put on that."

"I know it looks bad," I said.

"Can I ask you a question?" Grayson asked.

"You can ask me anything."

"Do you believe in love at first sight?"

"I do," I responded, grinning slyly. "So what are you telling me?"

"I'm saying I can see us going really far in this relationship. I know my timing may be terrible, but, Shauna, I've liked you for quite some time. I don't want to waste another minute."

"So are you saying you want to be in a relationship with me?" I asked.

"That's if you would have me," he said.

This man knew all the right things to say. I know this seemed like we were moving fast, but we were friends first, from back in the day. Why would I want to waste time when I could see if it could work with him?

"Do you think we are moving too fast?" I asked him.

"Not at all. No one knows when love will strike."

I smiled at Grayson and said, "I would love to have you in my life."

Grayson leaned toward me and planted his lips on mine. We kissed for what felt like forever. Grayson broke our connection to ask me, “Aren’t you going to be late for your meeting with your sisters?”

“I sure am,” I said, leaning forward to kiss him again.

Chapter 36

Serena

The gang was all here, aside from Dawn, who I didn't want to be here anyway for what I had to tell my sisters. It was still early in the day, so we were all dressed down in jogging pants and tees. Even Phoenix was dressed down in a pair of black-and-white geometric-print leggings and a long black top. She even had her hair still wrapped up. She was on Viv's sofa with her feet beneath her, lying down like she was getting ready to go back to sleep.

"Viv, you didn't cook breakfast for us?" Phoenix asked.

"No, I did not. Besides, it's close to lunchtime."

"Then you don't have any lunch made for us?" Phoenix griped sleepily.

"Again, no, I do not. How many fast food places did you pass on your way over here? You should have picked me up something to eat," Vivian retorted.

"I didn't stop and get anything because I figured you were going to cook."

"I've never cooked breakfast or lunch for you guys. You know we usually do dinners."

"You could have made an exception this time. Now what am I going to do? I'm starving," Phoenix said with her arms clamping down on her stomach like she had bad cramps.

"I got some leftover lasagna in there," Viv told her.

Phoenix jumped up with a quickness and ran to Viv's kitchen.

Viv looked at me as I shook my head and we both made our way to the kitchen. When we walked in, Phoenix was placing the lasagna on the counter. She also pulled out a bowl filled with tossed salad, along with taking out two different salad dressings.

"I guess you weren't lying when you said you were hungry," I said to Phoenix.

"Y'all know I'm not usually up this early on a Saturday. My body is not used to this," she said, taking the red plastic lid off the long glass dish. She retrieved a spatula and cut a nice-sized piece of lasagna, placing it on a clear glass plate. She then went over to the microwave above the stove, placed the food inside, and set the timer to heat for two minutes.

"Where's Shauna?" I asked, eager to get this little meeting started.

"Here I am," she said, walking into the kitchen. "I hope you don't mind I let myself in, Viv."

Shauna was the last to arrive and shocked the hell out of us when she came bopping her behind in there with a big bruise on the cheek. We all were ogling her, but she had the biggest smile on her face.

"I wouldn't be smiling if I had that bruise on my face," Phoenix blurted. "What happened to you?"

"It's a long story that I don't feel like discussing."

"You better tell us something," Viv retorted.

"Uhhh, you guys," Shauna said.

"Spill it," I said.

"Okay. Cal showed up at my place this morning and—"

"Please tell me that fool is locked up," Phoenix said, cutting Shauna off like she didn't want to hear any more details. "Because if he isn't, I'm going to call our cousins to handle this fool once and for all."

"Cal is locked up for violating his restraining order, and the man who came to my rescue is Grayson."

"Wait, wait, wait. Who in the hell is Grayson?" Phoenix asked with a frown on her hungry face.

"He's my boss and my new man," Shauna revealed, grinning from ear to ear.

The microwave beeped and Phoenix opened it to retrieve her heated pasta. The steam rose from it as she placed it down on the island. While Phoenix turned her attention to her food, me and Vivian went back to talking to Shauna.

"You can't be in a relationship with your boss," Viv said.

"Yes, I can," Shauna replied.

"Isn't that a violation of some code of ethics?" I asked.

"It might be, but we are keeping things cool until I find me another job."

"Shauna, did Cal hit you in the head too many times? Because you are talking crazy. One minute you down and depressed about this man beating your behind, and the next we know, you are in a new relationship with your boss," Phoenix said.

"Yes, pretty much, but Cal ain't beat me in the head too many times. Hell, maybe that needed to happen in order to find the man who is meant for me," Shauna explained.

All of us stood there looking at Shauna like she had lost her mind. I knew my mouth was open. She didn't pay any attention to me as her happy behind walked over to Phoenix.

"Ooohh, that smells good. Can I get some? I'm starving," Shauna said, reaching to take the fork out of Phoenix's hand to taste her heated food.

"Oh, no you are not. I don't know where your mouth has been," Phoenix said.

"It's been the same place yours has been," Shauna shot back.

"Which is the exact reason why you shouldn't be eating after me."

"Point taken. I'll fix my own," Shauna said, going over to the cabinet and retrieving a plate to fix her own lasagna to heat up in the microwave.

"Can we get this little meet and greet started before you heifers eat everything in my kitchen?" Viv joked.

We climbed up on the barstools at the island and watched Shauna fix her food and Phoenix eat.

"Okay. I called us together to tell you something I found out about our sister."

"What? She finally came to her senses and decided not to marry Corey?" Phoenix kidded.

"No. I haven't spoken to Dawn."

"Then what is this about?" Shauna asked.

"If you two motor mouths will shut up, I will tell you."

"Okay. Go ahead," Phoenix said with frustration as she squeezed ranch dressing on her salad.

"Our sister is a porn star," I blurted. I knew there was no other way to say it but to say it.

The room fell silent. I looked around at each of my sisters to see all eyes were on me. It was like someone had pushed a paused button on our life, and I was ready for the playback to continue.

"Did y'all hear me?" I asked.

"I think we heard you, but we are not sure if we heard you right," Viv said, looking baffled.

"Come into the living room. I have something to show you," I said, jumping down from my stool. Viv and Phoenix were right behind me, but Shauna was too busy fixing her food.

"Don't start without me," she yelled.

When I popped that disc into Viv's Blu-ray player and turned her television on, the same visual of our sister's room came on the screen. It wasn't long before my sisters were watching Dawn in action.

"You have got to be kidding me," Viv said in astonishment.

"I told you," I said, looking over at her stunned face.

"What does she think she's doing?" Viv asked.

"Well, it looks like she's getting hammered by some dude," Phoenix said with a mouthful of food.

"I can see that," Viv retorted. "But what is she thinking?"

"Evidently she's not," I said.

"And here we were thinking little miss innocent Dawn was a prude. She's the biggest freak of us all," Phoenix responded.

"Who knew she was a whore?" Shauna said, taking a sip of wine before putting a forkful of food into her mouth.

"How? What? Who gave you this disc?" Viv stammered.

"Tyree showed this to me. His boy brought it over to him after coming across it."

"So people have seen this?" Viv asked.

"Isn't that what porn is made for, for the enjoyment of others watching?" Phoenix said.

"I'm calling her," Viv said, getting up and going over to her phone.

"For what? She is on her way over here. Besides, what are you going to say to her?" I asked.

"I don't know," Vivian snapped.

"Don't get mad at me. I thought you guys should know," I said in my defense.

"What else is going to happen?" Viv asked no one in particular.

"Viv, you might want to sit back down before you make that call, because that's not all I have to show you."

The looks on their faces told me everything. They couldn't believe I had to reveal something else to them. Little did they know the next video I would be showing could permanently destroy the sisterly bond we were struggling so hard to maintain. For a moment I wondered if I should show it at all, but there were enough secrets among us. This needed to come out, although I hated to bring more damaging revelations to our slowly diminishing family.

Chapter 37

Shauna

All eyes were on me now. My fork was midair when all of a sudden I lost my appetite. A day that had started out great, turning ugly to end up amazing, had all of a sudden taken another dark turn down a road I was not ready to travel.

Vivian was standing across the room with her arms folded across her chest, watching with her mouth slightly open. Serena was sitting on the sofa, looking at me distrustfully, while Phoenix was still chomping on her food, glaring at me like she was waiting for an explanation. All of them were waiting on one, but I didn't have any words to say.

I reached over and put my plate down and replaced it with the glass of wine I had before me. I turned the glass up to my mouth and finished what was left in the glass. Lucky for me, I had brought the bottle into the living room with me.

I quickly poured me another and took a large sip before the silence between us was broken.

"Seriously, Shauna," Viv said, being the first one to speak. "How could you?"

I looked at Serena, who dropped her head in disgust, I guessed. The shame and humiliation was taking over.

"Say something," Viv demanded.

"What is there to say?" I finally spoke.

Nervously pivoting from one foot to the other, Viv said, "Explain yourself."

"What can I say? I was wrong."

Serena rolled her eyes as she crossed her arms across her chest. Both she and Vivian were blocking me out, while Phoenix was finishing up the last bit of her food.

"And y'all thought I was the whore," Phoenix said.

I glared at her.

"Well, it's true. All y'all were worried about how I get my money, and we had two sisters bouncing their ass for the world to see."

"You guys. I'm not a whore," I told them.

"Then what does this make you look like? You were so quick to call Dawn one a few minutes ago, yet your ass is up on that screen doing the exact same thing," Vivian said, pointing to the fifty-inch flat panel hanging on her wall.

I was just as shocked as they were to see myself appear on the television, but what made this revelation even worse was the fact that my debut performance was being performed with Dawn's fiancé.

"You slept with Corey?" Vivian asked.

"It was a few times," I tried to explain.

"What's a few?" Viv asked.

"I don't know. Ten. Twenty."

"That's not a few. That's an affair," Phoenix interjected, putting her now empty plate down on the coffee table.

"That's our sister," Vivian stressed.

"She's our half sister, okay? And one I never asked for," I said angrily.

"You didn't ask for us either," Viv shot back.

"True, but at least we came from the same people. She was created through deceit and mistrust."

"So that gives you the right to betray her?" Serena finally butted in.

"I tried to tell her he was no good," I explained.

"Why? So you could have him all to yourself?" Serena snapped.

"I didn't want him. We just had a sexual thing. I didn't want to marry him."

"Just sex, huh? Isn't that what it was for our dad?" Viv asked coldly. "Didn't he sleep with Dawn's mother for just sex?"

I couldn't say anything. It's funny because I'd never looked at it like that. Talk about a smack in the face.

"How are you any different than Dawn's mother?"

Hearing Vivian say that stung more than I was prepared to receive. I dropped my head in disgrace and clasped my hands in front of me, wringing them nervously. Vivian's words did hurt, but that didn't stop me from coming back at her.

"Dawn and Corey are not married, so what's the problem?" I asked angrily.

"But you were going to let her marry him knowing what you two had done together?"

"Would it have made a difference? I tried to talk her out of it. I mean, look at how many women Corey has been with and she stayed by his side. She accepted his hand in marriage for goodness' sake, so why should I care?"

"You don't think that if she knew Corey stooped so low as to sleep with her very own sister it could have changed her mind?" Serena asked.

"I don't know, and to be honest, I don't care. I'm tired of pretending I have been cool with Dawn joining our family. Looking at her every day reminded me constantly of the betrayal

Daddy did to our mom. She died with this burden on her heart. That could have been one less thing Mama had to deal with before she left this world."

"Mama was at peace about everything and you know it. If she weren't, she wouldn't have taken Dawn in as her own," Viv explained.

"How do you know? Mama could have died of a broken heart."

"Do you know our mother at all? That woman was so strong. She had the strength to forgive our father and raise the child he had with his mistress. You know Mama never faked anything for nobody, not even Daddy. When she kicked him out, she meant it; but when she took him back, she meant that, too. Mama left this world knowing she was going home to be with Jesus. Her main priority in life was to live the best life possible and treat people to the best of her ability. Mama was a great woman. She knew there was no need to hold grudges because that would hinder her from getting into God's Kingdom," Vivian explained.

I knew she was telling the truth. Mama's main purpose in life was to live right, because she wanted heaven to be her home once this earthly world was done for her.

"I think you can't forgive what happened, Shauna," Serena said. "You can't put this on Mama."

"Maybe you are right," I said.

"And that anger has allowed you to be another one of Corey's pawns," Phoenix said.

"I didn't know he was recording us," I said.

"If Dawn finds out about this . . ."

Chapter 38

Vivian

"Finds out about this . . ." was all I heard when I looked up to see my sister Dawn standing before us. In the midst of our squabble, none of us noticed her enter. And when she did, it was too late. The expressions on all of our faces were ones of shock. I didn't think my heart could take any more. Looking into my sister's eyes, seeing the pain radiating through her was enough to destroy me.

Dawn was glaring at the television as the visual of Shauna and Corey played on my flat screen. We all halted briefly when we saw her. Serena managed to gather her senses, picking up the remote to the television to cut it off.

"Wait! I want to see this," Dawn said coolly.

"Aw, hell," Phoenix replied.

Dawn walked deeper into the room as she watched Corey going in and out of Shauna. He was enjoying himself, and so was our sister. The way they looked at one another and kissed one another was enough to devastate me, and he wasn't even my man.

"Dawn, let me—" I started to say, but she held her hand up to stop me from talking.

"What should I do?" Serena asked. I hunched my shoulders.

"Well, you wanted everything out in the open," Phoenix said. "You got your wish."

"I didn't want it like this," I said.

"Sometimes the way we ask for something is not the way we get it," Phoenix countered.

I looked over at Phoenix, who was shaking her head, looking back and forth between Shauna and Dawn. I gave her a look to leave it alone, but I should have known better, because Phoenix began to speak.

"Y'all need to turn this off, because Dawn doesn't need to be viewing this. She's seen enough," Phoenix said.

Dawn snapped her head around and glared at Phoenix, asking, "Did you know?"

"Know what?"

"Know the two of them were sleeping together."

"No, I didn't know. We all found out about this today," Phoenix explained with a frown.

"Is this why you called me over here, Vivian, so you could humiliate me like this?" Dawn asked.

"You know I would never do anything as cruel as this," I explained.

"It's on the television. All y'all sitting in here watching it like it's some X-rated Lifetime movie," Dawn replied.

"You have to think very little of me to think I'm sick enough to gather our sisters together to watch Shauna in action. Heck, there's a disc on you too," I said, letting her know.

"What?" Dawn asked, confused.

"That's right. We know about your little extra-curricular activities. When were you going to tell us?" I asked.

"What I do in the confines of my bedroom is my business," Dawn snapped, pointing at me for emphasis.

"Well, it looks like what's done in the confines of your bedroom is Corey's and Shauna's business too," Phoenix quipped.

"Shut up, Phoenix," Shauna told her.

Dawn dropped her head when Phoenix said this.

I stepped closer to Dawn, saying, "Look, sis. I called you over here to resolve what's been going on with us. I don't like this friction we all have had lately. This is not us. This is not the Johnson sisters."

"She's not a Johnson," Shauna countered. "She had to come from our mother for her to earn that name."

"Shauna, please," I urged.

"Y'all wanted things out in the open, so here it is. Yes, I've been sleeping with Corey. Now what, huh? He caught me out there and taped our little escapades, and I will handle him on that note later, but for now, let's get things resolved," Shauna said callously.

"How could you do this to me?" Dawn asked Shauna, who was sitting back like she didn't have a care in the world. She seemed unfazed by the fact that Dawn just walked in to see her on the big screen doing her fiancé.

"It just happened," Shauna said nonchalantly.

"I swear if I hear another person say, 'it just happened,' I'm going to scream," Serena interrupted, walking across the room with her hands on her hips.

"Well, it did."

"Sex doesn't just happen, Shauna. If it were that simple, then you wouldn't be mad at Daddy and Dawn's mother for having sex either," Serena said.

"That was different," Shauna argued.

"How's it different? Sex is sex," Serena countered.

"Dawn is not married to him," Shauna said.

"And our parents weren't married either. Regardless of the fact that we didn't come from the same mother, we carry the same blood because we all have the same father," Serena retorted. "Mama was Dawn's mother too, so don't sit there and act like Mama would have had it any other way. When you talk like that, you are disgracing the kind act our mother did, so you need to shut your damn mouth about that," Serena said angrily as water filled her eyes.

Dawn began to speak. "I always felt like you hated me, Shauna. I tried to look past it and be the best sister ever. I was grateful for what Mama, your mother, did for me. I couldn't have asked for a better upbringing. I didn't ask for this path in my life. Our dad and my mother chose that for me," Dawn said. "Just like we can't choose our siblings, I couldn't choose my parents either. You've taken your hate and frustration out on me, when the person you should have taken it out on was our dad."

Shauna clapped her hands. "Bravo, Dawn. That was an excellent performance."

"This is not a performance," Dawn said, frowning.

"Come on, Shauna. You are being insensitive here," I told her.

"Has everybody forgotten about what this so-called sister did?" Shauna asked as she scooted to the edge of the sofa.

"Oh, here we go," Phoenix said under her breath as Serena turned her back on what Shauna was saying.

"Don't do this, Shauna," I warned.

"Why not? Isn't this what you wanted, for us to get everything out in the open?"

"Not like this," I said.

"Did you think it was going to go down calmly, with voices composed and smiles on our faces? Please. You know us better than that."

"Okay, Shauna. Let me have it. Say it. Say what Vivian's trying to stop you from saying," Dawn demanded.

Everybody in the room looked around at one another. I hoped Shauna wouldn't say it, but my gut knew this was the moment she'd been waiting for all her life. It was probably why she drank as much as she did. She was trying to forget about the pain our father brought to our family and the end results, which led to us losing our sister.

Chapter 39

Dawn

The words spilled out of Shauna's mouth so easily, like she longed to say those words to me but she had been holding them in for years.

"You killed Renee."

And there it was. The big elephant in the room was even bigger than the revelation that our father was unfaithful. Hearing Shauna say it with such disgust and rage was gut-wrenchingly hurtful. I could feel my throat struggling to close, as the will of my body fought against the anxiety that was setting in.

I nodded and said, "Yes, Shauna. I killed Renee."

I looked into Serena's face, which had tears rolling down her cheeks. Phoenix was on the sofa, leaning on the armrest with her head propped against her open hand. Vivian was standing near me with her back to me and her hands on her head in disbelief. Shauna was giving me a look that could kill me where I stood.

"Finally you admit it," Shauna said.

"I never denied it," I told her.

"But you never admitted to killing her either," Shauna said heatedly. "You let our sister Viv take the fall for you."

"You are right again, Shauna, but while we are coming clean, let's be clear. Not only do you resent me for being the illegitimate child of our father, but you hate me because I took Renee away from you."

"You damn right," she spat. "My sisters have been able to walk around like things within our family are okay, but I've never been able to forgive you for what you did. I've tolerated you for years because of Mama, may she rest in peace.; and I even continued to try to deal with you after her passing, but every time I see your face, I see my sister lying on that floor, struggling to take her last breath," Shauna said, choking on her words as she struggled to resist the tears from falling.

"I didn't mean to—" I started to say, but Shauna cut me off.

"What? You didn't mean to pick up the gun? What? Did it fascinate you after you saw how it blew your mother's brains across the wall, so you needed to see how it worked?"

"Come on, Shauna, that's enough. You don't have to be this heartless," Phoenix said.

"If she knew what guns could do, then why would she ever pick one up?" Shauna asked no one in particular, though she was looking at Phoenix.

No one had anything to say.

"Exactly. She should have known better."

"It was an accident," I pleaded.

I was twelve years old when I accidently shot Renee. I was fooling around in Dad's den and decided to pick up one of the many guns he had in the house. This one was in the gun cabinet, which was usually locked, but this day, it was open for some reason. There was a slight crack in the cabinet door. Being nosy as I was, I went over and picked up one of the handguns.

Renee walked in, saying, "What are you doing?"

Startled, I turned and fired the gun at her by accident. It took me a moment to realize I had even pulled the trigger. I didn't know Daddy kept bullets in the gun. I remember Renee looking down in shock as her mint green T-shirt became crimson.

She dropped to her knees and fell to the floor. Vivian was the first one to enter the room. She ran over to me and took the gun from my shaking hands, asking me what I'd done. Moments later, Daddy and Mom came running in the room, along with Shauna, Serena, and Phoenix.

Daddy tried to save her life. He applied pressure, while Mama called 911. Unfortunately for our family, the wound was fatal and Renee died right there in the den from the negligence of me playing with my father's weapon, resulting in a tragic end for our family.

For years, Vivian took the fall for that incident, saying that she had dropped the gun and it went off. Why I let her do that, I don't know. Maybe it was because I felt like I wasn't supposed to be in their home, and there I was an outsider who had taken someone who was already there and who had welcomed me with open arms. I didn't want anyone to be mad at me, because they were already dealing with the situation of my father and mother, and me having to move in.

It wasn't until Mama was on her deathbed that the truth came out. Mama always knew the story Vivian told wasn't the truth, and she wanted the real story, which Vivian gave her. Mama understood Vivian had taken the blame so the family wouldn't spend my entire life blaming me. Just like Vivian, she felt I had already been through enough tragedy. It still hadn't stopped me from blaming myself. I'd always felt like if I had never moved into their home, Renee would still be here today.

I knew this day would come eventually and I'd figured that with me being an adult now, it would be easier to deal with. But it wasn't. It was as hard, if not harder, than I could ever imagine. The sheer fact that Shauna was bringing it up and had resented me all these years for it hurt me more than I could put into words. I suspected this was why she took it upon herself to sleep with Corey.

"How could you live with the fact that Viv covered for you?" Shauna asked. "Our father was so angry with Vivian about that, because he felt like she knew better than to touch his guns. And she did. It was you, but he didn't know it at the time. Your carelessness cost my sister precious time with our dad, all because of you."

"Shauna, me taking the blame was my decision," Vivian admitted in my defense.

"Did Daddy not treat you differently after that?" Shauna asked.

Vivian didn't say anything.

"She could have spoken up and said it was her," Shauna said.

"She was a child already dealing with drastic changes in her life," Vivian said.

"It was drastic for us too, Vivian, but she had to go and make it worse by killing Renee," Shauna yelled.

"You act like she did it on purpose," Vivian replied.

"I don't know. Did you?" she asked me.

"I loved Renee. I never meant to hurt her," I explained.

"Yeah, just like your mother never meant to break up our happy home," Shauna retorted, leaning back.

"You know what? That's enough, Shauna. I'm tired of this. You need to let this anger go before it ruins you," Serena interjected.

"I'm fine," Shauna said with a smirk.

"Yes. I can see how fine you are. Beat up weeks ago by your crazy boyfriend for him to beat you up again today. You are sleeping with your boss, and then we find out you were trifling enough to sleep with our sister's fiancé. Yeah, I see you are doing real well," Serena scolded her.

"Don't judge me, Serena."

"I'm not judging. I'm stating facts. And here's another one for you: what if I didn't forgive you for sleeping with my man?"

Everybody's eyes widened with the shock of what Serena revealed. Even Shauna looked surprised, like she couldn't believe Serena had brought this up.

"She did what?" Vivian asked, dumbfounded.

"That's right. She did the same thing to me; and I'm your real blood. We have the same mother and father, and you betrayed me first before moving on to Dawn's fiancé."

Shauna glared at Serena angrily, not saying anything.

"With Dawn, you may have done it for revenge, but with me, what was it? Can you tell me why you slept with my man back in the day?"

"I can't believe you brought this up. You told me things were squashed," Shauna said furiously.

"It is, but you need a reality check, because you sitting here beating up on Dawn, when you are the one who's dead set on destroying our family," Serena shot back.

"Me!" Shauna yelled. "Oh, so our family is ruined because of me now."

"Serena didn't mean it like that," Vivian said, trying to ease the tension.

"Then how did she mean it? I didn't cheat, and I damn sure didn't kill anybody," she said, looking at me.

"But you drink and you've crossed the boundaries that never should be crossed when dealing with your sisters' men," Vivian explained.

"Wow! I see how y'all want to do me," Shauna said, picking up her glass of wine and guzzling it. "Since when did this turn into Gang Up On Shauna Day?"

"Since you decided to stoop so low as to disrespect your sister and disrespect yourself, for that matter," Phoenix told her.

"You know what? I don't have to deal with this," Shauna said, getting up from the sofa.

"Oh, so you are going to run," Phoenix taunted.

"I never run," Shauna replied.

"Looks like it to me," Phoenix retorted.

"You guys need to remember I'm your blood. She's not," Shauna said, pointing at me.

"We are all sisters," Vivian said.

"Dawn will never be any sister of mine. I put that on everything, including my mother's Johnson name."

All eyes widened when Shauna said that. She picked up the wine bottle, turned it up to her mouth, and finished what was left in the bottle. All my sisters shook their heads at her.

She put the empty bottle down on Viv's coffee table and headed to the door. Shauna opened it, turned, and looked at all of us before slamming the door behind her.

Chapter 40

Phoenix

As bad as things had been with my sisters, I was in a great mood. I was ecstatic that Tobias had to leave my home that day. When that officer told me I had to file an eviction notice to get this man out of my house, I was down at the courthouse first thing that Monday morning doing just that. Today was the last day he could legally stay in my home. I was all smiles as he sulked and held his head low, like I was going to feel sorry for him. Believe you me, I didn't. He had to get the hell up out of here so I could resume a lifestyle I was so accustomed to—living alone.

Tobias thought living together would make me fall for him, but after today, he would see I hadn't. There had not been one time I hid the fact that I wanted him out of there. He should have taken heed when I told him, but then I poured gasoline on the fire by having my men come through to lay a little, or should I say a lot, of pipe. And still this man refused to leave. Well, now he didn't have a choice. It was adios, sayonara, vamoose, skedaddle, and peace out.

Tobias toted the last of his bags to his car as I sat on the sofa sipping a glass of wine. He stared me down as he stood near the front door. I rolled my eyes and turned from looking at him. I was hoping he wouldn't say anything and walk his ass out of my house so I could get on with my life.

Tobias came around and sat on the chair in the living room and said, "This is it."

"You sure? Because I don't want you to have any reason to come back up in my house."

"No, I got it all."

"Good. I wish I could say it was nice having you here, but I didn't want you here in the first place, so good riddance."

"That's cold, Phoenix."

"Too bad. That's me," I said, crossing my legs at my ankles. His eyes landed on my exposed legs, since I was wearing a pair of cutoff shorts and a T-shirt.

"Why couldn't you just love me? I love you," he proclaimed.

"Look at you, Tobias. You are weak. No woman wants a weak man. The only thing you have going for you is money, and you don't have a lot of that."

"That's why you dealt with me in the first place, isn't it? Because you thought I had more money than I do."

"Yep. Money makes Phoenix come around, but only for a brief moment. Your money was good, but it's not like Diddy money."

"So you looking for a man who can take care of you the rest of your life financially?" he asked, leaning forward with his elbows propped against his knees.

"Yes," I said, nodding.

"What if I told you I could give you that?"

"Tobias, stop playing games. Just get your little briefcase and leave. You know and I know you don't have Diddy money."

Tobias smiled slyly, and I didn't like the way he was looking at me.

"Who hurt you, Phoenix?" he asked coolly.

"What?"

"I said who hurt you?"

"You hurt me by telling lies to stay here," I told him.

"You still have not recognized me," he said, smirking.

I looked at him, wondering what in the world he was talking about.

He reached to the floor and picked up his briefcase. Placing it on my coffee table, he opened it. I didn't say anything, because I was wondering what he was doing. He reached in and pulled out a newspaper clipping and handed it to me.

At first I was hesitant about taking it, but I did anyway. Staring him down, I waited a few seconds before my eyes landed on the picture. It was a photo of Tobias standing beside my ex-fiancé, Noah.

I frowned when I looked at him and asked, "Is this some sort of joke?"

"Not at all," he said calmly.

"Who are you?" I asked frantically, sitting up and placing the glass of wine on the coffee table.

"My name is Tobias. I was partners with your ex, Noah, at the firm he worked at before he moved away."

"I don't remember you," I said, going through my memory bank of all the different individuals I'd met when I was with Noah. Tobias never came to my memory.

"I was more of a silent partner."

"Did Noah put you up to this as some sort of sick, twisted joke?" I asked, glaring at him.

"No. He doesn't know I'm here."

"So you still keep in touch with him?" I asked nervously.

"We talk all the time," he said, wringing his hands together.

"Does he know you are here with me?"

"No."

"So when you got with me, you knew who I was?" I asked him curiously.

"Yes."

"But you decided to keep this bit of information to yourself."

"Yes," he said again.

"You know what? I need you to leave," I said, standing to my feet. This was some weird shit, and I didn't understand anything that was going on right now.

Tobias stood and walked up to me.

"Don't come any closer," I said, causing him to halt.

"I need you to calm down," Tobias said calmly.

"How can I calm down when you're friends with my enemy?" I said furiously.

"Phoenix, let me explain."

I held my hands up and walked away from him, saying, "I don't know if I want to hear anything else you have to say. I think it's best if you leave," I told him.

"Please, Phoenix. Just hear me out."

I paced back and forth, wanting an explanation but fearful of what this man had to say. This was some twisted shit I didn't understand but wanted to understand. If I kicked him out, I may never know the full story of how this came about, which would drive me crazy; so maybe it was a good idea to let him say what he wanted to say.

"Okay, Tobias. Explain yourself."

"I know this may sound cliché, but the first time I ever laid eyes on you, I knew I wanted you to be mine. I knew you were Noah's fiancée at the time, so I knew I couldn't cross that friendship or partnership line with Noah and betray him. I stood back and watched as he destroyed the good thing he had when he had you."

I didn't respond as he continued.

"I know about Noah leaving you for Emma. I know about this baby the two of them had together. And I know about the baby he made you get rid of that caused you never to be able to have children."

"How do you know this?" I asked, frowning.

"Noah would talk to me. I was mad when he betrayed you like he did, but he didn't care, because he was moving on with his life in a new country. I actually hated him for a bit for what he did to you. I also worried about how you were doing during this time. I used to drive by your house to see if I could catch a glimpse of you. I wanted to knock on the door and check to see how you were doing, but I knew I would have looked crazy because you didn't know me."

"You sound crazy now, because it sounds like you were stalking me."

"Maybe."

"So you admit it?" I asked, shocked.

"Every time I saw you, I got excited. I'd seen you in coffee shops and grocery stores, and not once did you pay attention to me. You always paid attention to those business types who looked like male models. I know I'm not a bad-looking guy, but I also knew I really wasn't your type."

"Yet, we got together," I said.

"Buying you that drink that night in the bar was the best moment of my life, because you finally saw me. You might have been looking at my money or the expensive attire I wore, but I didn't care because I was next to you," he explained sincerely.

I walked over and plopped down on the sofa due to my knees wanting to buckle from beneath me. I trembled at the memory, which had taken way too long to forget. Every time I thought about it or heard Noah's name, all of my heart-breaking past came flooding back, making me grieve a life I knew I would never have again.

Tobias came and sat on the coffee table in front of me so he was facing me. He clasped his hands in front of him as he stared into my eyes.

"I know it's hard for you to believe, Phoenix, but I do love you. I know I may not be the best-looking guy out there or have Diddy money, but I can take care of you. I've tried to show you that ever since I've been here. You don't know how hard it was to see you degrade yourself by sleeping with these men who used you for what you could give them. Each time, I wanted to run into your bedroom and snatch them up, throwing them out of here. I hoped you would see how much I cared by not tripping about what you were doing."

"Real men don't allow their women to sleep with other men. And as for me degrading myself, as you say, I don't see it as that at all. I was having fun. I was doing what I wanted to do, and I don't give a damn what you or nobody else has to say about it," I said to him.

"Phoenix, you care."

"No, I don't."

"Why did you allow Noah to change the vibrant woman you were? This is not you. I know this isn't you. You are trying to mask the pain of what Noah did to you by using others to make you feel better about yourself, and this is not the way to go."

"It works for me," I said.

"Why couldn't I work for you?" he countered.

I couldn't say anything.

"I know you call me dorky and wimpy and maybe even a punk, but those are things I can change. I'm not the best-looking dude, but I know I'm not a bad-looking one either." He grinned.

"Who gave you the right to try to save me?" I asked him.

"No one. I wanted to because I wanted you."

"Why?" I asked.

"Again, because I love you."

"You don't know me."

"Do I have to know you to love you?"

"Yes," I blurted.

"I told you: when I saw you, I wanted you. Something happened within my heart that told me you were the woman I wanted to spend the rest of my life with. I know it sounds crazy. I know it doesn't seem real, but it's my truth."

"You know what? This is too much," I said, getting up and moving from in front of him and walking over to the door. "I need you to leave, Tobias."

He lowered his head in defeat. Pursing his lips together, he pushed himself up. Walking over to his briefcase, he reached in and pulled out a manila envelope and placed it on the table for me. Clicking his briefcase shut, he picked it up and walked over to me by the door. I turned the knob and opened it.

He paused in front of me and then leaned down, kissing me on the cheek. I didn't move out of his way. He brushed his thumb against my face and then left. I closed the door behind him, leaning against it, trying to figure out what had just happened.

Then my eyes fell on the envelope he had placed on the table. I walked over to it and picked it up. Hesitating, I wondered what else Tobias was trying to show me. Curious, I opened it. Pulling out the documents, I sat down and began to read.

Chapter 41

Vivian

I was damn near in my birthday suit, having on nothing but a towel wrapped around my body, when Sheldon came walking into my bedroom. I didn't hear him come in. Usually he would be screaming my name from the front door, but today he walked in without so much as a peep.

I stood there gripping the towel around me like it was my lifeline. I had my hair up in a clip so it wouldn't get wet from the shower. Sheldon stared at me with his hands in his pockets, rocking his all-black jeans, tee, and sneakers, with a silver link chain around his neck. He had his dreads down today, and it wasn't long before the scent of his cologne caressed me. He smelled so damn good and looked even better.

Nervously, I said, "I didn't hear you come in."

"Do you want me to leave?" he asked tenderly, like he didn't want to go. Just the tone of his voice was causing my center to tingle.

"No, you don't have to."

Sheldon looked at me from head to toe, taking all of me in. I felt insecure, because I knew I didn't have the best body. Loving myself for who I was and what I had was still a struggle for me, but the way he was looking at me made me feel like the most beautiful woman ever.

He started walking toward me. We were supposed to talk today, and I knew if he came any closer to me, things could end up back in my bed again, even though that wasn't a bad thing. Trust me, I wanted him, but I knew we needed to deal with what had already happened. I felt vulnerable in this moment but managed to stand still until he was standing inches in front of me.

Our eyes locked, and I knew I was in trouble. Sheldon leaned down and kissed me gently on my lips. His dreads fell down around my face, caressing me as his soft lips tantalized me. His hands were still in his pockets and I was still grasping to hold onto the towel, which shielded my nakedness.

The kiss was succulent. I craved to have more of him but pulled away, taking a couple of steps back.

"What are we doing?" I asked him, still tasting the minty freshness of his kiss.

"I thought we were kissing."

"Is this what you came over here for?"

"Yes and no," he said with a smirk.

I frowned, and he began to explain.

"I've thought about kissing you for a long time. When we decided to take things further, Viv, I was in heaven. All this time I've been looking for a woman to fill my day, but I knew all the time I had already found her. I found that woman in you," he said affectionately, causing my heart to melt.

"But . . ."

"I know. We are friends, and you are afraid this will mess up the friendship we have. This could be true, but I'm willing to take the chance and take this friendship thing further. You are worth the risk. I would love if you would allow me to be your man."

The way Sheldon said that made me want to run to my bathroom and find my vibrating friend and use it immediately on myself. I closed my eyes, loving what he was telling me, but doubt hindered me from responding. I was still afraid this would ruin the only good thing I felt like I had in my life—him. He must have seen the doubt on my face because he continued.

"I know you are afraid because you've been hurt, and I can't promise I won't hurt you, but, Viv, I love you with everything in me. I've loved you for a long time now and reveled in the fact that we were great friends, when all the time I was wishing our friendship would become more. Making love to you solidified my feelings for you."

I looked down at the floor, not being able to take in his words. Sheldon removed his hand from his right pocket and used it to lift my face to meet his.

"As your friend, I know most of your fears. As insecure as you think you are, I love everything about you, Viv. I love your smile. I love your laugh. I love your body. I love you," he confessed.

He stopped talking as he gazed at me. I wondered if he paused to hear what my response would be, but I couldn't say anything.

"I hope you don't reject me. That's why I left the other night like I did, because I could not stand you not wanting me."

"It wasn't that I didn't want you. I did," I finally managed to say.

"Then why didn't you say so?"

"Just like you, Sheldon, I don't like rejection either."

"I'm telling you now I want you, but you haven't reacted."

I smiled, saying, "It's kind of hard responding when I'm standing in front of you with nothing but a towel on."

He smirked and said, "I see this as a good thing."

"Oh, you do?"

"You can't tell?" he said, looking down. I could see him holding on to his extension in his pants from his pocket. All this professing of his love didn't hinder his manhood from saluting me.

"I thought that was your hand."

"Do you want to shake it?" he said, removing his hand from his left pocket to reveal more of the stimulation that radiated throughout his body to create such a wonderful extension.

"I would love to," I said to him with a smile.

I stepped toward him and reached out to grip his manhood. Sheldon closed his eyes with my touch, and it felt like his length got even harder. When I let go, he opened his eyes to look into mine.

"I love you so much," he said to me.

"I love you too," I finally admitted.

Sheldon cupped my face with his massive hands and pulled me to his lips. He kissed me deeply this time. I let go of my towel to wrap my arms around his waist. I could feel the towel slip from my body and fall to the floor, leaving me exposed to whatever he was going to do. Never had I felt so comfortable with a man. This felt right with Sheldon. This was the feeling I'd been looking for all my life.

Once our lips disconnected, he looked down at my wonder. I didn't try to hide myself from him, and he smiled, I guess noticing the comfortable demeanor I had with him. He reached down and pulled at the hem of his shirt, pulling it over his head to reveal something I hadn't seen before.

"What did you do?" I said, looking at a tattoo on his chest.

"It's your name, Vivian."

"You did this for me?" I asked.

"I wanted you to see I'm not playing when it comes to my love for you. I know you are the woman meant for me, and I wanted to show you by placing your name near my heart. No woman has ever captured it like you have."

Tears welled up in my eyes as I reached out and ran my fingers over my name engraved in his chest.

"It's beautiful."

"Just like you," he said. "So would you do me the honor of being in a relationship with me?" he asked.

I smiled and said, "I would love to be in a relationship with you."

The biggest smile ever crept across his face, and he reached down and pulled me into his arms, hugging me tight. He rocked back and forth, holding me like he didn't want to let me go.

This felt good. This felt right, and I'd never been happier in my life.

When he let me go, he said, "I want to make love to you."

Hearing him say "make love" made my heart pulsate with eagerness. I had a man who loved me for who I was and everything I was about.

He leaned down to kiss me again as he backed me up to my bed. This was the moment when I knew I was going to spend the rest of my life with this man.

But like most perfect moments, it was quickly shattered by a phone call that would leave me stunned.

Chapter 42

Dawn

I was devastated. I walked into my home like I was a zombie as I replayed the visual of Corey and my sister, Shauna, on the big screen together. In addition, finally dealing with accidently killing Renee was way too much for me to handle. I cried all the way home. Vivian, Serena, and even Phoenix tried really hard to make me feel better about what had happened. I appreciated them being there for me, but Shauna's words had mutilated me. She had said what I'd told myself all my life: I was not an official Johnson woman. I was one by default, created by the sins of my mother and my father.

I walked into my kitchen to see if Corey was in there, but he wasn't. Nor was he in the living room. The next place I headed was our bedroom. I needed to talk to him about what I had just found out, and I wanted answers from him. How could he want to marry me if he was doing my sister?

When I got to my door, it was closed. I turned the knob and opened it only to get one more devastating blow. Corey was in our bed with some light-skinned woman with long, bone-straight black hair. He was hitting her from the back, and across the room was the camera, taping their little sexual escapade.

When he turned to look at me, he had the audacity to smile and wave me over to join them. Was he serious right now? Could he not see my face and tell I had been crying my eyes out? If he was my man, then one, he wouldn't be doing this; and two, he would stop what he was doing to run over to me and find out why I was upset. I guessed he was so deeply enthralled with his manhood being buried in this chick's wetness that he didn't notice my mood. He never stopped his stride. Was this because the camera was on, or was this because this man was playing me and was having his cake and eating it too?

My body trembled from anger, rage, and hurt. My world was crashing down around me, and I wanted the pain to end. My mother's face popped into my mind, and in that moment, I could understand why she gave up on life. I knew why she pulled the trigger and ended it once and for all. Sometimes it was better to not deal than to struggle with things that seemed to be out of control in your life.

I walked to our master closet, dropping to my knees in front of our safe, which was on the floor in the back of the closet. Turning the dial, I put in the combination. After putting in the third number, I pulled on the handle and watched as the safe opened with ease. In there were stocks, bonds, government documents, and some cash. And also in this space was a gun.

I picked up the cold steel and lifted it out of the safe. Bringing it to my chest, I hugged it, wishing it could comfort me in my time of sorrow. Tears streamed down my cheeks as so much pent-up pain released from me. It came in tsunami waves, crashing to the core of my being. I rocked back and forth and prayed to God to instantly take this pain away from me, but He wasn't hearing me. The pain was still piercing my soul.

I struggled to stand to my feet, looking around at all the clothes and shoes in the small walk-in closet. Material things meant nothing if I wasn't happy with myself and my life. Then I looked at Corey's things and wondered how I could allow this man to degrade me like this. What was wrong with me, for me to think this was okay? I had agreed to marry him, and I couldn't figure out for the life of me why.

I swiped at my tears and looked up to the ceiling, still praying for something to happen. I needed immediate satisfaction. I turned and walked out of the closet and back into my bedroom. Corey was still going to town on the woman. He didn't notice me enter the room again. I stared at him one last time before lifting the gun.

"God forgive me."

I pulled the trigger.

Chapter 43

Serena

Aw, hell naw, was my first thought when I walked into my home and found Juanita sitting on my couch. And who was sitting on the couch with her? Tyree. I was standing in my door with my keys in my hand, gawking at the two of them talking like they were old friends. I slammed the door, and Tyree stood to his feet.

"Hey, baby," he said like he didn't have the enemy sitting on our sofa.

"What is she doing in our house?" I asked angrily, glaring past Tyree at Juanita, who had this same condescending smirk on her face.

"Serena, stop yelling. Nevaeh and Zamir are sleeping."

"I don't give a damn. Tell me what is she doing in our home, Tyree?" I demanded.

"It's cool. She came to reconcile things with us," Tyree said dumbly.

"What?"

"She came over to apologize."

"She could have called. She didn't have to come to our home to do that." I looked at Juanita, who stood to her feet. I said, "You do know there is still a restraining order on you, right? You don't like abiding by the law?"

"Look, Tyree, I didn't come over here for all this," she said with an attitude.

"Serena, come on. Hear her out," he said to me.

Was he kidding me right now? Was I his woman, or was Juanita? I put my hands on my hips and said, "Get that bitch out my house."

"Bitch," she said, frowning at me.

"That's right."

"Don't get it twisted, Serena. Just because I'm pregnant with our man's baby and in your home don't mean I won't stomp that ass," she said, bristling up.

"Juanita, cool it," Tyree told her.

"You better tell her, Tyree," Juanita threatened him.

Tyree looked at me like he wanted me to chill.

"You know what? Both of y'all can get the hell out my house," I said, waving my arms and pointing to the door.

"Calm down, Serena," Tyree urged.

"I can't believe you, Tyree. You got your baby mama up in our house after all she's done. She's threatened me and your daughter. She's had you locked up by lying, and now she wants to apologize. Well, I'm going to tell you and her, I don't accept her apology. Now get the hell out my damn house," I yelled.

"You see. You try to do right and your trick-ass girl going to trip on me," Juanita said to Tyree.

"Trick-ass! Let's wait to see who that baby's daddy is," I said, pointing at her belly, "and then we will see who's been tricking."

"Yeah, we will see. I can't wait to see your face when you find out it's Tyree's baby."

Her words upset me because I was still trying to get over the fact that he even slept with the bitch. I thought things between us were working themselves out, but to see he had the audacity to allow Juanita in our home made me look at Tyree differently and wonder if he was really in this relationship fully with just me.

"Juanita, can you please leave?" he asked her.

"Gladly, but this will be the last time I try to work things out, Tyree," she said, wobbling her behind to my door. "Kiss our son for me," she said, looking at me and smirking.

Tyree looked at me knowing damn well she was egging me on by saying that. That's what that bitch did: she pushed you until you were ready to catch a damn charge from beating her ass.

Once that door shut behind her, I turned all my rage to Tyree. "What were you thinking?" Holding up my hands, I said, "Wait. You weren't. You never think. That's why she might be pregnant with your second child—because you didn't think."

"I wanted all this tension to stop, Serena. It's been going on way too long."

"It's been going on because she started it. She can't get it through her thick skull you guys are over. Or maybe you are not done with her. Is that it?" I asked him.

"No. We are done."

"It doesn't seem that way to me. You seemed to be more up her ass than being on the side of the woman who just gave birth to your daughter. You live with me. You are in a relationship with me, so you should have confided in me before you allowed her to step foot in our home."

"I tried to do a good deed for our kids."

"That woman wanted your child dead. Does that sound like somebody I'm going to forgive anytime soon?" I asked him. "Why would I accept her apology after all she's done?" I asked him.

"I just thought—"

"Again, you weren't thinking. You could have called me to see if I even wanted to consider talking with her instead of bombarding me."

"I'm sorry," he apologized.

"You sure are," I retorted angrily.

"It will never happen again," he said.

"I know it won't, because you are getting out of here today."

"What?" He looked at me, dumbfounded.

"Get your shit and get the hell out my home," I said sternly.

"You joking right?" he said, laughing nervously.

"Does it look like I'm kidding?" I asked him, looking more serious than I had at Vivian's house earlier.

"So you breaking up with me?" he asked.

"Yes. I'm done with you, because I can't trust you."

"Wow! I can't believe you right now," he said, walking away as he started to catch an attitude himself.

"You can't believe it? I can't believe I wasted my time with you, trusting you, loving you, for you to still find another way to hurt me, Tyree."

He leaned on the arm of the sofa, looking straight ahead. I continued.

"Give me a reason to continue this relationship, especially when I know one day I want to be married. You gave me an ultimatum before, so you know what? I've decided I'm done. I don't want to be with you anymore."

Tyree nodded and didn't say anything. He stood and started walking to our bedroom. I followed him to see what he was doing, and sure enough, when I entered, he was pulling out his suitcase and loading clothes into it.

I chuckled, and he looked at me, asking, "What's so funny?"

"You're funny. You were fighting harder for Juanita to apologize than you are to make us work. It's bit of an eye opener for me."

"I told you, Serena, if you want me gone, I'm not going to fight."

"Maybe if you did, then that would show how much you want to be with me, but I guess I'm not worthy."

"You are. I do love you."

"You've had a funny way of showing it."

He sighed and turned back to pack more clothes in his suitcase. Then he asked, "What about Zamir?"

"He can stay; that's if you and Juanita don't mind. There's no need to wake him. You can come pick him up tomorrow," I told him, knowing Zamir and our daughter were the innocent ones in this mixed-up situation.

Once Tyree had the majority of his things packed, he walked to the door and placed them all there. I sat on the love seat with my arms crossed, watching and thinking about everything that had transpired over the past few months.

"I got all my things," he said.

"Good."

He looked heartbroken, but I didn't care. As much as I looked like I was happy about our relationship ending, I was the heartbroken one here. I truly did love Tyree, but not enough to be used and abused by him or his baby mama.

"Are you sure about this, Serena?" he asked gloomily. "We can make this work. If you want me to marry you, I will."

My breath caught in my throat, and I got annoyed as I looked his way. "So you mean to tell me you want to marry me now?" I asked heatedly.

"That's what you want. Isn't this why you are doing this, to scare me into marrying you?" he asked.

"You're steady revealing yourself to me." I chuckled. "You think I'm doing this to make you marry me?"

He didn't respond.

"I'm doing this because I'm done. I am fed up with our bullshit; and for you to think I'm doing all of this so you can marry me further lets me know I'm making the right decision. Why would I want a man I had to force to be my husband? Think about what you are saying. I want a man who knows it's me he wants for the rest of his life with no doubt, and who doesn't base his future on the past of his parents," I said with certainty.

He dropped his head when I said this.

"So please trust, I don't want to marry you. I want you gone."

Tyree nodded as he picked up his duffle bag and slung it over his shoulder. Opening the door to leave, he picked up his suitcases.

Turning to look at me again, he said, "I love you, Serena."

"I love you too, Tyree."

And he was gone.

Chapter 44

Serena

One Year Later

Tyree kept his word when he said he was going to drop Nevaeh off early this morning, since our daughter and I had big plans today.

"Hi, honey," I said to my daughter, who grinned back at me. "What did Daddy get you?" I asked her, looking at her wearing a tiny gold necklace with matching bracelet and a new baby doll.

Tyree put Nevaeh down, and I watched as she took off running to her room. She looked so cute as her little head bobbed and her ponytails bounced. I smiled, amazed at how fast she was growing up.

"Thank you for dropping her off early. I know this is your weekend to have her, so if you want, you can spend some time with her tomorrow," I told him.

"It's okay. I will see her on Wednesday. I'm going to let her enjoy this happy occasion with you," he said coolly.

I thought after Tyree and I broke up that we were going to have issues with him wanting to see her and him not taking his responsibility seriously by paying me child support for Nevaeh. To my surprise, we'd worked things out between ourselves. Like adults, we talked and agreed that Tyree would get to spend time with his daughter every other weekend and every Wednesday. Concerning support, Tyree gave me $200 a month for her, and if I ever needed more from him, he didn't have any issue giving me what I needed. Plus, he brought her things all the time.

"You know she didn't need any jewelry, Tyree. She might break it."

"It's okay. I think it looks cute on her."

"It does," I said.

"You look beautiful," he complimented me.

"Thank you."

It was weird feeling awkward around the man I once loved and had a child with, but a lot had changed. When I kicked Tyree out of my place, I meant what I said by never allowing him back in my life. Concerning our daughter I had to deal with him, but pertaining to any intimate relationship between us, it never crossed that line after that day. Trust me; he wanted it to. Just the way he looked at me let me know he wanted me at times. Like now.

"Congratulations. I heard you and Juanita were getting married," I said.

Tyree dropped his head as he shifted uneasily. He couldn't marry me, but he proposed to the woman who made his life a living hell. I guess misery loves company. I was happy for them. I mean really, I was truly happy for him.

Tyree stuttered to say something, but I said, "It's okay, Tyree. I'm not mad," I told him.

"I knew you would find out eventually," he said. "I've been trying to figure out a way to tell you."

"You don't owe me an explanation."

"But I feel like I do," he said.

I giggled and said, "Tyree, it's okay. I'm happy for you. I know Juanita is happy too," I said.

"She is."

It was funny how Tyree went back to the very woman who caused so much turmoil in our relationship. Juanita got what she wanted, which was her children's father. Yes, the baby Juanita had did turn out to be Tyree's baby. She gave birth to another boy and they named him Shamar.

"Hey, baby, which tie do you think I should wear today?" my boyfriend said, walking into the living room holding up a red-and-black tie and a gray-and-blue tie.

"I like the gray-and-blue one. I think it's going to look better with your suit."

"What's up, Tyree?" my new man, Dorian, said.

Tyree nodded but didn't speak. I found this funny, because I could clearly see he had an issue with me moving on. I don't know why he had a problem. He made his choices and was with the person he wanted to be with. He had seven months to get used to seeing Dorian around. Dorian hadn't moved in with me, but he stayed over some nights. He had stayed over the night before because we had big plans, plus I didn't have Nevaeh, which gave us some time to spend alone with each other. We agreed to keep living separately to see how things went between us, and fortunately Dorian was a wonderful guy.

"I'm going to take my shower," Dorian said.

"Okay."

Dorian left the room. I turned to see Tyree clenching his jaw. He rubbed his head in annoyance and said, "I guess I should be going."

"Thank you again for switching weekends. I'll see you Wednesday," I said.

"Yes. I'll be here around six."

"Sounds great," I said, walking around him to open the door.

Tyree proceeded to walk out of the door but stopped directly in front of me, looking like he wanted to say something. When his face shifted, I knew he wasn't going to say whatever was on his mind.

"Good-bye, Tyree."

He pushed his full lips together before saying, "Good-bye, Serena."

Chapter 45

Phoenix

I'd never been so happy with my life. And you know why? I had gone on a man hiatus. That's right. I gave up men for a while. After Tobias put things in perspective for me, letting me know I needed to take a look at my life and how I was making detrimental decisions regarding myself, I had decided to cut all ties with the men I was dealing with. It took Tobias for me to realize I was putting myself out there like a paid whore.

I was celibate for five and a half months. Can you believe it? Me, Phoenix, didn't have dick for that period of time. It was like not having that animate object penetrating me allowed my mind to become clear as to where I wanted my life to go. That's when I decided to follow my dream and go to school to become a chef. I couldn't be happier with my decision. Becoming enthralled with something I loved, like taking different types of meat, vegetables, and spices and turning them into something magnificent, was enough to make me have an orgasm from the pure joy of it all.

Still, as fate would have it, I did end up with a guy in my life, and that guy ended up being Tobias. One day he just stopped by to check on me. I hadn't seen him in months. I guess instead of driving by my house, wondering how I was doing, he decided to park, get out, and knock on the door to see this time. I was surprised to see him, and I wasn't rude. I invited him in, and from there we'd been talking.

I realized there was more to being with someone than just money and nothing else to offer. I needed to be with a man who was willing to love me and give me the world. Lucky for me, Tobias was that man. The ironic thing was Tobias did have Diddy money. Those papers he gave me that night he had left revealed a lawsuit he'd filed against Noah, who had embezzled money from a company they were partners in. Tobias not only gained the joint venture company he and Noah acquired together, but he ended up winning a multimillion-dollar lawsuit against Noah, who was ordered to pay the money he stole back to Tobias.

Now, mind you, I had no clue about any of this. I had never been involved with how Noah made his money. Hell, I never cared how any man I dealt with made his money, just as long as he took care of me.

That was then; this was now, and I was a woman making her own money. Even though Tobias had Diddy money, I wasn't that same woman who felt privileged to this money. I liked that about myself now.

As irony would have it, Noah's baby mama left him for someone else when his money dwindled. I heard she took the baby and moved to France with her new man, and Noah was back in California living with his parents, so the child he yearned to have was still not in his life.

Don't you know he had the nerve to call me one day. He called to apologize and said he hoped we could be friends. I told him I didn't need any friends and to not get any ideas about trying to come back into my life, because I had moved on with Tobias. Needless to say, this was shocking to him, because he didn't have a clue I was with his once great friend. I can't lie; that shit felt good telling him that. I know it was wrong to feel great about him feeling bad, but I am human. I never thought the day would come when I felt like I got one up on Noah, but I did, and it helped me move on to develop a better relationship with Tobias.

"Phoenix, we need to go. You know we can't be late," Tobias said, looking handsome in his suit. That once-dorky man was looking way better than he used to, and that was due to me changing up his attire a bit. I think it was Dawn who told me you couldn't turn a whore into a housewife. I wasn't a housewife yet, but the fact that I could be with this man made me happy because now I knew that anybody could change.

Chapter 46

Vivian

I never thought I would see this day in my life. Looking into the long mirror, I stood in my wedding gown, getting ready to walk down the aisle to marry the man I loved. I had thirty minutes to be a free woman before I became Mrs. Sheldon Garrison. I smiled at my reflection, amazed at how far I'd come. Not only was I marrying the man I loved, but I'd learned to love myself more and be confident in the skin God had blessed me with.

Rubbing my hands down my waist, pushing out any imperfections, I turned right and then left to make sure everything was like it was supposed to be. My tiara on my head sparkled as ringlets of curls fell freely. My face was made up, nails were done, and the only thing left to do was slide on my five-inch heels and make my way to becoming a married woman.

"You look beautiful," Serena said, looking me over. She was holding Nevaeh's little hand, who looked cute with her white flower girl dress on and a ringlet of flowers around her little head. When I looked down at her, she smiled up at me with her little teeth and the dimple in her right cheek. She looked adorable.

"Hello, Nevaeh," I said in the baby voice I used with her, and she ran over to me and wrapped her little arms around me.

"No, Nevaeh. You are going to get Auntie dirty," Serena said, trying to stop her.

I said, "It's okay." I scooped my niece up in my arms and hugged her lovingly. Feeling her little arms around me felt wonderful.

"You better give her to me before she gets something on your dress," Serena said, reaching for her. Nevaeh went to Serena as she continued to speak. "You don't know how hard it is to keep this little one from getting anything on her. As much as this is your day, I can't wait until you walk down that aisle so I don't have to worry about her getting dirty."

I giggled.

"Are you ready?" she asked excitedly.

"I am. I'm so happy," I said joyfully.

"Here we were thinking Dawn was going to break the curse of the Johnson women, and now you are the first in four generations to get married."

"You know I never fed into that curse on the Johnson women thing," I told her.

"I know, but I did."

Phoenix burst into the room, saying, "You have ten minutes, Vivian."

I giggled and said, "I'm ready."

"I still can't believe you are getting married," Phoenix said.

"Me either, but I am happy I am, because I really do love Sheldon," I proclaimed.

Both of my sisters were wearing lavender-colored bridesmaid dresses with matching heels. It was so good having them both by my side today. Mama and Daddy crossed my mind, along with Renee, who I wished was there with me. I knew they were there in spirit, but it still made this moment bittersweet.

Shauna came walking into the room with her bridesmaid dress on, saying, "You should see all the people out there."

"Is it a lot?" Phoenix asked.

"You know it is. Sheldon has a huge family, and some of them brothers are fine as hell."

"We are in a church, fool," Serena said.

"Oh, my bad," Shauna said, covering her mouth.

If anyone had come a long way, it was Shauna. That night when my and Sheldon's moment was interrupted by a phone call, it was Shauna calling me from jail because she was arrested for reckless driving and DUI. That girl was a nervous wreck. I'd heard of karma, but she got it as soon as she left my home that day, and she had vowed she would never drink and drive again.

She didn't drink that much anymore. I think her being behind bars for that short stint was enough to scare the alcohol out of her. Here she was living in the past, not realizing she should have been working on how her future was going to be.

Another silver lining for Shauna was the fact that she was still with Grayson. Cal was finally out of the picture for good, since he received time for assaulting her and disobeying the restraining order. My sister couldn't be happier.

"Look, before we leave, I have something to show you guys," Shauna said, walking over to me. "I need you to sit down."

"Do you know how tight this dress is?" I said, laughing.

"Try anyway."

I did as she asked, and Shauna knelt down beside me as Serena and Phoenix stood behind me. Shauna took out her cell and pushed a few buttons until a video began to play. Dawn's face popped up on the screen, and my hand flew to my mouth with joy.

"Hi, you guys. Hey, Vivian, I heard you were getting married today. I wish I could be there, but you know I'm currently tied up right now," she joked. "I wanted you to know how happy I am for you. No one deserves this more than you. I'm there in spirit. You know I love you. I love all of you, and I can't wait until we have one of our sister-dinners again. It's going to be a while, but trust, it's going to happen. Congratulations, sis. You are marrying a wonderful man. Enjoy your day, and party enough for me. I love you," she said, putting her hand to her mouth and blowing me a kiss.

Tears streamed down my cheeks.

"How are you going to make her cry right before she walks down the aisle?" Phoenix asked, wiping tears from her own eyes.

I looked at all my sisters, and each one of them had tears falling.

The reason why my sister Dawn couldn't be here was because she was in jail for shooting Corey in the back. She had unloaded the gun completely before she walked back to her living room and sat waiting for the cops to arrive. This incident was made worse by the fact the camera was recording the entire incident. It quickly went viral all over the Internet.

She was arrested and charged with attempted murder. I say *attempted* because Corey ended up surviving. Unfortunately for him, he would be paralyzed from the waist down for the rest of his life. Again, there goes that karma. You can't do people any kind of way and not have to pay for what you've done. I don't agree his payment should have been him getting shot, but at the same time, you can't predict people a lot of times. I hated that it was at the cost of my sister's life, but she had to pay for what she did. She ended up getting a ten-year sentence, which was reduced due to the fact that she pled guilty due to being mentally unstable. She was getting the help she needed, despite the fact that she was behind bars. I missed her so much and tried to visit her as often as I could. Seeing her on the video made my day.

For Shauna being the one to show me the video, I knew this meant she had gone to visit her. She had blamed herself for Dawn snapping like she did, and she said she wished our last sister-gathering turned out better than it had. Shauna was dead wrong for what she did and realized her mistakes. I was glad she'd grown up to learn to be accountable for her actions.

She finally made peace with everything. I think both Shauna and Dawn had. Sometimes it takes getting down to your lowest points to help you rise above and beyond even what you thought you could achieve. This couldn't be truer for them. As Mama always said, "As long as you learn and grow from your mistakes, I'm happy."

"It's time," Serena said, looking at me.

I stood and walked over to my white blinged-out shoes and stepped into them. Phoenix held her hand out for me to hold so I wouldn't fall.

"Let me look at myself one more time," I told Phoenix, who helped me over to the mirror again. She dabbed at my face again, making sure my makeup was on point.

"Can't have you looking like a raccoon out there," she said.

I gazed at my reflection, knowing this would be the last time I would see myself as a single woman. I smiled at myself and tried my best not to cry so I wouldn't ruin the fabulous makeup job Phoenix did for me.

"I'm ready," I said with a smile. "I can't believe this is happening."

"Believe it, sis. You are marrying the man of your dreams," Serena said, coming up behind me and placing her loving hand on my back.

All of my sisters stood around me, and I looked at how beautiful we all were. Despite our ups and downs, we were still here, standing as one.

The curse on the Johnson women was mentioned earlier, and I had to smile, thinking I didn't know if it was a curse at all. Maybe it was just about the choices we made, especially the ones who settled for less than they deserved.

I thanked God in this moment for bringing me such a long way. He had blessed me with the man of my dreams. He blessed me with the gift of loving myself; and most of all, He blessed me with wonderful sisters. Life sometimes deals you a bad hand, but it is up to you how to play it. Each Johnson sister went about playing the hand they were dealt differently, but the one thing I was happy about was that we still remained close in the end.